STRICTLY BUSINESS

STRICTLY BUSINESS

KALLISTA KOHL

CHRYSANTHEMUM PUBLISHING

This is a work of fiction. All of the characters, organizations, locations, and events portrayed in this novel are either products of the author's imagination or are used fictitiously. Any resemblance to actual persons, living or dead, business establishments, events, or locales is entirely coincidental.

Copyright © 2022 by Kallista Kohl

All rights reserved.

No part of this book may be reproduced in any form or by any electronic or mechanical means, including information storage and retrieval systems, without written permission from the author, except for the use of brief quotations in a book review.

Cover design by Bailey McGinn

ISBN: 978-1-958991-00-8 (ebook)

ISBN: 978-1-958991-01-5 (paperback)

Library of Congress Cataloging-in-Publication Data Pending

To my Mom. Thank you for encouraging me to read anything and everything, including your romance novels.

To my Mom. Thank you for encouraging me to read anything and everything, including your romance novels.

One

IZABELLE

"Called it! I told you she would bring her suitcase to the bar. Pay up!"

Izabelle Green had barely pushed through the heavy wooden door of Buchannan's when she heard Sabrina call out the results of the weekly bet. Normally she wouldn't have been able to hear her over the din of the bar, but it was too late in the day for televised sports and too early for the rowdy regulars.

"As if my anxiety would let me do anything else other than bring it," Izabelle responded from the doorway, her eyes taking a moment to adjust to the dark. "I can't risk being late for my flight." In the dim neon light, she saw Sabrina stick her hand out toward Ava and Charlie, demanding payment.

Izabelle laughed. The bets were all part of their weekly tradition and had been their way to gamify who was paying for each of the rounds when Izabelle, Sabrina, Ava, and Charlie—her favorite people and the self-styled "Boss Babes of Buchannan's"—used to be broke and had just moved to the city. They were all doing well enough now that they didn't need to make excuses for who was paying for what, but the bets stuck around because Sabrina and Charlie liked to have a place to direct their competitive energy, and Ava and Izabelle hated to see traditions change.

Izabelle click-clacked on her heels toward where her friends were sitting, tucked back in their usual corner booth. She parked her roller bag against the dark wood paneling of the wall and made a motion for them to scooch. The maroon vinyl welcomed her with a familiar squish as she slid into her usual spot. Sabrina continued to hold out her hand in request for payment from the other two. Ava dug for her wallet with resigned acceptance, but Charlie, per usual, was treating this as a negotiation.

"I feel like I should be exempt from this one for saying she would be wearing business casual on the plane instead of leggings and a messy bun like the rest of the world," Charlie pouted. "I even called the heels."

"Well then, next time call the bet first Charlotte Ann. Pay up, or the whole round is on you," Sabrina said, perfectly resolute.

Charlie visibly recoiled at the sound of her formal first name, making an exaggerated gagging face. "Good god. I'll get this round and the next one if you promise not to call me that. You know how much I hate it."

"Sounds good to me," Izabelle quipped, playfully bumping into Charlie's shoulder. "I'll take a manhattan."

"Yeesh, no wine today?" Charlie asked, digging out her wallet, clearly surrendering to Sabrina's demands. "You really are anxious about this trip." She made a move to flag down Ed, their favorite grumpy bartender.

Ava interjected with a concerned look, "I thought going out to Sedona early was going to help ease your mind."

Izabelle shrugged. "That's the idea, at least. God help me if it doesn't." Izabelle could tell she needed a shake-up. She had hit a wall with her company, and she wasn't going to be able to grow any further without outside investment. That was the sole reason she had finally worked up the courage to apply to the EtaSella Investment Competition after all these years. It was the premier incubator for small start-up companies like hers, but they only took the best of the best. She had never expected to get in, but after adjusting to the shock of being accepted as a pitch presenter, she was right back at the same wall, trying to figure out how to convince investors that giving her their money was a good idea and trying to convince herself that she should accept it. After months and months, Izabelle had a bare-bones pitch presentation, all numbers and graphs but nothing that had any kind of attention-grabbing sparkle. Which made her even more stressed. She was now at the point where she was constantly ripping the presentation apart and putting it back together in the hopes of stumbling on something better. Izabelle was banking on the dual hope that going out early would spark some new creative energy and calm her nerves by getting acclimated to the environment before the rest of the companies and their presenters showed up. She wasn't sure what her plan was if that didn't work.

"Is it still the presentation part that's freaking you out?" Sabrina asked.

Charlie jumped in. "I've done a million pitch decks. You can do this easily. You get up there, razzle-dazzle them, and then you're done. I promise it's not so bad."

Sabrina picked up where Charlie left off. "She's really right. I have to pitch designs and themes to clients all the time, it's never as big a deal as I worry it's going to be."

Izabelle scoffed. "Easy for you to say! You literally do this for a living. It took me a month to figure out that a pitch deck was the same thing as a PowerPoint presentation. You guys know talking to big groups and trying to hype myself is not my thing. I spend all day with numbers for a reason."

Ava raised her glass with an understanding nod. She got it. As the other introvert of the group, she made it a point not to engage in confrontations. They gave her bad energy. Meanwhile, Charlie, as a manager at one of the largest sales companies in the world, thrived on it.

Charlie's expression softened. "I've told you a million times that I would be more than happy to help you practice. The offer is still open."

"Same. I can send you any of my client pitch templates or design you something completely new that fits your aesthetic," Sabrina followed.

"I know. And I appreciate it. But I've got it. I can do it myself. That's the whole point of Me-E-O, right?" Izabelle arranged her face into something that she hoped resembled a reassuring and confident expression, even if she didn't fully feel it. Her entire company was based on the premise that you could build a company all on your own. You could be your own CEO. You just needed to be connected to the right resources and be coached through the right steps. She had literally built her entire business model around doing it all yourself. After so many years of going it alone, the mantra of "I can do it myself" had infused itself into her personality as well. So she certainly didn't want to admit that the presentation portion of the investor competition was stumping her or that she was still nervous about bringing in outside investment at all. Thankfully, grumpy Ed arrived with their drinks, providing a distraction, and Izabelle let out a small, grateful sigh that they could move on. Her hopes were dashed when Sabrina picked right back up from where they had been interrupted.

"So do you have anything planned for when you get there?" She turned to the other women. "The resort is unbelievable. I would kill to host an event there. It's modern and romantic, settled in the hills outside of town, so much space and light to play with." Sabrina looked wistfully into the mid-distance. It was plain to everyone that she was getting lost in the daydream of whatever fabulous event she was planning in her head. "I am seriously considering getting some of my clients to do their retreats out there."

"No," Izabelle said. "I'm sure you've researched it more than I have at this point."

"I mean, I booked it for you, but I figured you would have investigated it past that. There is so much to do." The wistful look reemerged on her face.

"If you want, I can send you some articles about where to find positive energy vortexes near the resort. They are particularly strong there. It might help cleanse your thoughts," Ava supplied.

"I really appreciate it." Izabelle gave Ava's hand a soft squeeze across the table. "But I probably won't be leaving the room that much." She turned to Sabrina. "You confirmed that the room has a desk and that the hotel has room service. That's all I need to know."

"Iz. You really have to take some time for yourself. You haven't had a break the entire time I've known you. I know this is a business trip, but your mental health will thank you if you think of it as a vacation too. You deserve it," Ava said in her soothing yoga teacher voice.

"Agreed," Charlie and Sabrina said simultaneously and then clinked their glasses in a cheers. "Jinx."

Izabelle knew they were probably right. She had worked so hard for the last five years, rebuilding herself and building her company. But framing this trip as a vacation felt too indulgent. There was just too much riding on this pitch. She could push through a little longer. She would rest when Me-E-O was self-sustaining. "There is no possible way I can ignore work entirely, but I promise to do a few fun things while I'm there."

"I'll take that as a win." Charlie squeezed her arm. "All I know is that you've worked your ass off for this, and these investors will be falling all over themselves to get with you."

"Get with her? Oh, it's that kind of competition, then?" Sabrina asked saucily, winking at Izabelle.

"It's definitely *not* that kind of competition," Izabelle replied, laughing. "As if I have time to be sleeping around in the middle of this, much less with someone who would be there from one of the other companies."

"Good. Keep that mindset. You never know who is going to want to pull your head out of the game," Charlie said.

Ava rolled her eyes. "Charlie, lord. You and all the sports-ball metaphors. Sabrina already called the place romantic. I think we should be encouraging her to be open to possibilities."

Sabrina giggled. "Yeah, Iz. Be open." She made a gesture with her hands falling open and flopped them on the table

Ava blushed. "You know I didn't mean like that." She sipped her drink with a smirk. "Well, not exactly like that."

They all laughed as Izabelle continued. "If I haven't found a guy who supports me in the last five years, there is no way in the world I'm going to find one in the next two weeks."

"I mean, it's not like you had one that supported you five years ago either," Charlie quipped.

Ava and Sabrina whipped their heads around to look at Charlie with wide eyes that clearly telegraphed why-the-hell-would-you-bring-that-up-right-now expressions. They then looked to Izabelle to see how she was going to handle the mention of her ex.

"It's okay. She's not wrong," Izabelle said.

"Thank you," Charlie said, raising her glass with a self-satisfied nod.

"That doesn't mean you have to say it," Ava gritted through clenched teeth, lightly jabbing Charlie in the ribs.

"Really. It's fine. I'm over him."

"We know you are over *him*, but that doesn't mean that you have to pretend you are over *it*," Ava said.

God damn. How was it that she was always so on the nose when it came to feelings? Simon had turned out to be the textbook definition of a shithead. But for a time, he had been the people-person yin to her numbers-person yang. At least she thought that was what they were to each other. Bastard.

"I know," she sighed. "I know. But it's water under the bridge at this point. I've worked too hard to keep dwelling on Simon and all the ways he screwed me over."

Her friends looked between each other, clearly not wanting to move on after stepping on what used to be an emotional land mine. "Seriously, guys, I'm fine. See?" She gestured to her face. "Dry eyes. Now, please, god, can we talk about something else other than EtaSella and my nonexistent love life?"

Charlie looked left and then right, obviously unsure if she should move on or not, then gave a shrug. "Bet you can't guess who texted me the other night."

"Was it Mike?"

"Dave?"

"Samantha?"

"Hmmm. I see where I should have narrowed the question," Charlie chuckled.

The women all laughed at once. They all knew where this was going. Izabelle was more than glad that they had settled into their usual pattern. More than relived to move away from the quagmire that was her company and dating life. "Sounds like we're going to need another round."

An hour and a half later, Izabelle was outside on the sidewalk, waiting for her rideshare car. Her brow had unfurrowed, and the knots in her shoulders had loosened ever so slightly. It was amazing what a drink—alright, two—and the usual routine of gossiping with her friends could do. If she was honest with herself, it was only their friendship that kept her engaged with the outside world. The hours spent in their dark dive bar, with its sticky floors and 1970's beer advertisements, were pretty much the only hours of her workweek where she wasn't staring at a screen.

When she thought about it that way, it sounded a little sad, but that's just the way it was. It wasn't like she had spare time for anything else. She didn't need there to be anything else. She just needed this pitch presentation to go well. She needed an investor. The last five years were riding on it.

Glancing at her watch, she flicked open the rideshare app on her phone, checking the location of the car. It seemed like it was crawling across town, and traffic was starting to pick up. *I shouldn't have sold my car.* She clicked the phone shut with a sigh. She had budgeted plenty of time for happy hour and getting to the airport on time, but she absolutely regretted deciding to go with the shared option instead of paying more for the solo option. It was a variable that was out of her control, and whatever cash she might have saved was not going to be worth the price of being late. She sent up a prayer to the traffic gods that the rush-hour slowdowns had cleared by now.

Feeling her anxiety tiptoe its way up her spine, she clicked open her phone again. The car was just around the corner. *Fingers crossed we don't have to pick anyone else up.*

Five tedious minutes later, she plunked her suitcase into the trunk and plopped into the back seat of the car. As the sedan wound its way through downtown toward the 101 and San Francisco International, she instinctively started scrolling through her presentation on her phone.

She knew everything about Me-E-O. The numbers were right, and the business plan was rock solid. She had always been confident in her ability to plan and build a great company. She had done it before, and she had done it again here. But she hadn't ever had to be the one to sell it, and that was where her confidence faltered. Big-time.

She had spent every waking hour of the last few months

extensively researching how to structure compelling pitches, how to sound commanding when public speaking, putting together slides, working them and reworking them. Yet, she knew it was still missing that "special" something. Which was really a problem considering that the special something was supposed to be her.

But it was hard to feel much razzle-dazzle, as Charlie put it, with a giant pit in your stomach. Me-E-O needed outside investment; she knew that. She had taken it as far as it could go on her own. But bringing in outside investment meant giving up control, and that was the part that scared her. On the other hand, she was proud of what she had created, and she was just as worried that the fears about lack of control would be moot because no one would be interested in investing in her little company, leaving it to die on the vine. As a result, she waffled between being afraid of someone taking it and being afraid of not making it on pretty much a daily basis. It was an exhausting cycle.

Izabelle nervously picked at her fingernails as she flicked over to review the agenda for the competition. It outlined where check-in would be, when the networking mixers would be, and specified the half-hour time slots for the presentations. It was such a ridiculously brief description of an event with such massive implications. It didn't mention anything about the millions of dollars that would exchange hands over the weekend. The years-long mentorships that would be established between investors and participants. It didn't say anything about the sweat, tears, and carpal tunnel that had gone into Izabelle being accepted into the competition in the first place. Having to submit reams of company documents, business plans, and profit and loss statements hadn't been easy. Not to mention all those things had taken years to create and perfect.

The car slowed to a stop, and the driver hopped out, heading toward the trunk. She had been so absorbed in her worries it had only seemed like a few minutes had passed. *Guess we're here.* Gathering her work tote and triple-checking that she hadn't left anything else on the seat, she scooted toward the passenger-side door. She jumped when the door swung open on its own.

"Oh. Thank you," she said, looking up, expecting to see the rideshare driver and the terminal. "Oh!" Izabelle exclaimed again when she saw something entirely different.

Two

JAKE

"Cam, why in the hell am I getting in a car three hours before my flight?" Jake heard his assistant's chair squeak as she rolled herself into view in the doorway, making it clear that his question didn't dignify her getting up to give an answer.

"Okaaay," she said with an eye roll. "It's barely more than two and a half hours before your flight. You're better at math than that. And I did it because I'm the best assistant in the world who knows that you would rather have a drink and dinner in the first-class lounge than quickly scarfing something from the food court."

Jake shot her a narrow-eyed grimace from behind his sleek steel and glass desk.

"I'll take that as a begrudging 'you're right,'" Cam replied, getting up from her desk to lean against the doorframe. "Besides, the way this week is going, wouldn't you rather just go hide at the airport and I forward all of your calls to voicemail?"

Jake's grimace twisted up at the side, transforming into a

smirk. Cam did know him well. It had been a hell of a week. Jake had flip-flopped for months over the decision to go to EtaSella this year. He never felt like he had the time to step away, but Cam had browbeat him into thinking that it would be a good idea, insisting that he need a break.

And in this moment, boy, did he need a break. A break from the constant loop of people trying to network with him, call him, email him, and glad-hand him. Someone, or something, always needed his attention. Running from meeting to meeting, cocktail hour to cocktail hour, gala to gala, and always having to be "on" was starting to go from being a lot on his plate to being too much to manage. It wasn't that he was ungrateful—far from it. Starting out, he had wanted all of this. He had worked his entire life for it. The thrill he felt getting to call the shots, managing projects, and fixing problems had fueled him. Working side by side with his dad, he'd always wanted to prove that he deserved this, earned it, and that it wasn't just given to him because he was his father's son. But after his dad died, it just wasn't the same. Now, instead of side by side, he was the only man commanding the ship, and he didn't want it as much anymore, at least not like this.

For now, he just wanted a break. He didn't want to be R. Jacoby Masterson Jr., CEO of Masterson Holdings, every hour of the day. He just wanted to be Jake, without all the pressures and expectations. Hopefully, a week away would be enough time to decompress and get his head back in the game. *I don't know what I'm going to do if it isn't.*

The phone ringing jarred him out of his thoughts. He sighed, staring at it, planning to wait until the last ring to pick it up.

Cam looked at him with an exasperated expression. "Are you going to get that?" When Jake didn't make a move other than to frown at the ringing phone, she turned on her heel and dipped out of sight. "I got it!" Cam yelled from her desk, her annoyance with him clear before switching into an unnaturally cheery voice. "Yes, yes...definitely. Sadly, Mr. Masterson is going to be out of the office for the next week and a half or so. But I am sure one of our associates can handle the matter if it is urgent. I can gladly transfer you—uh-huh, yes, yes. I am sure he will want to hear directly from you. I'll make sure to get him the message. Bye now."

"You know your voice goes up an entire octave when you're on the phone, right?" Jake shouted through the open door.

"Of course I do. I have to play into some of these good old boys' expectations," Cam said, walking back into his office.

Jake opened his mouth. "You—"

"Yes. I know I don't have to do that here, but there are some habits like sounding 'phone pleasant' that are just too ingrained."

"I hate that," Jake responded.

Cam flipped her hair. "And I hate that people assume that a young, attractive woman's full name can't be Cam, and therefore they insist I give them my 'real name' over the phone. And yet, here we are." Cam motioned to the room around her with her hands spread wide, then interlaced her fingers.

"We're not that young anymore," he said glumly.

She shot him a withering look. "Jesus, you're a drama queen. You're in your midthirties. I just turned thirty, so agree to disagree." She walked toward the desk with a concerned expression. "Speaking of hate, did you forget to tell me you've suddenly developed a disdain for the phone ringing? When we first started working together, you used to get pissed at me if I picked it up before you did."

Jake rubbed at his eyes. Disdain wasn't the right word for it. Generalized anger that he wasn't what people wanted him to be, which had mutated into apathy, would have been better. But he didn't really want to wade into that with Cam right now. "I don't hate it. I just...I don't know."

"And this is exactly the reason that I pushed you so hard to get out of here for a little bit. I think you'll be amazed at what some interaction with the outside world will do to you."

Jake pressed his lips together as he narrowed his eyes. "What's that supposed to mean?"

Cam cocked her head at him. "Oh? Was I not being clear? I meant it to mean all you do is work, all you talk to is work people, and all you think about are work problems. You need to step out of the bubble, or else you're going to end up weird."

"That's not true." Cam raised her eyebrows questioningly. Jake wanted to contradict her but was racking his brain to come up with a solid example. "I go to the gym."

"The gym?" Cam asked, not lowering her eyebrows even a millimeter. "That's what you're going with as evidence here?"

"Yeah, the gym."

Cam rolled her head to her other shoulder. "The gym that is in the building? The gym you go to only because I hired you a trainer and sent you approximately one hundred and six articles about how exercise increases work productivity? That gym?"

Jake knew he was cornered. "Okay, fine, but just because I work a lot doesn't make me weird."

Cam grimaced. "I'm not so sure about that. You weren't exactly Mr. Suave at last month's shareholders meeting."

Now it was Jake's turn to raise his eyebrows. "Now, what the hell does that mean?"

Cam glanced down at her watch. "We literally don't have time to unpack all of the reasons why, but let's start with the fact that when Greg Litchfield was trying to tell you about his kid's soccer team, you asked if he was keeping a detailed log of his stats, and when Greg said, 'Uh, he's four,' you tried to transition to talking about last month's reports. So, yeah, what little touch you had, you are losing."

Shit. He had hoped that conversation had only been painful on the inside. Apparently, it was painful to watch as well. He dropped his head and sighed. "Please tell me you did something to smooth that over."

Cam waved her hand dismissively. "Of course. I said we would sponsor the entire soccer league next year and that you loved hearing about how much his son was enjoying it."

Jake sighed. "Thank you."

"You're welcome. And I know this is a bad moment to pile on, but I have to tell you something else that you aren't going to like."

"What's that exactly?" Jake said, now taking his opportunity to roll his eyes.

"Welllll, since you were thinking about investing in a rideshare company, and since most people take rideshares to the airport as opposed to company town cars, I scheduled one to pick you up for your flight. It says it will be here in fifteen minutes."

"Mmm," Jake grumbled, the grimace returning.

"And it's a shared ride," Cam said, scampering away.

"Cam!"

First thing I would change about these rideshares is that you don't have to stand on the street corner. Jake looked up and down the block with an irritated expression. The thing was taking forever to get here. Two separate people had stopped to "ask him something real quick" and "just pick his brain for a second" on the way out of the lobby. In the moment, he had been irritated that they were going to make him late; now he was irritated that he had the time to give them a fuller answer and hadn't. The irritation was compounded by the anxiety that maybe this vacation wasn't such a good idea after all.

Clearly, people needed him at the office and EtaSella had been running fine without him. Maybe he didn't need the break or the memories of how going out to Sedona used to be. The competition had always been his dad's passion project, but Jake hadn't really ever grasped why. While the trips and time spent with his dad had always been fun, he never understood why his dad would voluntarily take so much time away from their primary business to go work on something that didn't make them any money. So, after his dad had passed, he hadn't been back to the competition. He had always made a point to briefly make an appearance at the livestream event in the office, but he never stayed to watch the pitch presentations, and he had been entirely hands-off in running any part of it or choosing companies to compete for the better part of a decade.

Jake sighed as he checked his watch again, his frustration

growing. He was just going to end up coming back to a mountain of emails and things that had gone off the rails while he wasn't paying attention. If he wanted to stay on top, he had to keep his foot on the gas, and waiting on a street corner for a vacation he shouldn't be taking was not keeping your foot on the gas.

His phone pinged, alerting him that the car was arriving. *Finally.* As soon as the sedan pulled up, he stepped off the curb and yanked open the door. He nearly lost his balance when he saw a woman looking up at him instead of an empty seat.

"Oh!" she exclaimed.

Damn. Cam did say this was a shared ride.

Her face was warm, cheekbones sprinkled with freckles. But what was even more startling than her presence was her eyes. They were a deep green—emerald—and were evaluating him in a deeply appraising way. Her lips parted, her mouth opening as if to say something and then closing when she decided not to.

"Are you getting out?" Despite his tone being terse he sincerely hoped not. But he was very much in her way if she was. She continued to stare at him. Jake wasn't sure what to do next. Normally this kind of silence and indecision would drive him insane, and yet he didn't mind this particular stasis, each of them looking at the other.

"No. Uh. Airport." She shook her head slightly as if clearing a thought. "I'm going to the airport."

Her voice was so smooth, a warming honey that slid over him, slowing his thoughts, smoothing over the layers of irritation that had built up while waiting for the car. "Should I go around or..."

"Oh, uh. No. It's fine. I'll scooch," she said, sliding out of sight across the back seat of the car.

He folded himself into the seat after her. Ordinarily, squishing himself into a compact car was not his idea of a good time, but today was an exception. Jake registered that the driver had pulled away and was headed in the general direction of the highway. He was in the habit of modifying the directions from the GPS, telling the driver a more efficient way to go, but at the moment, he couldn't think of a single thing to say. He sat there with her in silence, stealing a glance in her direction and then feeling her gaze on him in return. He finally decided that he should just ask her what she was traveling for when the car turned onto the on-ramp for the 101, and his shoulders shifted, brushing against hers in the cramped back seat.

"Do you have enough room? I don't want you to feel like I'm on top of you." *Shit.* That hadn't been what he wanted to say. He wasn't trying to make it sound like an innuendo, but it definitely could have been interpreted that way. Thankfully, she met the question with a hint of a smile.

"No. You're fine."

Jake bit his tongue to stifle the unexplained impulse to say, "*Well you are more than fine.*" Good god. He talked to people all day, every day. Why was his brain glitching like he was fourteen years old? It dawned on him this was what Cam had meant when she said he was starting to go a bit weird. He scrambled to find a conversation starter. "Business or pleasure?"

"What?" she responded, a look of mild confusion on her face. Which was fair considering he dropped that cliché out of nowhere. Good grief, he was beyond rusty at this. He should be able to make small talk with a stranger outside of a business context, even if they were an exceptionally beautiful stranger, without being this awkward. *Let's try and put together a full sentence this time.*

"You said you were going to the airport. Are you traveling for business or pleasure?"

Her stare shifted from bemused interest to something he couldn't place. "Strictly business." Her lips zipped into a straight line as she looked away.

"Makes sense."

She gave him another look and then turned back to the window. He still couldn't fully read the expression on her face, but she didn't seem pleased. She was wearing a pencil skirt and a blouse. It wasn't like she looked like she was headed to Hawaii; it looked like she was coming from work or going to work. Or at least that's what he had meant. *This is going poorly.* He looked at her, trying to figure out what to say next to salvage this interaction while simultaneously second guessing everything he had blurted out thus far. She probably thought his "makes sense" had been some kind of dig, and now she was just sitting there, silently stewing about this stranger commenting on how she presented herself. He was trying to find a more eloquent way to say that when he heard her question.

"You?" She turned her eyes, meeting his, and Jake was caught off guard all over again.

"I don't know." He sighed. The sigh was deeper than he anticipated, the weight of his months-long ambivalence making itself known.

The woman restrained a confused chuckle. "Okay then."

Jake felt something bubbling over inside of him. "Had you

asked me an hour ago, I would have said 'to relax,' but now I feel like it's work."

The confusion on her face grew. "I'm not sure I understand."

"I mean, I'm supposed to be going on vacation, ostensibly to get away from work, because I feel burnt out, or at least I'm told that I look like I feel burnt out, but I'm not expecting to enjoy it because I'll probably just end up thinking about work the whole time and then show back up at work with a bunch more work I didn't do while I wasn't enjoying myself, and end up more miserable than I left."

This time, she let out a genuine laugh. "Now that I understand." Her smile was wide, and it crinkled the corners of her eyes.

"You do?" Jake was incredulous that anyone would understand that word salad he had just tossed out.

"Deeply." She gestured to her bag. "That's why I just take my work everywhere I go. Nothing to come back to if it's always with me."

Now it was his turn to laugh. "Well, in that case, I don't know whether I'm glad there's at least two of us in this club or sad there is someone else who lives this life." He was mostly relieved he hadn't sounded like a total raving lunatic but he left that part out. "I'm Jake, by the—"

"You've arrived," a disembodied voice interrupted him.

They both snapped their heads forward at the sound of the metallic voice. It took him a minute to remember that "you've arrived" meant they had pulled up to San Francisco International. Half an hour couldn't have gone by. It had only felt like five minutes.

"Are you getting out?" she asked.

"Hey, that's my line," he replied. It garnered a small chuckle from her as she got out of the car and headed toward the trunk. Jake scrambled out after her. He made a move to get her suitcase out of the trunk. "Here, let me—"

She held up her hand, stopping him short. "I've got it," she said as she hauled her own bag out of the trunk.

Unsure of what to do, he reverted to the business version of himself and held out his hand. "It was very nice to meet you. Hopefully, I'll see you again sometime."

She looked at him again, her shining emerald eyes boring into him like they had before. She took his hand in a firm, practiced way. A perfectly businesslike clasp, and yet it didn't feel that way. They lingered like that a moment. Her eyes twitched down to their interlocked hands and then back up at his, her face fixed with a small wisp of a smile. It wasn't the eye crinkling grin of before but something much more somber, any resemblance it had to a smile deflating as she dropped his hand.

"Probably not." And she turned and walked off toward the airport.

Well, that was...something. Jake leaned back in the upholstered lounge chair, sipping at his cocktail and staring out at the tarmac. Despite planes coming and going, the only thing he saw was a replay of the conversation in his mind. He had no other option than to alternately laugh and cringe at his ham-handed attempt to seem like a normal person, much less attempt to flirt with a woman who he found attractive. Cam was right—he had been in his work bubble for too long. He would have loved to say he was just rusty, but the truth of it was he had always been all about work at the expense of his personal life.

Growing up, he had been laser focused on doing things that would help him become just like his dad one day. That meant that the only things he cared about in school were getting good grades and padding out his extracurriculars with things like Future Business Leaders of America. Any moments that weren't allocated to that pursuit involved him following his dad around like a shadow, and his dad had been thrilled to oblige.

Richard Jacoby Masterson Sr. had taught him everything about his business. Since it was just the two of them, his dad had treated him like a mini-executive, just as much as he treated him like a mini-me. Jake had been along on every work trip and had been in way more board meetings than a kid had any right to be. His dad ensured he was outfitted in tiny suits, had his own fountain pens, a miniature briefcase, business cards, and even his own kid-proportioned leather office chair that raised up extra high so that he could see over the giant conference table. He still kept the chair in his office. Jake laughed at the memory of his dad starting EtaSella twenty years ago. *Thank god I talked him out of calling the competition Tiny Chair.* The reminiscence felt like a faint glow, something he hadn't looked back on in so long that it was starting to dim. Jake wished he could call his dad up in this moment and tell him about today. Hear his laugh again when he told him how bumbling he had been and get his advice. *I wonder what he would say.*

Through the years, they had talked about everything—stocks, profit and loss statements, networking, and even capital adjustments—but they definitely hadn't talked about girls.

Hell, after his mom died, he hadn't seen his dad interact with any woman romantically, so in his quest to be just like him, young Jake had thought that he shouldn't have an interest in girls either, which lasted roughly until late high school, at which point he realized that girls might be something other than schoolmates and rivals in young-entrepreneurship competitions.

But as interested as he was, things never really worked out. He was always business first, which meant he upset just about everyone in his life who wasn't a shareholder, a board member, or an employee, and particularly the women who had been in his life. In the last few years, business had gotten even crazier, which meant he had gotten even busier, so he had just stopped trying. He could only stomach disappointing so many people at a time.

Yet, meeting this woman today reminded him of two things. The first was that he was still a very awkward kid at heart, and the second was that maybe there were beautiful women out there who would understand where he was coming from and wouldn't begrudge him being busy. But clearly, nothing was going to change anytime soon. He chuckled, shaking his head in resigned acceptance. *Just my luck that the first woman I meet outside of work is the last woman I am ever going to see again.*

Three

IZABELLE

Backspace. Backspace. Backspace. Izabelle smacked at the keyboard in frustration. She sat staring at her screen, furiously clicking on her trackpad, deleting the graphics she had just added to her pitch. They just didn't look right. None of it looked right.

Coming out here early was supposed to help break my mental block, not make it worse. She couldn't even count the multitudes of things she had added and deleted from the slides at this point. All the numbers were there, but she couldn't for the life of her decide on the best way to present them to the investors.

Dropping her head in frustration, Izabelle shifted her gaze from her screen on the small wooden desk to the subtly chevron-patterned carpeting. Hanging her head pulled at the knots that had formed in her shoulders. That's what she got for having them hunched up around her ears all morning while she typed. She rolled her head side to side, looking at the room that was serving as her temporary dining room, office, and bedroom. It was certainly more stylish than her apartment.

Hand-hewn beams accented the ceiling and complemented the mission-style furniture that concealed the minibar and housed a 4K TV. Ultra-fluffy duvets of crisp white linen were capped with hand-woven Navajo blankets perfectly draped at the foot of the bed. The effect clearly communicated southwestern luxury. But the chic iron-and-leather chair beneath her butt didn't feel like luxury. It was much more fashion than it was function. She considered grabbing a bed pillow to sit on for the fifth time today. *Come on, Izabelle, keep grinding.* She rolled her head backward and forward, trying to work the knots loose. *Just push. One slide at a time. You can do this. Ergonomics of this chair be damned.*

The buzzing of her cell phone interrupted her half-hearted internal pep rally. She had placed it on the nightstand, away from the desk, in order to avoid distractions. Now it was just annoyingly far away. *Damn.* She hobbled over to it, her legs half asleep thanks to the world's worst office chair. She got the phone on its last ring, sliding it open as she flopped on the bed.

"Do you miss us yet?"

"How is it going?"

"We hope you're not just working!"

Izabelle heard all three of her friends shout through the receiver at once, clearly trying to overcome the noise of a restaurant. The low din of patrons and plates was clear along with the sound of something that sounded like...parrots? "Where are you guys right now?"

"After talking about your vacation yesterday, we were jealous, so we all decided to take a long lunch and go get some vacation-y drinks at Paper Umbrella," Sabrina supplied.

Paper Umbrella? It sounded vaguely familiar. "Wait. You mean the tiki bar downtown?"

"Yep!"

Explains the parrots. "They're open for lunch?"

"Yeah! We figured that is as tropical as we're going to get without leaving the city. Did you know there's a full-size pool in here? They have a floating stage on it sometimes," Sabrina said.

"Where are you right now?" Ava asked.

"I'm in my room. The bed, specifically," Izabelle replied, throwing a hateful glance at the chait.

"Please tell us it's a man that has you in bed in the middle of the afternoon," Charlie said.

With a simultaneous laugh and sigh, Izabelle responded, "Sorry to disappoint, but there isn't anyone here."

"Damn. I had a long-shot bet on 'met a sexy stranger on the flight and fell into bed with him immediately.'"

Izabelle's mind flashed to her ride to the airport. His face appearing in her mind easily. The image of his dark hair swooping back from his forehead, the light blue eyes, the cut of his jaw, covered in light stubble. It was as clear as if he were sitting in front of her. "I did sit next to a very attractive man in the rideshare on the way to the airport."

"How hot are we talking?" Ava asked.

"Hot enough for me to actually look up from my phone and admire the view rather than my pitch presentation for a few minutes," Izabelle responded.

"Jesus. I didn't know a man could be that hot," Charlie quipped. "Did you get his number?"

It wasn't worth going into the details about the ride. How it had been layered with levels of interest, awkwardness, and brief connection over their work-life balance. Like they had both been caught off guard by the other and weren't fully sure how to act. Trying to explain how she knew it wasn't going to go anywhere but had spent last night dreaming about something other than spreadsheets and slides for the first time in a year was way more complexity than she wanted to get into right now.

"Nah. I knew there was no chance I'd ever see him again, so I didn't even bother."

"There is definitely no way you're going to see him again with that mindset," Ava said.

"And that is exactly how I like it," Izabelle replied, putting a period on that portion of the conversation. There wasn't much use in worrying about what *could* have happened when she was already so worried about what *needed* to happen. This call was distraction enough. It wasn't like she needed a man to add to it. She paused, not wanting to hang up but knowing she should. "Alright, I have to get back to it. I was just taking a break to answer your call. It was the first time I stepped away from the project since I got here."

"What?" Sabrina asked, incredulous.

"I said I'm just—"

Sabrina immediately interrupted. "No, I *heard* you. It's lunch, for god's sake—it's not like any of us are drunk. But why the hell are you working in your room right now? I'm personally offended that you aren't enjoying the resort as we speak. We're looking at a pool we can't swim in, in a dark bar, in a very foggy and cold city, while on a break from work. You need to go outside for all of us."

"Well, I have to—"

"Have you even *seen* the pool?" Charlie asked.

"No, I—"

Ava picked up where Sabrina and Charlie had left off. "Have you even been *outside*?"

"No. I got here late, it was already dark, and then I've been working in the room because I have to—" Izabelle couldn't even finish her defense before Sabrina cut her off.

"Errrr. No. Stop. Wrong answer. What you have to do is put on your bikini and get your ass to the pool."

"Besides," Charlie chirped in the background, "you're looking too pasty anyway. You'll present better if you have a little bit of color." Izabelle thought that was particularly rich coming from Charlie's Irish Catholic ass but decided not to engage. She knew she wasn't going to win this one over the phone.

"Put sunscreen on!" Ava screamed from the background.

"All in favor of Iz going to the pool and drinking for us in spirit, say 'Aye.'"

"Aye!" they all shouted in unison.

Izabelle could hear how pleased Sabrina was in her voice. "See? We've voted, and we insist that you go get a drink at the pool."

"Pics or it doesn't count!" Ava said.

"Good god. Are you all thirty or thirteen?" Izabelle laughed.

"Pool! Pool! Pool! *Pool*!"

She could hear them banging the table on the other end. "Fine! I give in. Just stop terrorizing the bar!"

"Okay, go now!"

"Love you!"

"Bye!"

She heard all of them yell over each other before hanging up. They were probably right. Her eyes were starting to cross from staring at the screen and her butt could use the break. If she was going to spend all this money to be here, she might as well go take a lap and see what she was paying for. *I'll just go take one picture to placate them and come right back in.*

∼

Twenty minutes later, Izabelle was blinking rapidly, pleading with her eyes to adjust quickly to the natural light outside. She recognized it was tough on them to look at anything other than an LED screen, but she only had so much time. It had taken her longer than she thought to dig out her bikini, decide that she wasn't ready for the bikini, proceed to dig out her cover-up, and walk down to the pool. She had used even more time taking a detour through the lobby to snag a book as a prop in the hopes of making this fake-break photo look convincing, so she really need to wrap this up.

Eyes finally adjusting to the light, she stepped out onto the pool deck, taking in the scenery for the first time since she arrived. She was immediately overwhelmed. *Google really doesn't do this place justice.* She would have normally described scenery as "it's nice" or maybe, if it was particularly notable, "super-pretty," but this was on a different level. The interplay between the hotel and the surrounding landscape wasn't just complementary; it was a dance. The modern hotel took its cues from the ancient rock cliffs that surrounded it. The burnt-orange adobe of the hotel curved and undulated as it mirrored the ochre red of the rugged canyon. The cool blue of the cloudless sky mimicked the serene turquoise of the pool. Modern glass reflected jagged peaks, the matte-black steel supports a partner of the deep rust colored bands in the sandstone, and wooden accents echoed the incredible greenery that she hadn't expected to be so dense in a desert. It was only the perfectly positioned chaises, stretching out in an orderly row around the pool, that interrupted the seamless effect between the wild desert and cultivated luxury.

The girls were right. I really was missing out. She slid off her sandals and eased back onto the terry cloth-covered slats of a chaise. Izabelle sighed as the sun embraced her in its warmth. After days, or rather, years, of hunching over a keyboard in front of the perpetual blue light of a screen, stretching out in the golden light of the Arizona sun felt like an indulgence. Izabelle sighed again and closed her eyes. Between the travel and the fruitless effort on the presentation today, her energy was more zapped than she cared to admit. She was fighting the urge to go back inside and stick to the grind just as much as she was fighting to enjoy herself in this rare moment of relaxation. The tension was exhausting.

She opened her eyes to see a hotel employee in white embroidered polo tucked into navy shorts, pressed to perfection, holding out a menu. "Would you like something to drink?"

She took the perfectly timed interruption as a sign. She could let herself enjoy a few minutes in the sunshine before she went back inside. "You know what? I would. I'll have...something...vacation-y." She chuckled, thinking back to Sabrina's use of the phrase.

"Vacation-y?" the waiter said with an expression that pleaded for something more concrete.

"Fruity. Something with a paper umbrella." She suppressed a smirk, knowing that he wouldn't get the joke.

"Of course. Would you like me to get it for you now, or will someone be joining you?"

This question was why she always got takeout instead of eating in a restaurant alone. The dreaded "table for one" question. She never had a good answer, so she went with the first thing that popped in her head. "I'm afraid that my life choices have pretty much guaranteed that someone won't be joining me."

"Oh," he said, visibly taken aback. "Okay, well, I will be right back with that, then."

The poor kid clearly hadn't been expecting that one. It was heavy-handed in the existential dread department, but it was true. Izabelle settled back into the chair, glancing down at the phone in her hand, then leaned her head back to catch a couple more rays of sun. *One sip, a quick photo, and it will be back to business as usual.*

Four

JAKE

Jake reached over and took his phone off the charger, checking the screen. Nothing. It was unnerving that he hadn't heard the ever-present "ping" of his email notifications since he had left for the airport the day before. He clicked on the mail icon; there had to be something. But there wasn't. *Hmm.* He padded over to his bag and pulled out his laptop, returning to the couch. He scoured through his inbox. Nothing new. Nothing that needed him. Nothing marked URGENT. Suspicious, he fired off an email to Cam.

Subject: No Incoming Messages
Cam,
Is the network down? I'm not getting anything in.

The second he closed the laptop, he heard the familiar ping from his phone.

> **Subject: re: No Incoming Messages**
> The network is up and running. Business as usual. You, however, are not supposed to be. You are on vacation. Be on vacation. The emails are being diverted. I promise that the business can still run without the boss-man.
> -Cam

Grumbling, he began typing out a message but was interrupted by a new email notification taking over the screen.

> **Subject: re: No Incoming Messages**
> Save your fingers. I know that the email was about to start with 'Cam!' and then dribble on about how you need to be apprised of everything that's going on because it's your name on the door… blah blah… Responsibility… blah blah… I'm a workaholic and can't admit it… My entire identity is centered around my work…blah blah.
> I know for a fact the pool is great. I know that because you told me about it. Multiple times. Go there. I will continue to hold your emails hostage and keep you locked out of the network no matter what you say. You need this break. Take it. If anything goes sideways, you'll be the second to know. As always, I'll be the first.
> -Cam

"Well then," Jake sighed. "I guess that's that." He sat back into the couch, staring idly at the slowly rotating ceiling fan. It bothered him a bit that Cam had locked him out, but he knew she was trying to get him to actually unplug. It came from a place of caring, even if it was inconvenient. But no matter how inconvenient, he knew better than to dig in with Cam. She had proven time and time again she wasn't going to budge. She'd been especially insistent he take this trip and actually try and enjoy it. So, enjoy it or not, without access to the network, there wasn't much he could do.

There was one big problem though. *I'm not sure I know what to do with myself without work.* He sat there, absorbing the reality of vacation. He was at a resort, alone, with a big pile of nothing to do. *Shit. It's going to be a long week.* Was this what people called relaxing? Relaxing to him was having only four meetings and a few dozen emails to respond to. Having absolutely nothing to do hadn't crossed his mind since he was five years old. Not having to work was stressing him out—he should have at least brought a stack of books. He had heard the new one about the Dassler brothers was good, that it really detailed how their falling-out led them to create rival businesses in Puma and Adidas.

Cam's likely right about me being a workaholic. Even the books I want to read are about corporations. He was not looking forward to ten days of this. *I need a drink.*

A short stroll through the gardens later, he unlatched the gate to the pool and sauntered toward the nearest group of loungers. His butt had barely made contact when a waiter approached.

"Hello, Mr. Masterson, so glad to have you with us. What can I get you?"

He sat up formally at the sound of the name. It had taken

him a while after his dad passed to realize that when people said "Mr. Masterson," they now meant him, not his father. In the years since, he had learned to respond, to put his hand out and make introductions, but he couldn't say he had ever really gotten used to it.

"I appreciate you trying to be formal, but Mr. Masterson was a better fit for my father. Please call me Jake."

"Absolutely, Mr. Ma—" The waiter visibly caught himself. "Jake. I can let the rest of the staff know your preference if you would like."

"That sounds great. Thank you." He had to give it to this place. The service was always top-notch, and the people were always a class act. Dad knew how to pick 'em.

The waiter nodded in understanding. "Can I interest you in a drink? We have soft drinks as well as beer, wine, and cocktails."

"Let's start with a beer. And we'll see where we go from there."

"Absolutely. I'll be right back."

Jake leaned back into the lounger and surveyed the scene. The red rock around him was familiar, and the familiarity was calming. He shouldn't have been surprised. The canyon cliffs hadn't changed in thousands of years; it wasn't like they would have drastically changed in the last five or so. But still. Knowing that this resort, the view, and the warm sun hadn't changed when so much of his life had was more comforting than he would have guessed.

Yet, as interesting as the landscape was, it couldn't hold his attention for every hour of the next two weeks. As much as he was itching to go to the concierge and have them order him a stack of books, he decided he should at least try and stick it out at the pool until his drink came back.

He chuckled to himself. *I should attempt small talk with a stranger again since it's clear I need the practice.* It was a ridiculous thing to think, but clearly, it was true. That car ride yesterday made it plain as day that after years of not socializing outside of work, he barely remembered how to do it.

He scanned the rest of the resort-goers, looking for someone approachable, but the pickings were slim. There was a couple holding hands on side-by-side loungers, who were so into each other he doubted they would even notice if he approached, much less want to chat with a random guy trying to be an impromptu third wheel. There were two older men who appeared from their hand gestures to be armchair quarterbacking a football game from last week. Traditional sports weren't his thing, so that was going to be a pass. His eyes settled on a brunette woman about his age who had a death grip on her cell phone and a tote bag with the logo of a Silicon Valley cryptocurrency company. *Now, that's much more my speed.*

He stood and headed across the patio area. He smoothed back his hair, hating that he felt nervous. *You talk to people all the time. This shouldn't be this big of a problem.* But after bungling the interaction yesterday, he wasn't keen to make a repeat performance. But as he got nearer to her, he stopped up short.

No. Fucking. Way. It couldn't be, and yet he knew. He recognized the face. A face that was burned so deeply into his mind he would have recognized it anywhere. *It's her.* Somehow, the universe was giving him a chance to redeem himself.

"Hi," he said, standing back a bit from the foot of her

chaise. She didn't say anything. "Looks like we're sharing a hotel as well as a back seat." He again got nothing but silence. *I deserve that.* He tried again. "I apologize for being so awkward in the car. I feel like we might have started off on the wrong foot." He took another step forward, crouching slightly to see if he could catch her eye behind her sunglasses. It was then he realized he wasn't going to catch her eye at all. They were closed. She was asleep.

He stepped back, resurveyed the scene, and laughed. He really should have noticed she was asleep well before he had. The drink next to her, which seemed like it had been some sort of fruity concoction, had melted and separated. It was now more science experiment than cocktail. A book had fallen off the chair onto the ground beside her. Her grip was still tight on her phone, but she clearly wasn't looking at the screen. Her sunglasses had slid up her face, where they were stopped by her eyebrows, and her head had slightly flopped to one side.

Emboldened, he stepped directly next to the chair and loudly cleared his throat. "Excuse me, miss. Can I get you another?"

Five

IZABELLE

Izabelle woke up with a start at the sound of a voice next to her and with the terrible feeling that she had no idea where she was. Backtracking in her mind, she alternated winking one eye open and then the other. She must have fallen asleep on the pool deck, hard.

"What?" she asked, disoriented.

"Can I get you another?"

The voice was male. Deeper than the last voice that had been here but undeniably pleasant, sexy even. *Jesus. How long was I asleep?* Blinking, she slowly tilted her head to the left to see the melted remains of what looked to be a frozen daiquiri. *I guess it was a while, then.* More awake now, she rolled her head toward the flip-flopped feet to whom the voice must belong. *I should probably answer him before he asks again.*

"Considering that I didn't even start that one—" Izabelle's sentence and eyes came to a halt so fast she was sure she heard the squealing noise of brakes outside of her head as well as in it. It was him.

"It's—It's...*you!*" Izabelle looked around, verifying that she was actually still awake and that her dreams from last night hadn't bled into her catnap, because good lord did he look dreamy. His linen shirt was unbuttoned at the collar and rolled up to the elbows, showing off a much more muscular physique than she had originally guessed. His hair was more tousled than yesterday and his scruff a bit more apparent.

"Yes! Hi." He pointed at himself. "Jake. We met in the rideshare yesterday."

As if I would forget the hottest guy I've seen in ages. "Yes, I remember." She paused, running the last few moments back through her mind. Remembering that when she woke up, she had thought he was a waiter. "Do you work here?" She had thought he said he worked in San Francisco and he was going on vacation, but perhaps she had misunderstood what he had meant in the car.

"Um, no," he said.

"Didn't you ask me if I wanted another drink?"

"I did." He shifted his weight uncomfortably. "But I don't work here."

"Oh." Izabelle was still confused. "So, what are you doing here?"

His face took on a chagrined expression. "Funnily enough, I thought after bungling the conversation with you in the car yesterday that I should work on my small talk with strangers. I saw your bag and figured I would have something to talk to you about, not realizing you were *you*. But then I saw you were asleep, and somehow, inexplicably, the only thing I thought to do was to pretend like I was a waiter? Instead of just—I don't know—walking away, or saying hello, or asking if you wanted a drink like a normal person?" He ran a frustrated hand through his hair. The awkwardness she had seen in the car becoming apparent again. "I'm realizing now that I'm completely shitting the bed on this conversation, yet again, and this entire idea was not well thought out." He ended his speech by resting his brow bone in his hand, obscuring his face.

Izabelle laughed. She got the distinct impression that he desperately wished he was playing this more cool. But she had to admit, it was incredibly charming. Seeing a man this handsome get this caught up in his streams of thought was the opposite of what she would have expected. He didn't give off that overly practiced vibe so many people she met in the corporate world did. Between his overshares, his palpable frustration, and his verbal missteps, he came across as one of the most authentic person she had met outside of her friends. And she couldn't lie, it was working for her. "I meant what are you doing at this resort, but good to know why you came over to chat." She couldn't help but giggle as she unfurled a smile.

Jake shook his head, tilting it back slightly as he laughed in return, his smile flashing wide as some of the tension seemed to roll off him. "I don't know if it's you or me or what. I mean, it's definitely me, but I swear to god I didn't use to be this bad at talking to people." He gestured to the lounger next to her. "May I sit?"

Izabelle nodded. "Of course."

He sat on the lounger, keeping his feet on the ground so he could look directly at her as he spoke. "If you would be so kind as to let me start over, and I mean all the way over, I would really appreciate it."

She nodded, amused at his earnestness.

He held out his hand. "Hi, I'm Jake."

She looked at his outstretched hand, the memory of their handshake at the airport snaking into her mind. She placed her hand into his, and just like before, she felt an uncharacteristic zing at the way his hand wrapped around hers, his strong knuckles encircling her palm. "Izabelle."

"Izabelle." He repeated her name as he glanced down at their hands, then back up to her face. The warmth of his gaze matched that of his grip. "It's really great to see you again." A recognition flashed between them that they were both holding on to this handshake just a little too long. He dropped her hand and continued. "Anyway, I'm here at this resort because I used to come here back in the day. My assistant convinced me that I needed to try and unwind from work, which thus far has been a miserable failure. How about you?"

Izabelle couldn't help but smile in return. "Ha. I'm the opposite. I'm here trying to get my head into work and thought a change of scenery would help. It has similarly not been particularly successful so far." She glanced down at the phone in her hand, and her stomach sank when she realized how much time had passed. "Which reminds me, I should really get back to it."

"Oh," Jake responded with a twinge of what sounded like genuine disappointment. "I'm guessing that means you don't want another drink, then." Izabelle shook her head. He gave her a small smile in response. "Would it make a difference if I assured you that a qualified professional would be getting it and not me pretending to be one?"

Izabelle laughed. "It's not really so much that I don't want to, it's that I can't. I was just out here to take a quick photo to placate my friends." Jake looked at her quizzically. "They were on my case about doing something fun while I was here, so I was going to show them I actually did go out to the pool at their request."

He nodded. "Ah. I understand."

Izabelle stood up from the chaise to leave, an unexpected feeling of disappointment registering with her too. Turning down invitations had become so automatic at this point that she didn't even process any details about the invite before she answered "no." The words "I can't. I have to work" had become de rigueur, and that didn't usually bother her. But this interaction and, come to think of it, the one in the car before were...different.

"You did say this trip was strictly business," Jake said as he stood up, pulling her focus. "But it was a pleasure meeting you, Izabelle. Both times. If you happen to take any other breaks..." He shrugged. "Well, I just hope that I see you around again."

Him saying her name and pleasure in the same sentence jolted her body into action. She heard herself say, "I do have to eat though," as if she was suddenly a disembodied voice and it wasn't her own throat making the noise.

"What?" Jake responded.

"I-I can't have a drink now. But I do have to eat dinner, eventually. Do..." Now it was her turn to be bashful. "Would you like to have dinner with me?"

"Yes," Jake responded without a second of hesitation, his smile lighting up his face again. "Which restaurant?"

"Just the one here at the hotel."

"This hotel has three restaurants."

"Oh." She really hadn't googled this place enough before coming here. "Well, whatever is quickest is fine."

A brief moment of heat sparked in his eye. "If I'm only going to get one more shot at this, I would rather not make it quick."

Oh. Izabelle's body certainly caught and appreciated the look, even if her mind wasn't fully on board. "Oh, I wasn't—" She was about to say, "intending this to be a date" but then stopped up short, because maybe she actually did want it to be a date. Maybe not. Did she?

He must have sensed her hesitancy. "I just meant that I seem to be less awkward the longer we talk and that I will gladly take as much time as you have to give. But I'm not looking for anything other than that."

"Okay, where do you want it to be?"

"Cliffside. Eight o'clock."

Turning to leave, Izabelle's body took over for her mind again as she threw Jake a look over her shoulder. "It's a date."

Six

JAKE

Jake swirled the amber liquid in his glass, clinking the ice around and around. He was early. He had already confirmed he was early by checking his watch a dozen times. But it didn't hurt anything to check again. 7:45. *Shouldn't have made it 8:00. This is way too long to wait.* He drummed his fingers against the smooth wood grain of the bar. He replayed their interaction by the pool this afternoon as a way to pass the time. He smiled into his whiskey at the memory.

"Thank god you didn't stand me up."

Startled, he turned toward her voice. He shifted his frame and his chair to make room for her at the bar. As he did so, he saw her in full.

Holy god. Here she was, wearing a dress that looked like it was melting off her, with nothing but the thinnest of straps holding it up. "You're stunning," he said, meaning it, deeply. She smiled a close-lipped smile, shrugging off the compliment with a dip of her head.

"You're early," Izabelle replied.

"Seems like that's a shared state."

"You know what they say, if you're not early—"

"You're late," Izabelle finished for him. They stared at each other, a mix of heat, flirtation, and a dash of awkwardness swirling between them. Izabelle's eyes flicked to the bartender, who was now staring at them as they stared at each other.

The glance jolted Jake from his reverence. "Can I order you another daiquiri? I think that's the poor drink that you neglected earlier."

"Ha, no. It's really not my style."

"You gave me a second chance. Why not the daiquiri?" he asked.

"To be fair, I zonked out before I even had a sip of the thing. So, it got neither a first nor a second chance. You, on the other hand, are on your third chance. But I'll take a manhattan if your offer extends to other drinks."

"Of course." Jake turned to the bartender, who nodded in response.

"Can you deliver it to our table, please?" Izabelle asked the bartender. "I was promised dinner," she said, grinning in Jake's direction.

"And dinner you shall have," Jake said, rising. "After you." He couldn't help but sneak a look as she walked away, making a mental note that the back of her dress was just as flattering as the front. *I don't know what I did to get this lucky but thank you universe for the second chance.*

Arriving at the table, he stepped behind her to pull out her chair. He was very aware of the fact that he couldn't start stream-of-conscious talking at Izabelle like he had done in their last two interactions. She may be great, but there was only so much anyone could take before he came across as truly weird. And after Cam's comments in the office, he had apparently been closer to that line than he thought. As he came around to his own chair, she asked him something from across the table. Her sentence took a second to land amid the swirl of thoughts in his head. "Uhhhh, sorry, what?"

"Did you manage to get any relaxing in after I left?" she repeated, looking up from her menu.

"Oh god, no. I had a full early afternoon of being anxious about a client deal that I didn't wrap before I left, a late afternoon of frustration that I couldn't get my mind off said client deal, and a jam-packed early evening of worrying that I would be too worked up about both of those things to be in the right headspace to see you again, which culminated in me getting ready too early and sitting at the bar, waiting for you to arrive." He hoped that wasn't too much to say, but her laugh was reassuring. "How about you? I genuinely hope that you had a more productive afternoon than I did."

Izabelle screwed her face up. "Eh. Not exactly. I was hoping to a be a lot further along than I am."

Jake felt a bit crestfallen. As excited as he was to get to know her better, she had clearly said this was a work trip, and he knew the feeling of being pulled away from a project. "I'm sorry. If you want to keep this short and get back to it, I understand."

"No, no." She looked down at her menu again. "I spent hours staring at it this morning without making any progress, so I can hardly blame you for not making any headway this afternoon." She caught his eye. "I also might have been a little nervous about tonight."

Jake was surprised by that. Up until this point, she had

always been the self-assured foil to his self-conscious mess. He had literally come to the bar forty-five minutes early in the hopes of smoothing over the rough edges of his nerves, but he didn't get that vibe from Izabelle. "Really? Why?"

Izabelle cast her gaze around. "Ummm."

"You don't have to answer if you don't want to."

"No, it's just—I haven't actually been on a date in a while, and...I guess I'm kind of embarrassed to admit that."

Relief washed over him. "Izabelle, please do not be embarrassed. I haven't been on a date in three years."

"Seriously?" He could hear the incredulity in her voice as she looked at him in disbelief.

"Seriously. Clearly, I don't do much socializing outside of the office." He gestured to himself with his hands, a rueful smile playing at his lips. "Hence the rambling sentences and thoughts."

Izabelle let out a giant exhale, her head falling all the way back. "Oh, thank god. I haven't been on one in two years, and I have no idea what I'm doing."

They looked at each other for a long moment and then cracked up. She was clearly just as relieved as he was. The tension he was holding all over his body started to unwind.

"But seriously. Three years? I find that extremely hard to believe. You're—I mean, look at you."

Jake could feel Izabelle's gaze run over him in a way that made him wish it were more than just a gaze.

"Oh, believe it. Literally an hour before I met you, my assistant, Cam, had a conversation with me that I was turning into a weirdo because all I talk about is work." He saw Izabelle snort into her glass at that comment. "I assure you that her bringing it up did not help the matter. Hence all the word dumps I've put on you in all of our conversations. I've been really in my head since she said that."

Izabelle smiled at him. "The good news is I always knew what you were thinking."

Jake smiled back at her and the warmth that was building between them. "But what about you? It's equally hard for me to believe that men aren't falling over themselves to take you out."

Izabelle visibly blushed at that. "It's not that no one has tried. It's just that every time I put myself out there, they inevitably get upset that I'm so focused on my work and in the words of every guy I've been with 'I don't have time for them,'" Izabelle said with a sigh, resting her head in her fingertips. "Scheduling things is a nightmare."

"Exactly." Jake felt an immediate connection to her words. "I always end up in the same argument where they are upset I have to spend time outside of 'work hours'—which to me aren't even a thing—doing business-related things and just straight up working, and therefore can't be with them all the time."

Izabelle leaned forward. "I don't get how I can explain to people that this is the way I pay the bills, and this is the time commitment it takes to make it work, that I've put my entire life into it. So I'm not just going to stop because you want to watch TV on a random Tuesday night."

Jake was incredulous at how similarly he felt. "It's like you're pulling quotes straight out of my head."

Izabelle sat back in her chair again. "Wow, it's so nice to talk to someone that gets it."

"You have no idea." As strange a topic as this was for a date, Jake couldn't be more glad they were talking about it. It was the same connection they'd had in the car sparking up again. The first sparks he had felt in as long as he could remember.

Izabelle held up her glass as a toast, still giggling from their revelation. "To absolutely shitty work-life balances."

"I'm not going to toast to that," Jake said, raising his glass but holding it back from Izabelle's. She tilted her head in confusion. "To all the people that didn't understand before, and to finding ones that do."

A huge grin broke across Izabelle's face, and her eyes twinkled. "I will abso-fucking-lutely cheers to that." She enthusiastically clinked her glass against his.

After the revelation about their similar lack of dating prowess, the entire mood of the evening shifted. The conversation felt freer. Jake didn't feel like he had to be so on edge or constantly worried about saying or doing the wrong thing. They were able to chat through the regular small talk, order their entrées, and eat without the awkwardness that had plagued him earlier. Jokes about San Francisco stereotypes and bad dates flew back and forth with ease. Trips they had taken because of work and trips they hadn't taken for the same reason.

"So how many times have you been here?"

Jake sat back with a slow exhale. "At least a dozen. I used to come here roughly once a year with my dad for his work, and then eventually for my work, so I'm finding it increasingly ironic Cam thought it would be a place where I could actually unwind."

"That does sound like a rather uphill battle."

"I suspect that's why she locked me out of the network."

Izabelle looked at him quizzically, setting down her glass.

"I'm sorry, what? What do you mean locked you out of the network?"

"She manages my passwords, and she changed them so I can't log in remotely." Jake rested his head in his hand.

"And you're okay with that?" Izabelle asked, her voice ticking up.

"I, reluctantly, have to say she was in her rights to do it. Cam's title is technically my executive assistant, but she should really be titled half best friend, half VP of Operations and Management because I wouldn't be able to fully function without her. She knows better than anyone how rough it's been lately, and she was pushing me to take a break. So, it may sound like an extreme measure, but clearly she thought it was necessary, and she is rarely wrong."

"Good lord. That sounds like my nightmare." A visible shiver ran over her. "To be clear, not the friends looking out for you part but the someone locking you out part. I work alone for a reason."

"How alone are we talking?"

"Like one-woman-show alone."

Now it was Jake's turn to be stunned. "Really? All by yourself?"

"Really." She nodded, her face a mix of pride and apprehension.

"Well, color me impressed, then," Jake said, lifting his glass in a toast.

"Thank you, thank you." She dipped her head in a mock bow, pleased. "I do get the need to contract and work with good, reliable people though. That's pretty much the entire concept of my business, actually. It's a one-stop shop for entrepreneurs to learn essential business skills, connect with vetted outside professionals, and manage things like invoices and payroll, with the hope that by teaching people what it means to build and run a business they can avoid a lot of the common pitfalls and shady people that prey on those that don't know any better."

"Oh, that's really cool. Do you do the coaching part yourself? Through recorded seminars or something?"

Izabelle screwed her face up into something resembling a slow-moving wince. "I'm more of a numbers person than a people person. I'm trying to expand more into that territory, which from my projections would really grow the business, but it's not something I'm comfortable doing myself. Which is why the presentation I'm working on is both wildly important and pretty much my worst nightmare."

"Oooo, now we're talking. I may be locked out of my own work projects, but no one said anything about digging into other people's. I would love to insert myself into whatever problem you're trying to work out. Heck, if you just want to give me the whole thing, I'll take it over completely." Jake laughed but immediately stopped when he saw Izabelle visibly stiffen and the smile tumble off her face.

"No," she said, her voice both edgy and hollow.

Jake sighed internally. *Well, there goes that hard-won rapport.* "Oh. Yes, of course. I'm sure I wouldn't be of much help anyway. But it sounds really cool."

"It is." Izabelle nodded curtly. She started to look around the room as the conversation died. She twisted the napkin in her lap around in her hand, no longer making direct eye contact with him. "I should probably wrap up soon. I do actually have to get some work done tomorrow." She looked directly at him, an emotion he couldn't quite place dulling her previously twinkly eyes. "This was really nice though."

Jake had known exactly how he had messed up in every conversation moment prior to this one. But now, he was confused. Clearly he had stumbled onto something that upset her deeply for her to be having this reaction, but he didn't know exactly what. "Izabelle. I—" She continued to look at him expectantly. "I'm sorry if I've said or done something wrong. It wasn't my intention. I didn't mean—"

She put a hand up to interrupt him, then moved to scratch her head, flustered. "I just have a lot going on right now. And I just—I should just be focusing on work right now." She stood to leave. Jake hurriedly scrambled out of his seat, taking a step toward her. She smiled hesitantly as she continued. "I let the host know on the way in to have the meal charged to my room. So...yeah." She put her hand out as a handshake. "I really hope you get to unwind a bit while you're here."

Jake took another step toward her, taking her hand and running his thumb over her knuckles. "If the only unwinding I do this trip was this dinner, then it was more than worth it." He knew it was laying it on a bit thick, but it was honest. He had felt more like himself in the past hour than he had in the past year. Despite any early awkwardness, Jake didn't want this to end or her to go and he especially didn't want either of those things coupled with Izabelle being upset.

She bit her lip as she looked up at him. Everything in his body suddenly wanted to see what her lips tasted like.

"Jake." She paused, and he could see the feeling in his body reflected in hers. She hadn't let his hand go, and she hadn't broken their gaze.

"Izabelle?" He wanted to know where she wanted this to go. She inhaled sharply, leaning toward him, but then stopped. When she dropped his hand, he knew she didn't want it to go where he did. He accepted defeat. "It has been a pleasure to get to know you, Izabelle."

She looked up at him with visible sadness in her eyes, paired with a closed-lipped smile. "Good night, Jake." And she walked away from him for the second time.

Seven

IZABELLE

As soon as Izabelle shut the door to her room, she knew she had made a mistake. *What the hell kind of idiot doesn't kiss a man like that?* She looked at herself in the mirror, ruffling her fingers through her carefully curled waves. *This kind of idiot, apparently.* The hair, makeup, and dress she had agonized over had been appreciated, just like she'd hoped. Her stomach had involuntarily zinged at the first words out of his mouth: *"You're stunning."*

She couldn't have written an ad for her dream man any more clearly than Jake was delivering. *Female CEO seeks man who understands her schedule, isn't full of himself, and is transparent about his thoughts and feelings* would have summed up everything she could have wished for. But to have it all wrapped in a blue-eyed, brown-haired, broad-shouldered package was nearly too much to comprehend.

And yet, here she was, back in her room alone. As much as she'd enjoyed dinner tonight, all the parts of her that had felt warm and fuzzy taking in Jake's boyish charm had gone ice-cold when he said, "...give me the whole thing, I'll take it over completely." It had taken everything in her power not to throw up. She knew he had meant it as a joke, but he didn't know that exact scenario had been very real for her. Because that was exactly what Simon had done.

God, she had been so naïve then. From the moment she had arrived at college, she had felt so out of her league. She couldn't connect with anyone else there on what prep school she'd attended, where her family "summered"—a verb she'd quickly figured out meant to take a fancy months-long vacation—or what firms she had interned with in high school. Therefore, she spent most of first semester just trying to hide on the edges of rooms, hoping to blend into the wall.

Simon had approached her at a networking event for people interested in entrepreneurship. He had seemed so put together, so suave, so self-possessed. She had been so attracted to his unflappable confidence. He came from a family of high-powered corporate types and was clearly comfortable working a room full of strangers. He was everything she wished she could be at the time. He would laugh and exclaim how rare she was, and she thought it was because she was funny and that they were connecting. She opened up to him about her ideas for the business she wanted to start, and his interest only grew. She hashed it all out to him, and the desire in his eyes was clearer and clearer.

He had said she was brilliant and that they would make a perfect team. She could do everything behind the scenes, and he would do all of the public-facing things she wasn't comfortable with. The more time they spent together on it, the closer they grew. It made perfect sense when the personal and the professional started to overlap. They were in love, and they were in business, a perfect fifty-fifty team, each person playing to their strengths. But the reality was he had just been playing her. And boy oh boy, he had played her like a fucking fiddle.

It was a year or two after they started dating that they first started looking for more investment. She could still hear his voice in her head. *Okay, so I have an investor who is interested, but obviously, that would mean expanding the board past us and going from fifty-fifty to forty-forty-twenty.* Which of course she had agreed to. That was basic business. Brining on investors meant giving up some control. What she hadn't realized was the person they were expanding the board with was Simon's fraternity brother and a proxy for whatever Simon wanted to do with the business. He moved to expand the board twice more over the next six months with his patsies, each time reassuring her, "*Belle, this is incredible. We're expanding, and people are interested in what we're building. Isn't that what you want? For us to grow?*" He would smile away her worries and make it seem like everything was fine. But she should have known when he came to her a year later. "*You are never going to believe who I just got off the phone with. Coastal Capital. And they want in.*" It had been incredible news. They had put in enough of her savings and his money to get off the ground. Their first investor had given them high six digits; the two they had brought on after that had gotten them into the low millions. Now Simon had Coastal Capital on the line for tens of millions, if not hundreds of millions. "*The only thing is that they want to do a stock split before they'll come on, and they're asking for two board seats.*" Which was unusual. A stock split would give them more shares so they could have more flexibility, but Izabelle hadn't been certain about it. Her percentage had been diluted enough already, and the board had already expanded to five. Which seemed plenty big for a company of their size. Getting Coastal Capital's investment would be a feather in the cap of any company, much less their fledgling one, but why were they eager to invest so much? She had told him something didn't feel right about it. *"Think about it from their perspective, Belle. We are a new company with tons of growth potential. And when it comes to the stocks, they don't want one share for one hundred dollars. They want ten shares for one hundred dollars. It would be like trying to buy a candy bar with a hundred-dollar bill. No one wants the hassle, and they need the flexibility. It's just how these venture capital guys work.* Izabelle laughed to herself darkly. Sure, it made perfect sense when the venture capital guy was actually your uncle and you were setting a trap. But she didn't know that. All she knew was that it felt like they were making big moves together, and that was what she wanted, so she had agreed. She had never assumed someone she trusted, someone she loved, would ever be setting her up.

She only discovered the kinds of big moves he had been making the day it all blew up. He had come to her apartment to pick her up for a fancy dinner. He had told her it was going to be at a swanky restaurant. Now that the business was taking off and it was their six-year anniversary, she had thoughts that maybe he was going to propose that night. He had looked so concerned when she got in the car. He was silent until they pulled up outside of the restaurant. *"Belle, we have to talk. The board is uncomfortable with our relationship."* Which of course it was, seeing as "the board," legal as it may be, was just his college buddies and extended family. She had asked him what that meant. *"They don't want our personal relationship to cloud our professional one. They're threatening to start stonewalling all future decisions."* She had been so blindsided that she didn't know what to do. Stonewalling meant everything they had worked for would start to crumble. A hostile board was every company's worst nightmare. They would just refuse to approve any decision and the company would be paralyzed. At this point, Simon and their company were her entire world. She felt like she couldn't lose him or what they had built. In a moment of romantic stupidity and desperation over the threat of the company stalling, she offered to quit. *"You would do that for me? You're quitting?"* Yes. She wanted this to work so badly that she blindly charged ahead and sacrificed herself for the good of the company. Right there in his stupid car. To prove her love to him and her dedication to her company, to the board. She would never be able to unsee the way the concern melted right off his face. *"Wow. That's incredible. That works out so well. I was going to have to find some sort of pre-textual reason to fire you after I dumped you. This is awesome. Now I don't even have to give you a severance."*

It was an icy, hard slap. She remembered vividly how the world seemed to slow, how her thoughts felt like they were freezing over and locking up. She had asked what he meant. *"It's all so convenient, Belle. I mean, we've had a great run, but you aren't the kind of person that can make it at the top. You had a promising idea, but I'm the one who actually made it a company."*

It hit her then that she had been set up. He had led her by the hand to give away her ideas and her ownership and her entire life up until this point. He had taken everything, and he had done it legally. He had lied to her, manipulated her, but he hadn't broken the law, so he was going to get away with it. She got out of the car and threw up at the valet stand. It crashed into her consciousness what their years together had meant. Nothing.

It still made her sick to her stomach to think about it all. But her rage had fueled her. She created Me-E-O to help educate other start-ups and entrepreneurs on how to protect themselves, how to connect with the right people, how to navigate the business world, and ensure that this kind of thing wouldn't happen to other people. But clearly, the hurt was still there. And she had clammed up at dinner because of it.

She sat down in front of her laptop and sighed. "Still have you though, don't I?" She powered it on, sat down, and clicked into her presentation. "You're just too jealous to let me have any other relationship, aren't you?" She clicked mindlessly through the pitch slides. "If you're going to prevent me from having any kind of human contact, how about you start thinking about being the big spoon at night, huh?"

It was the same dumb series of jokes she always said when dates went bad. She had started doing it after the first date she went on after things ended with Simon. After that "get back on the horse" date tanked, she had come home a little sad and a little drunk and proceeded to flop down on her couch and get more of both with a bottle of rosé. It was that night she first made the joke about being in a relationship with her work, talking to her laptop as if it was a jealous partner. She had kept it up in the years since, and even if it made her seem a touch crazy, it did always make her feel a little better.

Except this time it wasn't working. Her fingers stopped

their aimless scrolling on the trackpad. She let out a deep sigh. *That's because this time it wasn't a bad date.*

～

Roughly seven hours later, Izabelle rubbed her bleary eyes as she placed a pod in the coffee machine. She couldn't exactly say she ever went to sleep last night; it was more like she went into screen-saver mode for a couple of hours, her thoughts bouncing from corner to corner in her brain. Thinking about Simon had stirred her up, but it bothered her even more that after all these years, she would still have the kind of visceral reaction she'd had at dinner. All fun and smiles until the icy-cold remembrance settled over her, the result of an innocent, unknowing joke. She had insisted to her friends that she was over it. But just like Ava had pointed out, as much as she was over Simon, that didn't mean she was over what he did. And based on the involuntary shutdown that happened last night, those wounds still hadn't healed.

It panicked her to think she was at a competition with the goal of bringing investment into her business, and yet when Jake had even joked about giving up a little bit of control, she had freaked out so hard that she had to leave. A large part of her wanted to blame the fact he had said it while they were on a date. A date in which she was very much enjoying herself. After everything that happened with Simon, she'd vowed she wouldn't ever mix love and business again. Jake had gotten too close to that boundary for comfort last night. Yes, that was definitely part of it. But it wasn't all of it.

The coffee machine sputtered out the last of its steaming

hot coffee into her mug. She gathered it up in her hands, feeling the warmth radiate through the cup. Izabelle took a sip, considering the problem in front of her. Variable one: Jake. He was a distraction she didn't need but increasingly wanted. It was a major inconvenience that after all of the time she had wasted dating, she would find someone worth her time when she had none of it to spare. Which brought her to variable two: the presentation. She had put it together and ripped it apart so many times she didn't know up from down with the damn thing. So, now, all she did was stare at it for hours and hours every day. It was a variable compounded by the ticking clock of the competition. Every hour she delayed was another hour closer to when she would have to stand on stage and convince someone to give her and her company money, at the cost of giving up a percentage of control, so she could turn around and hire more people, which would mean giving up even more control. A pattern that Simon had taught her was not in any way ideal, even if she knew it was necessary. It all seemed like too much, and no matter how she arranged the variables, she couldn't get the equation to balance.

Her stress spiral was interrupted by the buzzing of her phone on the dresser. She grabbed it and saw a text from Ava.

Call me when you get a chance. Need to get into your apartment asap.

"Shit." Izabelle dialed the number immediately. "Hey. Ava, what's up? Is everything okay?"

"Yes, of course, why?" Ava answered.

"You just texted me that you need into my apartment."

Izabelle could tell she was speaking more tersely than normal. The coffee hadn't kicked in yet, and she really didn't need a crisis with her apartment right now.

"I know." Ava sounded completely unconcerned. "You sound frustrated. Is everything okay?"

"Ava, what's going on? Did something go wrong or..." Izabelle felt pinpricks of anger starting to form.

"Ahhh. You forgot I volunteered to water your plants, didn't you?"

Shit. She had completely forgotten. Izabelle sighed as the tension unwound from her spine. "I'm sorry, Ava, you're right. I completely forgot. You need the code to the lock, don't you?"

Ava laughed. "Yes I do. Unless you want all of the great progress you made with your fiddle leaf tree to be completely undone in a week."

Izabelle chuckled in response. "God, no. I just got that thing to like me." She shook her head. "Such a temperamental little bitch."

"You're lucky I know you mean the fiddle leaf." They both laughed. "How are you doing, girl?" Ava asked.

"I'm fine," Izabelle lied.

"I'm sorry, but Iz, I'm not buying that. Especially after you just got so spun up over a text."

Izabelle sighed. "There's just a lot going on here."

"I'm walking to the studio. I've got time."

Izabelle blew out a long exhale, considering just how much she wanted to say. "I just—I'm just not making the progress I thought I would be at this point."

"That doesn't mean you won't though. What have you been doing?"

Izabelle put her head in her hand. "I mean, I've been doing what I've always been doing." She paused. "And it's always worked before."

"And I take it now it's not?" Ava asked.

"Not as much as I would like." *By which I mean not at all.*

"Iz. I don't want to overstep here, but as you know, you are the reason I ever had the courage to open my own studio, so you know I already think you and Me-E-O are great. But if everything you've been doing isn't working, then it seems like you're going to have to try something new."

Ava's voice was gentle, but it was hard for Izabelle not to feel defensive. "That's the problem. I don't even know what that would be," Izabelle said.

"You're surrounded by new things. All you have to do is be open to the opportunities they offer."

"As lovely as that sounds, the problem is with every new opportunity there is an opportunity cost. I can't take a bunch of time away from working on my pitch presentation."

"I'm not saying you shouldn't work on it. I'm just saying you may find your muse somewhere other than your desk."

"Hmmmmm." Izabelle knew Ava had a point. She had spent the better part of the last year adjusting, drafting, grinding, and letting the days until the competition dwindle without any real progress. She still had the same slides and the same numbers, just rearranged with different backgrounds and in a different order.

"All I'm saying is that you may need a little more balance than you've been giving yourself. You've been pouring your heart and soul into this, but you haven't been pouring anything into yourself to refill. You can't run on empty forever."

"I wasn't planning to run on empty." Izabelle sat back up in her chair, glowering. "Just fumes."

Ava laughed. "I think we both know there isn't a difference there, but at least you're admitting you're running low."

"Your psychology degree is showing today," Izabelle responded.

"It makes a showing every day, and I know you're just trying to deflect."

Jesus, she's spooky good at that sometimes. Izabelle could hear Ava rummaging around in her bag. "Alright. I'm at the studio now. I'm sorry I have to go, but I do hope that you permit yourself one indulgence today. I think you would be surprised about the impact it has on your productivity."

Izabelle was sorry to hear she had to go. "Thanks, Ava, I'll keep it in mind."

"That's all I ask. Don't forget to text me the code for the lock, okay?"

"I won't. Bye, girl," Izabelle said.

"Bye!" Ava hung up.

Izabelle stood up, processing what Ava had said about running on empty. Her body decided to underscore the point by rumbling with hunger. Izabelle shook her head. "Well. It seems like my indulgence of the day is about to be a big plate of bacon."

Eight
IZABELLE

Now, this is a breakfast buffet. Izabelle made a beeline for the row of silver chafing dishes. They were serving up all of the greatest breakfast hits, along with some less common options that were absolutely her favorite. She piled her plate high with an omelet from the omelet station, a fluffy golden-brown make-your-own waffle, freshly whipped cream from a bowl instead of a can for the waffle, a coffee cake muffin, some fruit salad that blissfully didn't contain any goopy melon, and of course, a mountain of bacon, not too wiggly and not too crisp. As far as indulgences went, this was working out pretty well. She snagged a fresh-squeezed orange juice from the juice bar and then turned to the sunny breakfast room to find somewhere to sit and enjoy.

Spotting a table near the windows, she made a move for it, looking forward to sitting in the sun. Just as she was about to set her plate down, she saw him, two tables over. He was sitting hunched over the table, fingers interlocked, shoulders bunched, and head hanging, taking in a large semicircle of glossy, colorful brochures laid out on the table in front of him. Izabelle froze, unsure of what to do. She had left their dinner—er, date—last night in such a weird place. He hadn't done anything wrong, yet she didn't really want to explain the entire saga that had led to her reacting the way she had. It was a lot, and she didn't know if she could drag it all back up again while maintaining her composure. She still had an emotional hangover from last night and didn't really feel like crying in front of a sexy-semi-stranger-friend today.

Izabelle glanced over at him to see if he had noticed her. He hadn't. He was still staring at the tabletop intently. She could easily take the plate, turn on her heel, walk out of the restaurant, and never say another word to him. She wouldn't have to talk about her company or her Simon baggage, and she could keep working away, distraction-free, and internalize all the lessons that she should be taking away from this fiasco after the presentation when she had some time. Mind made up that slinking away was the right thing to do, she nodded resolutely and took one last, lingering goodbye look at Jake.

He unlaced his fingers and placed his head in his hand, a visible sigh raising his shoulders and dropping them as he exhaled. He hadn't touched a single brochure. She felt an involuntary tug at her insides. *Shit.* Izabelle knew she couldn't just walk away from this. If she did, it just meant Simon was continuing to win. Ava was right. She couldn't keep doing what she had always done and expect anything to change. As the cliché went, that was the definition of insanity. If she went over and talked to Jake, she could prove to herself she was able to work past all these stupid Simon hang-ups. Which was mission critical, considering that if any of those hang-ups boiled up during the presentation or while she was talking to investors, she could pretty much kiss her chances of winning any investment goodbye. Plus, Jake made her laugh, which could count as an indulgence under Ava's refill-your-cup advice, which would in turn help her be more productive later on. Yes. It was definitely one of those two things and not the fact that he looked a little sad sipping at his coffee that made her walk over to him.

"Is this seat taken?"

Jake's head snapped up at the sound of her voice. "Izabelle! Hi," he sputtered into his mug.

"Mind if I join you?" Izabelle asked tentatively. She didn't want to force herself on him after running out last night.

He beamed at her, setting down his coffee mug. "God. Yes, please." Izabelle broke away from his warm gaze to look down at the brochures on the table. She didn't want to mess any of them up if she set her plate down. Jake took in her hesitancy and swiped them all off the table with his arm. "Here. Please. Ignore those."

Izabelle laughed as they fluttered to the floor. "Finally embracing your vacation?" she said, taking the seat across from him.

"I wouldn't say that exactly." His features fell back into the melancholy expression he'd had when she walked up. "Izabelle, about last night."

Crap. She had really been hoping they could ease into this.

Jake rubbed the back of his neck before he continued. "I really wanted to call you and apologize. But then I didn't know your last name or your room number, and I seriously doubt that the front desk was going to give me your room number based on my description of you, so—"

Izabelle cut him off. He looked torn up over this, and she couldn't take it. "Jake, please don't apologize. I'm the one who needs to apologize."

"What?" Jake looked genuinely confused.

Izabelle took in the tortured look on Jake's face. Despite not wanting to address anything from her past, her explanation tumbled out of her mouth. "I don't really want to get into all the details, but suffice it to say, I have a couple of hang-ups lingering around from when people screwed me over in the past, and they flared up last night. I'm trying to work through them, but I suck at it. I know you didn't mean it, but when you joked about taking over my presentation, it hit a nerve. I made a vow to myself that I would keep my personal and professional lives separate. That's why I got upset and left, but that has everything to do with me and nothing to do with you. So please don't apologize for it."

He took her in with a measured look. "I am still deeply sorry. I really had no idea."

Izabelle desperately wanted to push past this. "Thank you, but I'm fine, and I was hoping that we could just forget the whole thing."

Jake's expression immediately hardened. "No."

The floor of Izabelle's stomach dropped out in response. *Shit.* She should have known he wouldn't want to revert to the way things were. Coming over here was a mistake; she should have just taken the bacon to-go. "Oh, yeah, well..." She was readying herself to leave quickly when he interrupted her.

"Izabelle." He said her name in a way that made her now floor-less stomach flutter just a little bit. His gaze pinned her to her chair. "That was the best dinner I've had in years. I'm not going to forget that a single minute of it happened."

"Oh." Izabelle could see the flicker in Jake's eye. She blushed. It seemed like they might be able to get back to fun and flirty after all. "Okay then."

Jake smiled at her. "Okay then."

She looked down at her plate, feeling suddenly bashful. As she did so, the faces of helmet-clad people on zip lines stared up at her from the brochures scattered on the floor. "Soooo, have you decided on what you're going to do today?" Izabelle ran her eyes over the picture of an off-road jeep crawling over a rock. She leaned and picked it up from the floor, setting it on the table. "Seems like you were doing some pretty serious research for someone who's been here as many times as you have."

Jake picked up his coffee cup slowly, like he wasn't ready to change topics just yet. "You aren't the first person to invent holing up in a hotel room and working all day." He took a sip and shrugged. "I haven't seen as much of Sedona as you would think. Especially not as an adult."

"But you said you were here as a kid. With your dad, right? I'm sure you did something other than work." Izabelle took another bite of her bacon. "Unless your dad was big into violating child labor laws."

"Hmmm." Jake sat back in his chair with a long exhale, raising his eyebrows in thought. "It's a good question, actually."

He stared out the window with a glazed expression for a significant period of time. She saw him chuckle at whatever he was remembering. She waved a hand to get his attention. "Hello? Earth to Jake? Did I lose you?"

Jake shook his head like he was clearing it as he leaned

forward in his chair again. "Your question reminded me of something I haven't thought about in a long time. You were right—my dad and I did use to go somewhere near here."

"Based on the look that was on your face, it must be pretty special," Izabelle said.

"It really was." Jake nodded. He looked at her squarely. "You should come see it."

"I don't know..." Izabelle broke off her own sentence, conflicted.

"I know you have a lot going on, and I don't want to pressure you. But I would love to make up for last night. I promise I won't ask about your project, and it isn't far from here, but it is really pretty. We can just take a look and come back. It would take an hour and a half, tops."

Izabelle weighed it out. An hour and a half wasn't that much in the grand scheme of things, especially compared to the hours she had wasted with her lagging productivity. Ava's advice about indulgence echoed through her thoughts. Maybe she could work this morning, and they could go later. She could have a little of each. That was balance right?

"Okay. But I can't go now."

Jake grinned. "When it comes to you, I have all the time in the world. When would you like to head out?"

"I need to work this morning. I'm generally most productive in the first half of the day, so how about..." She paused, thinking of a number that didn't sound too ridiculous. "Two?"

"Two is perfect. It's better to go when it's a little bit warmer anyway," Jake replied.

"Great."

"Great." Jake continued to look at her.

Izabelle felt like she needed to get out while the going was good. They had reestablished something here. She couldn't say exactly what it was, but it was good, and it was something, and she was highly interested in more good somethings. He said he wasn't in a rush when it came to her, so she didn't need to rush either. But she did need to work. At least for the next couple of hours. She stood up with the remnants of her breakfast feast. "Alright. I will see you later, then."

Jake's face lit up. "It's a date."

Nine

IZABELLE

Damn. These shorts are doing wonders for my ass. Izabelle glanced at her reflection, then the clock, then her reflection again. Twisting side to side in the mirror, she was simultaneously thinking, *I'm so glad that Ava made us do all of those squats in her barre classes* and *I can't believe I'm actually listening to her and knocking off early to go hiking.*

But Izabelle was now fully ready to admit she needed to shake things up. She hadn't been able to make any forward progress in the hours since breakfast. She had really been hoping that some waterfall of productivity was suddenly going to bubble up and pour forth into her laptop, but the unfocused, hen-pecked edits she had made were much more like a leaky faucet in need of a fix.

Whatever flow there had been trickled out and dried up well before her "Get Ready for Hike" alarm at 1:15. So instead of working, she had spent an inordinate amount of time brushing, braiding, unbraiding, and then rebrushing her hair before finally settling on a ponytail. *That looks like the right amount of trying without looking like I'm trying to try.*

She glanced at the clock again, anxious and yet excited to get to the lobby. Luckily for her, the indecision about what to wear, coupled with the multiple attempts at a hairstyle, had run out the clock. She checked herself, and the time, once more and headed toward the lobby.

In her rush to get out of breakfast this morning, she hadn't really clarified where they were going or what they were doing. Izabelle had the passing worry that they were about to wander out into the desert to do a live reenactment of *127 Hours*. On the other hand, this wasn't the wilderness of Utah, and Jake had said that whatever they were going to see was nearby, therefore it wasn't that likely that they were going to have to saw any limbs off to escape a rock fall this afternoon. So she wasn't concerned about where they were literally going. Where they were going metaphorically, however, was a slightly different concern.

Her attraction to Jake was complicated in light of everything that was going on. Actually, no, the basis for her attraction wasn't complicated. It was simple. Jake was hot and nice, his initial awkwardness was endearing, and the more he relaxed, the sexier he got. She was drawn to him. And that was the part that was complicated. Where was she going with this? Was this a vacation fling, a potential one-night stand? Or just an afternoon between friends? A person to make herself talk business with? To prove that she could? To prove Simon wasn't living rent-free in her head all these years? She had no idea. But she knew when she was with him, she felt something other than stressed and anxious, and for now, she was just going to keep following that feeling to give her poor brain a break. Just keep following the good. She could figure out the rest later.

Izabelle stepped into the lobby and immediately saw Jake. His back was to her as he was speaking to the concierge. *God damn.* Looking at him made her mind blank out in the equivalent of a wolf whistle. Until this point, he had been mostly covered in sweaters and collared shirts. From the glimpse she saw at the pool, Izabelle knew he had a decent body, but now she really got a look at the structure of his shoulders and lats hulking under his thin athletic shirt. Izabelle's mind flashed the image of her grazing her teeth and lips along the muscular ridges that ran from his neck to his biceps. She wanted to be much more than friendly with that kind of musculature. *God, who knew I was into backs?*

As she came around him, she couldn't help herself. She ran her hand over the ropey sinew of his shoulder blades, hoping that it came off as a casual greeting.

"Alright, Mr. Hiker. What's on the itinerary?" she asked.

"Are you still down for a little adventure?" Jake asked, a hopeful look on his face.

"Absolutely."

"Well then, milady, after you," Jake said, gesturing toward the doors that led to the parking lot. They strolled through side by side, but when Izabelle turned toward the self-park area of the parking lot, Jake didn't follow.

"Didn't you park your car over there?" Izabelle asked, pointing at the parking lot, where she had self-parked the rental car she drove from the airport to here.

Jake held up his hand, where a key fob was dangling from his fingers. "I did. But I figured we would borrow one of the resort's rides. They're a little nicer than your average rental." He swung the key into his hand and clicked the Unlock button. A shiny new Volvo SUV chirped in response.

"This place has cars?" Izabelle asked. *Sabrina was right. I really should have looked into this resort more.*

"It's a new thing they started. I thought it would be a fun addition," Jake said.

As they approached the car, Izabelle swung around to the passenger side. "Should I sit in the back like a rideshare?" she joked as she opened the door to get in.

"I did meet a beautiful stranger in a rideshare once," Jake said, catching her eye.

Izabelle felt her stomach zing at the look. "So weird. That happened to me once too." The zing doubled down when he winked at her in response. She climbed into the passenger seat. "So where are we headed?"

"It's a surprise." He looked at her with a sense of mischief. "But it's not far."

With a shrug, Izabelle resigned herself to the fact that wherever they were going, she wasn't going to know until they got there. They pulled out onto the road that wound down toward Sedona proper. It had been dark when she drove this road up to the hotel from the airport. She could only make out shadowy ridges against the sky at the time. But now, in the full light of day, it was spectacular. The view of the resort spread out 360 degrees around her. She bent down toward the dashboard to take in the tops of the mountains through the windshield. Jake saw her fold herself in half and then clicked open the button for the moon roof.

"Here. So you can see better."

She leaned back to take in the blue sky. "Wow, it's beautiful everywhere here. I really had no idea." The rugged peaks of sandstone still dominated the skyline, but she was most surprised by how dense the greenery was. It was much more forest than it was desert. The road wound through a natural valley and was flanked by ponderosa pines. These trees were tough and gnarled but still thick with pine needles. She looked over to Jake. Another view she was more than happy to take in.

He smiled at her in return. "It's one of my favorite places. I didn't know how much I missed it."

"You said you came with your dad, right? Did you guys always stay at the resort?"

"We did. But it wasn't anything like it is now. Everything around here has been built up a ton since we first started coming." Jake turned left into town. "There certainly wasn't a Whole Foods in the early days. There is one thing that is the same though. I always thought this was the coolest as a kid." Jake pointed out the window at a McDonald's just ahead.

"You thought McDonald's was the coolest?"

Jake let out a small chortle. "Well, actually, yes. I was obsessed with fast food and collecting happy meal toys. But specifically this McDonald's because it was different." He pointed again at the restaurant. "Notice anything?"

Izabelle stared past Jake out the window to where he was pointing. It looked different than your standard McDonald's in that it was a stucco building with a flat roof, but then she saw it. "The M is blue!" The golden arches of the McDonald's M were a bright turquoise blue as opposed to their typical sunny yellow.

"Only one in the world," Jake responded. "The town thought that the yellow would clash with the rock."

"Huh. I guess it would."

Jake gave her an excited grin. "Whether that is true or not, I always insisted that we go there at least once while we were in town. The place we're headed is the other stop I demanded we make."

"What is your dad up to now? If he's like you, I doubt he's retired."

Jake laughed a dark chuckle. "Actually, he's not up to much. He died almost six years ago."

"Oh. God, I'm so sorry." *Way to go, Iz.* She glanced over at Jake's face to see the excitement on it dim into something more distant. She knew the feeling. But it was clearly fresher for him than it was for her at this point.

"Thanks." Jake sighed quietly. "I miss him. But you're right. He would not have taken to retirement well."

Izabelle let them continue on in silence for a bit. She wasn't sure she wanted to get into her backstory and how she related to him on this level. It felt too intimate. But she knew from experience that sometimes it was nice to just sit with your feelings for a moment.

"I actually haven't been back here since he died," Jake said.

Now, that was interesting. "On purpose? Or just by happenstance?" Izabelle asked.

"Hm." Jake tilted his head, clearly weighing her question. "Probably a little of both." He kept his gaze straight out of the windshield. "When he died, I took over the family business, and I got so busy...I think I just let it fall to the wayside. There were so many other things that needed my attention." Jake smiled to himself and was quiet for a moment. "I thought that he had taught me everything about the business and that I could step into his role at any time. What I didn't realize was that stepping into a role is not the same as filling someone's shoes." He glanced over at Izabelle. "He was much, *much* better with people than I am."

Izabelle leaned over on instinct and squeezed his arm. She sensed this wasn't something he talked about often. "You're too hard on yourself. You aren't bad with people."

Jake folded his hand over hers, pinning it to his forearm and running his thumb over the back of her hand. Her stomach flipped at the touch. "I am certainly glad you're so delusional." He gave her hand a playful squeeze.

"Hey!" Izabelle pulled her hand out to give him a playful smack on the bicep.

"Oh, trust me, it's not a criticism. I would still be back there bumbling on the pool deck if it weren't for you," Jake said with a laugh, lightness returning to his demeanor. "And guess what?" He directed her attention out of the windshield. "We're here."

Izabelle read the white letters on the classic brown park entrance sign as they passed. "Slide Rock State Park?"

"Yeah!" Jake said as Izabelle glanced over at him. The excitement was back and vibrating off him as he looked into the canyon in the distance. "This is going to be so awesome. I haven't been here in fifteen years. It's way more official now." Jake paid the day pass rate and pulled into the parking lot.

It wasn't two seconds after he put the car in park that Jake was out of the car, backpack in hand, and coming around to her door. He opened it and extended a hand for her to get out.

"I can't wait to show you."

Izabelle took his hand despite being perfectly able to get out of the car herself. His energy was infectious. When their hands linked, it was as if he transfused the excitement he was feeling into her. She was suddenly thrilled to be seeing this place she didn't know existed until three minutes ago. She hurried to match his pace as he pulled her by her hand across the gravel parking lot toward some scrubby trees.

"Alright, if I remember correctly, this entire valley used to be a farm, and this was the apple orchard."

"Huh. I didn't expect there to be an orchard in the middle of the desert. How do you remember all this stuff?"

"I read anything and everything when I was younger. Including making my dad wait while I read every interpretive sign in the park."

It warmed Izabelle's heart to think of Jake as a little kid going to each of the signs in the park while his dad looked on. "Well, wait, if this is what we came to see, shouldn't we go see some of the buildings, read some of the signs or something?" Izabelle asked as they quick-stepped past some structures that appeared to be part of the historical site.

"I normally would, but I really want to show you the rest of it."

"Rest of it?" As they blazed past picnic tables, Izabelle couldn't help but wonder what else there was to this place. The beauty of the red rocks mixed with the green of the apple trees was more than enough to designate a park for. But as the path extended before them, she saw they were coming up to a set of stairs that descended. Just as they reached the top, Jake let out a triumphant "*Ta-da!*"

About fifty feet down was a creek that cut through a breathtaking canyon. The rocks sloped sharply down to it with a small flat plateau that made a natural stone deck around the narrow creek. Then she saw what was unique about this canyon compared to all the others.

"Slide rock! You slide down it! Like a natural water park." Jake's voice was staccato with excitement. "It's exactly like I remember. Well, they put in better stairs, and there are actual bathrooms now, but other than that, still the same!" The excited little-kid energy from the car was growing stronger now that they were here.

Izabelle looked down at the people sliding through the canyon. They were laughing their heads off like they didn't have a care in the world. She was deeply envious. Plus she was starting to sweat. She wasn't used to being out in the heat. "Damn. I wish you would have told me to bring a swimsuit."

Jake looked crestfallen. "I know. But I know you have to get back to work, so I didn't want to dominate your afternoon. I figured we could just take a look, and then I would take you back."

Izabelle looked down at the canyon and heard the echoes of laughter again. It sounded like more fun than she'd had in a long time. "Well, I don't want to go back right now. So can we go in in our clothes?"

Jake's expression lifted. "Yeah, of course you can. I actually never wore a swimsuit as a kid because I didn't want to tear it up."

"Jesus, how rough is it?"

"It's not, I promise." He sheepishly raised the backpack he was holding at his side. "And if it helps, I brought towels just in case."

"Well, in that case." Izabelle looked at Jake, the creek, and then back again. "It's a race!" She took off down the stairs, leaving Jake and his delighted laugh behind her.

"Last one in buys dinner!" Jake called as he passed her, stripping off his shirt and dropping his backpack on the rocks.

"Who said I'm going to have dinner with you?" Izabelle questioned as they reached the flats and were jogging up toward the top of the slide.

"Is my company that intolerable so far?" Jake said, turning around and jogging backward.

Jesus Christ. Izabelle's eyes delighted in the visual of Jake's body unencumbered by a shirt. To say he was cut was an understatement. She had gotten a preview of the great shoulders and a peek at some sculpted pecs, but the rest of him was ridiculous. Her eyes couldn't help themselves as they raked over his pecs down toward abs that were basically cobblestones on the heavenly highway that was his torso. His hips even came with their own muscly arrows that formed a V, directing her eyes on a nice Sunday drive down south. The only response Izabelle could muster was "No. No it isn't."

"In that case, are you ready for this?" Jake asked, nodding toward the creek.

"Born ready." Izabelle jumped in with both feet and felt all of the air leave her body as her head went under. She felt the wave of Jake jumping in next to her as she bobbed up. "*Holy fucking shit this is cold!*" she yelled, breaching the surface.

"Thank god there aren't any kids around," Jake cackled, looking left and right, taking in about a dozen kids and their families within earshot.

Izabelle was too cold to care. "Why the hell didn't you warn me!"

"I recall something about you declaring it a race and that you were born ready," Jake said, pushing his hair out of his eyes with a smirk, seemingly unaffected by the rivulets of icy water snaking down his chest.

"F-f-feeling v-v-very wimpy. Very not ready!" Izabelle shivered out, crossing her arms over her chest and locking her fingers under her armpits.

"You'll get used to it. Besides, what did you expect? It's a mountain stream."

"I was thinking that this is Arizona, and that it's hot here, and that maybe it was a hot spring or something," Izabelle said, half-annoyed, half-giddy from the cold.

"Trust me, one slide and you'll forget about the cold." He turned away from her and shouted, "Bye!" as he launched himself down the slide.

Having no choice but to follow, Izabelle did the same. It was exhilarating. The water pushed her along just like you would expect on a body slide at a water park. The rocks, worn smooth by the water and untold numbers of visitors before her, allowed her to glide along the top of them. The curves of the creek made natural banked turns, and before she knew it, she plopped out into a catch pool of sorts at the bottom of the slide.

"That was so fun!" she yelled at Jake, understanding his giddiness now and all the screams of delight she had heard at the top.

"Right!?" he responded. "I'm so glad you liked it."

"Let's go again!" Izabelle yelled as she pushed herself up and over the lip of the creek to walk back toward the start.

Jake and Izabelle went slipping and sliding for the next

hour. They were about to hop in again when Izabelle felt her shivers turn into full-on quakes.

"Hey, Jake. I-I hate to br-break up the party, but I th-think I have to call it quits. I can't stop s-sh-shivering."

Jake looked over at her dripping, shaking form. The look of concern on his face was immediate. "Oh no. I'm so sorry. Hold on just a sec," he said, jogging to retrieve the backpack from where he had dropped it earlier. He reached into the bag and pulled out a towel. Izabelle didn't think she had ever been so relieved to see a towel in her life. She expected him to hand it to her, but instead, he opened it up with both hands. "Come here."

She stepped toward the striped terry cloth and immediately collided with Jake's chest as he enveloped her. It was like curling into a bed with sheets straight from the dryer. The towel had been warmed by the sun through the bag, and she could feel his body heat through the fluffy fabric. The firm pressure of his arms around her intensified the warming feeling. She closed her eyes and leaned into it.

"Good god, Iz. You are cold. You're shaking like a leaf."

Izabelle smiled. "My friends call me Iz." Izabelle felt Jake's body tense slightly.

"Am I your friend?" he asked, rubbing her arms and back slowly.

"You can definitely call me Iz," she responded, and she felt him squeeze just a little tighter in response. "You were right," Izabelle said directly into Jake's chest. "Once we got going, I forgot about the cold."

Jake's voice was slightly huskier. "You mentioned earlier you were hoping for a hot spring. I can't deliver that exactly, but my room has its own hot tub if you want to warm up in there."

"Yes." Izabelle nodded emphatically against his pec. "Yes, please."

"Alright, let's get you out of here." He pulled her in for one last squeeze before he wrapped his own towel around his waist, and they walked toward the stairs.

While she had sprinted down the stairs and across the rocks on the way in, the way out was a different story. Izabelle's legs felt so numb that halfway up the stairs, she tripped when she didn't manage to lift her foot high enough.

"Ope!" Izabelle said, shooting her free hand out to catch her fall as she careened forward. Jake caught her hand before it hit the stairs, halting her fall. He interlaced his fingers with hers and didn't let go. They continued to drip-dry, hand in hand, along the path without saying a word. The pleasant warm sun and the heat radiating from his hand were replacing her cold shivers with a very different type of shiver in a hurry.

The only problem was now that she wasn't so cold, she was absolutely ravenous. A fact her stomach made known with a very audible gurgle.

"Was that your stomach?" Jake stopped abruptly, releasing her hand. It felt like a loss.

"The cold makes me hungry. I also might have skipped lunch."

He looked down at her with a mix of humor and concern. "I'll be right back," he said before jogging off toward one of the newer buildings near the picnic area.

Okay then. Izabelle took the moment alone to reflect on what the hell was happening here. *Today was a really good day.*

Then she realized that when she said today, she only meant the last couple of hours. The morning had been just like every other morning, but this afternoon with Jake had been something else. She shuffled in her towel over to one of the nearby picnic tables to sit.

She couldn't remember when she had last felt a rush like she had from that freezing water. But even more shocking was the rush she felt pressed up against Jake, having his hand wrapped around hers. It was foreign. It had been ages since she had been interested in anything but work and even longer since she had been interested in a man. Now she was shucking off work to hang out with one. A man who wanted to take her somewhere that was special to him as a kid. A man who understood what it was like to be busy with work. She still hadn't talked about her company with him, but she was actually starting to feel like she could do so and not freak out again. Which was weird but also exciting.

She heard the crunching of the gravel behind her and knew it must be Jake approaching.

"I was last in the water. So, as wagered, Ms. 'It's-a-race-born-ready-definitely-not-a-wimp,' dinner is on me."

Jake plopped down across from her with a cardboard box lid full of food. He had two of everything. Two hot dogs, two Cokes, two boats of french fries, two slices of pizza, two trays of nachos, and two soft pretzels. It was absolutely perfect.

"I have never loved anyone more than in this moment," Izabelle blurted out. *Shit. That is not what I meant.* Well, it was what she meant, but not like that. It wasn't capital *L* love. She searched his face for signs that he suddenly thought she was bizarre for spastically declaring her love for him after two dates. She was relieved when it didn't even seem to register.

"I wasn't sure what you would want. So, I got some of everything."

"Good. Because I am going to eat some of everything," Izabelle said. "I'm starving."

"I know it's not gourmet, but..." Jake said apologetically.

She waived him off. "Shhh, this is exactly my kind of dinner. Pass me the nachos."

He handed over the boat of chips and molten cheese with a chuckle. "Thank god I thought to stop. I'm worried you might have gnawed my arm off in the car."

"Swerisfy, thwanc you, Jafe," Izabelle said, mid-chew of a bite of hot dog.

"Was that a thank you, Jake?"

"Mmmhmmm," she nodded emphatically.

"Thank the Slide Rock Market. They provided in this time of need," Jake said, laughing between bites of his pizza.

Izabelle swallowed in order to get her thought out in a more ladylike manner. "No. I mean more generally. Thank you for bringing me here."

"Was it worth playing hooky for?"

"I had my apprehensions," Izabelle said, taking a bite of the nachos. "But it was more than worth it. The snacks are really putting it over the top."

Izabelle caught Jake's eye over the table. He smiled back at her with a contented expression. They proceeded to work through their feast, recounting the afternoon in the chilly water. As the sun started to set, the red rocks bounced golden light off the planes of his face. She felt her breath quicken just looking at him. It was like staring into the sun; she could only stare directly at him for so long before she had to look away. And when she did, his face was there in inverted colors behind her lids. She shuddered at the intensity.

"Come on. You're still shivering. Let's get you back."

"Don't think for a second that I'm leaving these snacks behind."

"Oh, I didn't think for a second that you would. I'll drive so you can keep eating."

Izabelle trundled back to the car. Jake had been kind enough to carry the remnants of dinner, seeing that she would have been forced to make the choice between keeping her towel tightly wrapped around her and saving the soft pretzel.

Once at the car, Jake opened the door for her. Once she had settled and resumed control of the soft pretzel, he reached over her to buckle her in so she could keep clutching onto the towel for warmth. Jake climbed in and started the car, turning the heat to full blast. Izabelle could feel herself drifting in the warmth. She looked over at Jake, who flashed her an easy smile. She felt fully relaxed in a way that she hadn't in a long, long time.

Ten

IZABELLE

"Are we back?" Izabelle said, feeling the car rumble to a stop.

"You fell asleep before we left the parking lot," Jake replied.

"Nahhh. I at least made it a quarter mile down the road."

Jake chuckled. "Good news is you kept a death grip on the pretzel."

Izabelle looked down at the squashed pretzel in her lap, still being gripped by her left hand. Her hair had dripped on it, turning it back into the soft dough from which it came. The whole scene wasn't a good look for her or the pretzel. Desperately wanting to divert the focus away from the soggy tragedy on her lap she hoped out of the car before he came around to open to her door. Turning her back on Jake, she brushed the soggy bits off her lap and hucked the remaining solid piece into the bushes. Satisfied that she had mostly covered up the evidence of her crimes against pretzel-kind she headed around to Jake's side of the car. "I had a really great day. Thank you."

"Umm, well, I guess you probably want to head back to your room," Jake said, rubbing his neck unsurely.

"Yeah, I just have to grab a bathing suit real quick, and then I can meet you..."

Jake's expression was one of hopeful surprise. "You still want to come?"

"You promised me hot water, and I am absolutely holding you to that," Izabelle said.

He rolled his head back, letting out a low whistle. "I am so glad to hear you don't want to get back to work. I had definitely braced myself for that possibility."

The way he was outlined against the pinkish sky of the setting sun was something to see. He was relaxed and genuine, wanting to spend more time with her but understanding that might not be a possibility. Something told her he wouldn't have complained if she said she had to go. He understood her, accepted her for who she was. Which made it easy to decide how she wanted this evening to go.

"I figured if I'm already being this bad, I might as well go all the way."

She knew her words hit in the way she wanted because Jake's eyes visibly darkened. "I'll go wherever you tell me." He stepped toward her and then stepped back again, stuffing his hands in his pockets. "But my room is 1102."

Izabelle turned to head inside. "I'll be right over."

~

Izabelle dug through her suitcase with abandon. If this was going to be her best chance for pure indulgence, then she was going to give it everything she had. Which in this instance meant slithering into her favorite bathing suit—a one-piece cut high on the hips and low on the chest that she knew showed off her curves in the most flattering light. It had passed the modern-day crucible of actually looking good under the harsh fluorescent lighting of the dressing room when she tried it on, so she knew it looked damn good in real life.

She rushed past her desk to the closet to grab a robe to walk over with. She glanced at her computer, thinking how she hadn't thought about her pitch for hours. It hit her that not only was that a minor miracle, but it also felt amazing. After today, she was feeling lighter, freer. This felt like the right track. Or at least like something new, and that was good enough for now.

Popping on a robe from the closet, she headed out to find room 1102.

Ten minutes later, she had walked the length of every single hallway in the hotel and couldn't find it. *What the hell?* Feeling her frustration rising, she headed to the front desk to see if 1102 was actually a real room number or if Jake was pulling her chain.

"Hi," she addressed the front desk concierge. "I'm looking for the mystical room 1102. Can you tell me where that is, if it exists?"

"Oh yes, ma'am." The employee nodded. "It's out past the main pool in the casita section of the hotel."

"What?" *Casita* wasn't a word that Izabelle recognized right off the bat.

"The casita section."

Izabelle looked at him, confused.

"The casitas are individual units that aren't connected to the main building. If you follow the pathway with the red pavers, it will lead to 1102. It will be individually marked."

"Thank you," Izabelle said while simultaneously thinking, *Well, I'll be damned*. It had taken her a minute to process that casitas were the southwestern equivalent of villas or cottages. Then it had taken another minute to register that they had those here and another minute to process that Jake was staying in one.

As she exited out the back of the hotel, the cool night air lapped at her skin under the robe. She wandered along the red paver pathway, noting the tasteful yellow lights lining each side. She saw the laser-cut metal sign that read "1102," directing her through an opening between two giant agave plants on its own dedicated pathway. A short walk through a rock garden full of cacti and other succulents, mixed with the various trees she had seen on the drive today, led to an adobe building with Spanish-style tiles lining the roof. It had its own front porch, and through the paned windows, she could see Jake sitting at a kitchen island. Much to her disappointment, he had put a shirt back on.

He was sitting on a barstool at the high-top counter, jiggling his knee on the footrest, looking at two empty wineglasses and two full bottles of wine, one red, one white. When she rang the doorbell, he jumped, nearly taking out the glasses in the process. She grinned, watching him settle them and putting his hands out in a "stay" motion like you would a dog as he walked away from them. He opened the door with a smile.

"Uhhh, Jake. You really held out on me. I thought that my

room was nice, but holy shit." Izabelle walked past him through the door. "How in the world did you snag this?"

"Um—" He looked over his shoulder. "I got an upgrade."

"Remind me to get on that person's good side." Izabelle took in this "hotel room," which, considering it had multiple rooms and was larger than her apartment, was aptly named a casita.

Turning from the kitchen to the rest of the space, she took in the full kitchen, dining room, living room, game table, and what she guessed was the bedroom in the back. Light-colored stucco walls set off the rich dark wooden beams on the ceiling and sturdy mission-style furniture. Beautiful woven rugs lined the floor and highlighted the dominant feature of the open floor plan, a round adobe fireplace tossing out warm, crackling light.

"Would you like some wine?" Jake asked behind her. "I have red and white. Or if you would rather have a cocktail, I'm sure I could whip up a manhattan—"

"Red would be great," Izabelle interrupted. "I only have manhattans when I'm nervous." She slowly let her eyes roam over him in a way that communicated she was anything but nervous. "Now, about this hot tub."

"It's out back. I'll bring your wine."

Izabelle loosened the belt on her robe, shrugging it off one shoulder as she turned, letting it slide down her back as she gave her best attempt at a sashay. Based on the audible groan behind her, the calculated move had its intended effect.

Opening the french doors to the patio, she saw the hot tub, which could be better described as an in-ground hot pool. The thing was massive. And incredibly private. Looking out past the light of the villa, Izabelle couldn't see anything other than the silhouette of the mountains against the stars.

"It's a beautiful view." Izabelle spun to see Jake behind her, wineglass in hand, looking at her with an intensity she hadn't seen before. He set her glass down on the edge of the pool near her and then moved to the other side of the pool with his own. He eased himself onto the ledge opposite her.

Izabelle slowly waded down the stairs, allowing herself to adjust. She sighed as the warm water encircled her. "It's heavenly."

"I'm happy to provide," Jake said, watching her closely.

"I'm just happy I asked the front desk where this was. I was about to give up."

Jake chuckled. "You're braver than I am."

Izabelle cocked her head. "Why is that?"

"Like I said at breakfast, I wanted to come to your room last night but didn't know your last name, so I couldn't go ask where you were staying." He took a slow sip from his glass. "Figured the front desk wasn't going to give room info out to a guy looking mildly desperate asking for Izabelle. 'You know, Izabelle—brunette, funny, infectious energy that I am compelled to be around, Izabelle.'"

She laughed, sliding the rest of the way into the water. "It's Green, by the way."

"Hm?" Jake questioned.

"My last name is Green."

"Like your eyes."

Izabelle gave him an arch look. "It's dark out. You can't see the color of my eyes."

"Do you think I didn't notice them the first time you looked at me?"

Izabelle felt her stomach flip. She remembered that initial encounter. And the ones since then. Any initial awkwardness they had between them had been slowly burnt off as the heat between them continued to rise. She was feeling the full-on flame now.

"Are you trying to charm me?" Izabelle asked.

"Is it working?" Jake's eyes continued to burn into her.

"Do you want it to?"

They stared at each other. Neither one made a move to interrupt their tête-à-tête. A smirk unfurled across his lips. "There are actually quite a few things I would like to do."

"So how about you come in?" Her eyes bored into his.

Jake held her gaze. "I'm easing in. I don't like to rush. Trust me, you won't want me to be in a hurry."

She rose from her perch in the corner and waded toward him. Her swaying hips caused the water to ripple out in small c's around her, and a low groan emanated from his chest. "Nothing I can do to speed you up?"

He picked up his glass a took a leisurely drink. "Why are you in such a hurry, Izabelle?"

Izabelle laughed, her voice thick with anticipation. "I guess I'm not. But I've only got just over a week before EtaSella starts, so I'm hoping that you make a move before then."

Jake jerked his head. "Eta—what did you say?"

Izabelle took another step toward him, biting her lip. "The business thing I'm here for. The presentation that I've been working on—it's a competition called EtaSella for companies to win investment. But that's not really the point."

The glass dropped out of Jake's hand. It didn't break, but red wine spilled all over the pool deck. "Shit. Uh. Shit. I'll be right back."

Before Izabelle could say anything, he hopped off the ledge and ran back into the casita. Izabelle spun in a circle in the pool, her confidence faltering as she blew a few stray hairs out of her eyes. "Huh. So much for not being in a hurry."

Eleven

JAKE

Fuck. *This has all been a mistake.* How had he not even considered this as a possibility? He had made way too many miscalculations. Now they had all added up to him coming inside, ostensibly to refill a wineglass, when really he was trying to think of an exit plan. He sat on the edge of the bed with his fingers balled in his hair, reviewing how the fuck he had gotten himself here.

Anyone could have overlooked that they were both going to the airport at the same time. That was just pure coincidence. The fact that they both worked in business could also be easily written off as coincidence. Tech, business, and law were pretty much the only things people did in San Francisco.

Where he really should have drilled down was when she said she was here for a work project. But the thought hadn't crossed his mind at the time. EtaSella only paid for competitors to be here for the nights of the competition. He had come out here early specifically to avoid any presenters or companies and relax before the competition wound itself up. He never would have guessed that she was here for more or less the same reason. Plus, she had said she was a solo entrepreneur. EtaSella hadn't had a company that small win a spot in years, as far as he knew. Participants in recent times had huge teams backing them and hired marketing firms to do their presentations. If Izabelle had gotten herself here all by herself, then she was an absolute rock star. Even in his anguish, Jake's heart swelled with admiration, and that was the fucking problem.

If the first set of miscalculations regarding Izabelle was missing the fact that she could possibly be an EtaSella participant, then the second was how he would feel about her. His attraction to her in the car on the way to the airport was one thing. People see other attractive people all the time. But their dinner together started to change things. He had desperately wanted to kiss her and was crushed when he upset her. When she had agreed to come with him to Slide Rock, he had been elated. What sane man wouldn't want smart, talented, understanding Izabelle to spend more time with them?

He expected it to be a fun activity—something unique to show her—a nice little piece of his own nostalgia. He hadn't expected to be so excited to turn into the familiar parking lot, and he *really* hadn't expected to feel a crushing longing when Izabelle asked about his dad. The wave of emotion had hit him completely flat footed. And she just gave him the space to feel it. She had been incredible.

Incredible. That was the feeling he'd had when she'd taken off toward the top of the slide, so game to jump in. He had expected she would need to get back to work and wouldn't want to go. He had brought the towels on the off chance she might want to slide once. But instead, she had relished it just as much as he had. And that made him feel even more things about her.

The way her wet clothes had clung to her body was the singular reason he hadn't felt cold the entire time. But he was goddamn pissed at himself for not factoring in how cold she must have been before she announced it. Once he had stopped ogling her and actually looked at her, the slight tinge of blue in her lips made his heart ache. He couldn't stand the sight of her standing there shivering, each drop of falling chilly water leaving a goose bump behind. Instinctively, he had wrapped her in the towel and pulled her into his chest to warm her up. When she tucked her head against his chest, he had prayed she couldn't hear his heart hammering through his ribs.

He had let her go only because he realized that unless he did, she was going to start feeling a lot more than just his heart. But he hadn't wanted to. Later, when she tripped up the stairs, he had reached for her hand because he didn't want her hurt. He told himself that he had continued to hold it because he didn't want anything to happen to her the rest of the way up the slippery stairs. But in reality, it just felt good. When he had let go of her hand to go get dinner, it felt like he was letting go of something bigger. When she had fallen asleep in the car, he had wished it had been in his arms, and when he heard the slow breaths of her sleeping, he felt his heart lurch. And those were just the miscalculations from the afternoon. He flopped back on the bed, trying to calm the fuck down and think.

He'd had to hold on to the counter earlier when she slipped

her robe down her back on her way outside. When he walked out with her wine, it took everything in him to not drop the glass when he saw her outlined by the light of the moon. He still couldn't believe he managed to say something cliché about the view instead of immediately moving to press his body against hers. If he got back into that hot tub with her, there was little to no chance he would be able to hold off again. Which was a *massive* problem.

She's a presenter. There weren't any hard and fast rules about investors and companies fraternizing before the competition, but it was also kind of the entire point of EtaSella that they didn't. His dad had created it so that companies would have a shot at an investments they wouldn't otherwise have. One that was based on merit and not whose dad played a round with who at the local country club.

But then again, he wasn't actually an investor. Masterson Holdings sponsored the competition and hosted the weekend, but they didn't actually invest in any of the participants themselves. It was possible he could just stay super hands-off this year and... But then he thought about Izabelle, and his stomach clenched. He had already made so many miscalculations he couldn't risk another one right now.

He was just going to have to leave. It was the only way he was going to be able to stay away from her. He didn't need to be at the competition. It could run perfectly fine without him. It had done just fine without him for the last five plus years. Anything that came up, he could answer remotely. He doubted anyone would actually miss him.

He sat up on the bed, put his hands on his knees, and took a bracing breath. He could do this. He could sit on the opposite side of the pool and just admire from afar. He would tell her he had to leave tomorrow. They could simply chat, she could finish warming up, he would walk back all of the things he had insinuated and hoped for, and that would be that. Friends. No lines crossed.

Having steeled himself with a new level of resolve, he grabbed his wineglass and went out to meet Izabelle. "I'm probably going to regret this."

∼

"Did you have to go into town for that refill?" Izabelle joked when he reemerged from the casita. She had settled back into her seat at the far side of the pool.

"Something like that," Jake responded. "Sorry for the wait."

Izabelle gave him a look that fully communicated she was ready to resume where they had left off. "You're worth waiting for."

Hearing her voice was enough to make him want to launch across the water at her. He should have never come back outside. He should have just left without a trace. This was going to be impossible. He eased himself into the water, hoping he could play this off as casual.

"So, tell me more about EtaSella. How did you first hear about it?" He sounded like one of the people from his marketing department. Which was good in that everyone knew how-did-you-hear-about-us surveys were the least sexy thing ever.

Izabelle raised an eyebrow. "You want to hear about EtaSella? Now?"

He stretched his arms out to either side of him, mentally gluing them to the pool deck. "Yeah. You mentioned it. Seems like a pretty nifty thing." *Nifty?* Jake wanted to punch himself in the face. He was often awkward by accident, but being awkward on purpose was even more painful.

Izabelle blew out her cheeks with a slow exhale. He heard her mumble under her breath, "Of all the times—" She looked up at him. "EtaSella is a big investment competition where companies pitch their businesses to investors and then —" She circled her hand. "—you know, hopefully get investments."

Jake took a slightly less constrained breath. This was certainly pulling the release valve on the sexual tension. "I know you said you've had some people screw you over in the past. Have they been part of the competition?" This was a desperate, petty move, but talking about her past businesses had iced down their conversation before, and he was hoping it could work again.

Izabelle tilted her head, giving it a slight shake. "I did say that, but I didn't think you would want to hear about it right now."

She stood up and inched toward him. He watched rivulets of water run down her neck and chest. "I want to hear everything you want to tell me, Izabelle," he said thickly. *Shit.* He was losing his grip again. He flexed his fingers on the concrete as a reminder of the goal. He lightened his tone, trying to deflect. "You know. Just one friend to another."

"Friends, huh?" Izabelle smirked and moved toward him slowly. *Jake, do not move your arms from the side of this goddamn pool.*

"Now I'm the one that feels a bit awkward," Izabelle said, inching closer to him.

"Why is that?" He could hear the strain in his voice as he fought for the will to not reach out and yank her toward him.

"Because I really didn't think that we were friends." She ran her fingertips over the top of the water, and his mind went fuzzy, imagining how those delicate fingers would feel skimming over him instead of the water. "At least, I don't want to be *just* friends."

Jake had to shut his eyes and tilt his head back at that one. He was starting to feel light-headed, and it wasn't from the heat of the pool. "What is it that you want?" He shouldn't have asked. But god damn did he want to hear her say it.

"See, that's where it's awkward because I really want to kiss you, but it's always awkward when you have to ask." She had fully closed the gap between them and was standing between his spread legs. He had to shift his hips as his arousal tightened against his shorts. Time seemed to slow down as she leaned down to his eye level, her hands moving to his shoulders as she leaned her weight onto him.

Holy fuck. He wanted this. He wanted her. He wanted to pull her onto his lap and have her feel exactly how much. Then he remembered why he wasn't doing that at this exact moment. *Fuck.* He could feel the warmth of her body and her exhale. She was so close when he pulled the rip cord.

"Izabelle, I can't. I can't do this."

She straightened up so fast that the water created a vacuum from the speed of her backing up.

"Oh. Uh. I'm so sorry. I thought—"

"No, no you're right. You thought exactly right. I..." Jake

racked his brain for any plausible excuse. "I'm just leaving tomorrow, and I—"

"Oh. Well, that still leaves tonight if you want to..." She looked at him hopefully, taking one of her hands and moving through the knuckles, cracking them.

You can't even imagine how much I do. "I really shouldn't. It wouldn't be fair to you." The words he was forcing out were hard to hear over the throbbing of the blood in his ears.

"Oh. Yeah, um..." She glanced around her. "Well, I don't want to keep you up, and uh, I'm warm now, so I guess I'll head out." She hopped out of the pool, heading for the front door in a hurry, snatching her robe off the ground as she passed it. She had her hand on the latch when he caught up.

"Izabelle. Wait."

She turned around with her eyebrows raised, an expectant look on her face, clearly waiting to see what he was going to say. He was inches from her. That fact alone was enough to scramble his thoughts. He just didn't know how to explain this entire thing. He opened his mouth and then clamped it shut again, looking away in indecision. That was enough to prompt her.

"Well, Jake. It was really nice to meet you. Thank you again for a nice day." She looked up at him, her eyelashes clumped together from the moisture of the pool. It was hard to keep her face in focus. All the blood in his body was rushing out of his head. He raised his hand to cup her face but stopped halfway.

Izabelle saw him hesitate. Her head slumped, and her lips went from gently parted to twisted to one side. He couldn't tell if his arousal or her disappointment was going to break him first. He stepped back from her to adjust himself. It was painful being this close to her.

"Ummm. I guess if you need anything, I'm in room 105."

"Iz. I—"

"Goodbye, Jake. Maybe I'll see you around sometime." She turned and walked away so fast it was nearly a jog.

He tapped his fist to his forehead. He couldn't bring himself to say "probably not."

Twelve

IZABELLE

Izabelle had walked back to her room, showered, slipped into a fresh robe, done her overly complicated skin care routine, and still hadn't been able to work out what the hell had just happened. There was heat between them. *Good god almighty, there was heat.* She knew it. He had said he was drawn to her. That she hadn't read the situation wrong. So she wasn't sure why the hell he had pulled away. Why he shut things down when she could tell he was turned on.

She would have killed to take things further. She wanted it so badly. She wanted *him* so badly. To feel his chest without a towel in between. To run her hands over him. To taste him. She was mere inches from running her lips over his. She had made it clear she was into him. *Must have been too clear, Izabelle. You probably turned him off. What were you thinking with all of that "Now I feel awkward" stuff?* That would show her for trying to force a fling. This was why she didn't date. Even when she thought the signals were crystal clear, she still managed to misinterpret them.

It was a deep irony that Jake had opened the door to talk about her company and EtaSella, and then she had shut it down because she wasn't in the mood for shop talk. She was in the mood for lots of other things, but not for that. Good grief. This was all unbelievably bad timing.

Bang bang bang! The noise of the door being rocked in its frame startled her so badly that she slipped on the bathroom tile, catching herself by grasping wildly for the counter. *What in the ever-living hell?* She walked the few steps to the door, ready to rip it open and lay into whoever just scared the shit out of her. Whatever they wanted, it could not be that urgent. The fire alarm wasn't going off, for christ's sake.

When she wrenched open the door, the breath she had taken to shout went right back out of her lungs. *Jake.* The light of the hallway was entirely replaced by the shadow of his body. Both arms were pressed high against the frame, his shoulder muscles bunched, transferring the weight of his torso to the wall. His chest was heaving. His hanging head snapped up, and his eyes bored into hers, a fire in them hotter than she had ever seen.

"I need you. Now," he said, a roughness in his voice that she had never heard before.

"I—I thought you had to leave tomorrow," Izabelle stammered out. "That you didn't want to—"

"Izabelle, I have wanted to pretty much since the first time I saw you. I was an idiot to think that I could stand you walking away again." He paused, not dropping her gaze. "Do you want me?" His voice was strained, as if he could barely keep a hold of it. His forearms flexed as his grip tightened on the door.

"Yes," Izabelle responded breathlessly.

"Do you want this now?"

"Yes," she repeated.

"Because if you tell me to go, I'll go. If you tell me to stop, I'll stop. But if you say yes again, I'm coming in there, ripping off that robe, and running every part of me over every part of you."

"Ye—" Izabelle wasn't able to finish the word before her mouth was owned by Jake's. One of his hands gripped the back of her head to keep her where he wanted while the other slipped into the V of the robe at her neck, then slid down her chest and around her waist. He pulled her into him with enough force that she could feel the length of his hardness against her hip. She gasped against his mouth, his tongue taking the opportunity to lap against hers.

She could feel the strength of his fingers gripping the flesh of her hips. He broke the bond of their lips and slid his hand from her face into the damp hair at the nape of her neck. Pulling head back to bury the scruff of his jaw into the crook of her neck, nipping at the skin there.

"What do you want, Izabelle?"

She wasn't sure she could even form thoughts at this point. She wanted it all. *God, please, anything, just yesss.*

"I want to hear you tell me what you want," he said.

"I want whatever you want to do to me." It was an honest answer. She was so turned on she couldn't even consider formulating an actual request. She wanted him to surprise her, to intuit what she needed.

"In that case, I'll just start at the top and work my way down." His hands glided from their positions to grab her by the waist. Bending, he picked her up. She wrapped her legs around him, causing her robe to open at the bottom, and the sweetness of her inner thighs to feel the taut skin of his hips where they met the fabric of his shorts.

He easily walked her to the bed, lying her down onto the fluff of the comforter, and flinging away the flimsy terry cloth belt. He slipped his hands into each side of the robe, opening it wide with the backs of his hands as his thumbs grazed over her nipples. Izabelle felt them harden immediately at the burst of cold air and his touch. She closed her eyes, arching into the feeling. When she felt him back away, she blinked them open again.

Jake was at the foot of the bed, staring down at her naked body. His look one of awe. Normally she would have covered herself in embarrassment, but the look on his face dissuaded her.

"Holy fuck," he rumbled. "You are beautiful."

With a ragged exhale, he brought his body down to hers, pinning her between his arms, but Izabelle felt the opposite of trapped. He started where he had left off at the crook of her neck. The heat radiating off his muscled torso was palpable. The warmth of his mouth on her skin felt like fire. His mix of scruff, lips, and tongue worked down her body, his powerful hands sliding in correlation with his kiss. Izabelle sighed in anticipation of him reaching her breasts, but instead, he kissed his way between them, pausing just long enough to run his tongue under the crease. Her sigh changed to a disgruntled groan when she realized he was moving on so quickly.

"You didn't say what you wanted, Izabelle. So, I'm doing what I want." He breathed into the softness of her stomach, kissing at her waist, her belly button, and the ridges of her hips. When he ran his tongue over the line where her hips met her thighs, her legs opened to him reflexively. "Seems like we want the same thing," Jake said, running his cheek down the inside of her thigh as his arms reached around her. Grabbing her by the hips and pulling her toward the edge of the bed, he expertly maneuvered himself so that her legs were draped over his shoulders while his hands continued to grip at her hips and waist.

Oh, fuck yes.

"You still haven't said what you want, Izabelle. Is this it?"

"Yesssss, please, Jake." Her body felt simultaneously like jelly and a taut rubber band.

"Yes to this?" he asked as his tongue flicked across her clit.

Izabelle gasped as a shock wave rippled up her body. It had been so long, and his tongue felt so unbelievably good. Her core clenched, and she bit her lip.

"I want to hear you, Iz."

"Yes, god, please don't stop."

"Don't stop this?" He began working her with his tongue in earnest. She curled her legs as the tension in her body grew, causing Jake's skilled mouth to be pulled in even deeper. Her arousal climbed higher and higher.

"Yes." Izabelle was nearly panting now. "More."

"I'll give you as much as you want," Jake rumbled as one of his hands slid from her hip to her mound, his fingers raking across her stomach while his thumb began to rub her clit in smooth, even circles. He moved his tongue lower to tease at her opening.

Izabelle gyrated in circles of pleasure. *Holy shit, he is fucking amazing at this.* All her thoughts were centered on the expert ministrations of Jake between her legs. As his pace picked up, her breathing and her heart rate followed in lockstep. He was pushing her toward a cliff, edging her closer and closer, and good god was she ready to swan dive off it.

"I want you inside me," she said.

Jake, not losing his rhythm for a second, moved from teasing her labia to sliding two of his fingers into her hot center. He worked her, gliding them in and out, taking her wetness and slicking it across the rest of her, alternating his tongue and his fingers on her clit. Her moans and whimpers of pleasure grew closer and closer in time.

"I can't wait to see you come," he breathed into her.

The thought of Jake wanting her that much sent a jolt through her body. She arched as if there was an electrical current pulsing from her toes to the crown of her head. When Jake groaned, she could feel the vibration deep in her core. Each lap of his tongue added to the tension deep within her.

"Oh. Fuck. Jake!" Izabelle's orgasm hit her all at once. Her thighs quaked at the sides of his head as her calves pulled him in deeper. She brought her fist up to her mouth to keep from screaming out. Jake enthusiastically responded and didn't let up, causing wave after wave to crash through her. It was only when the shock waves started to abate from a cymbal crash to a flutter that Jake backed off.

"Holy shit, Izabelle, you are incredible," he said, resting his forehead against her inner thigh. "Just..." She felt him exhale against her soft skin. "Wow."

Izabelle raised up to her elbows to look down her body at him, blowing a loose curtain of hair out of her eyes. "Wow is right," she said. "Like god damn. I can't even hold myself up. I'm still shaking." She flopped back down on the comforter.

"That's why you're so hot." Jake gave her clit one last flick of the tongue, which caused her entire body to contract with one last involuntary jolt, and she sucked a gasp through her teeth.

"Jesus. Are you trying to kill me?" Izabelle asked, laughing.

"Trying to do the exact opposite," Jake said.

"Mmmmmm. Mission accomplished." Izabelle lay back, savoring the feeling of relaxation that had washed over her. She laughed at the thought that popped into her head. *I feel the same way as I do when I'm floating down a lazy river.* Stretched out, lounging, going with the flow. Jake crawled up the bed and scooped her body into his. His forearm locked her in tight against his chest. For the second time today, she felt completely relaxed.

Thirteen

JAKE

Jake woke up feeling like his back was in a freezer, his chest was pressed against a radiator, and his hair was covered in hair. Cracking an eye open, he realized a few things in rapid succession. His back was cold because the air conditioner was cranking at full blast, his chest was hot because he had fallen asleep with Izabelle tucked in against him, and the hair in his face was hers and not his. It smelled like oranges. He squeezed his eyes shut and relished the moment.

When Izabelle had walked away from him last night, he'd gone immediately numb. He collapsed into the couch as the thought struck him that numb was how he generally felt. It was only in these last couple of days that he felt anything other than apathetic or angry. Since getting in the car with Izabelle on the way to the airport, he had felt awkward, cringey, embarrassed, sad, nostalgic, lustful. But most of all, and especially in this moment, he felt happy. And as that feeling spread over him, he knew he had made the right choice to stay. To soak up whatever minutes Izabelle had and provide whatever entertainment or comfort or stress relief she needed.

He was going to leave before the competition. He still had to. Since she didn't want any part of his help with the presentation, it eliminated the risk he would contribute in any inappropriate way. But the risk that someone would see them together, or see him here at all, increased as they got closer to the competition. There were too many moving pieces, and no matter how he arranged them, there wasn't a scenario in which he was here for the presentations. But that was fine. He wasn't looking forward to it anyway. But that didn't mean that he had to leave today.

He blinked his eyes again, incredulous that the sun was up. *I can't even remember the last time I slept through the night.* The thought was shocking to him. He craned his neck to see what time it was on the nightstand. *9:30. Jesus.* He hadn't slept past 7:00 since he was in high school. Being able to sleep through the night and lie here with Izabelle made it all the more clear to him that he had made the right choice. She felt so perfect against him.

The clock check must have awoken Izabelle because she began shifting against him. He heard a small "mmmm" as she scooched her ass more firmly into his lap. *Yes, please.* She continued pressing herself closer until she abruptly stopped and reached her hand back to his thigh, patting around wildly at the fabric of his shorts.

"Holy shit, how do you still have shorts on?"

Jake chuckled sleepily into her wonderful orange-scented hair. "Umm, because I never took them off."

"You—we..." He could hear the recognition dawning in her voice. "Ohhh. I fell asleep on you, didn't I?"

"Not on me, precisely, but next to me." *And it was incredible.*

"I'm so sorry, I must have been tired. I've been super stres—"

"Izabelle, are you apologizing for not having sex with me last night?"

"Yes?" she said questioningly.

"Please don't." The last thing he wanted was for her to be apologetic.

"Okay?"

Jake could tell she was confused. "Don't apologize for enjoying yourself and then falling asleep in my arms. I said I was going to do what I wanted to do, and I did." Every word was true. Her moans and writhes of pleasure had been a dream. One that he got to live all over again when they fell asleep together and one he was looking forward to recreating soon.

"You are unreal."

Jake chuckled. "In a bad way or..."

"No, in a good way. Like in the that-is-pretty-much-the-hottest-thing-I-have-ever-heard way."

As Jake laughed, he could feel the echo of his rumbles in Izabelle's body.

"It's barely sunup, so I think we have time for some things that I want to do," Izabelle said, rolling to face him.

The expression on her face was all heat. He definitely liked where this was going. "It's not sunup, but I am certainly ready for it," Jake replied, his arousal beginning to physically manifest.

"Wait, what?" Izabelle said, rolling away from him with a jerk to look at the clock. "Oh shit! I haven't slept in this late in ages! I'm usually deep into work by now."

That makes two of us.

"I'm sorry, Jake. I can't do this right now. I have to get working. I can't ignore my pitch for another day. When does your flight leave today? I do want to at least see you again before you go."

"Izabelle, remember what I said about apologizing?" Izabelle laughed, and he moved his lips to the warmth of her neck. "Maybe the next time around, I can be good enough to have apologies fall out of your head too." He could feel her pulse where he kissed her; it was picking up in lockstep with his own.

"I'm certainly open to that possibility," Izabelle said with another little shimmy against him.

"But in terms of leaving..." Jake was fishing around for yet another plausible excuse. "My plans changed suddenly. That's why I broke down and came over last night." Which was true. Mostly. The full truth was his will to stay away from her broke down, which then caused him to change all of his plans about leaving. But that was semantics. "I'll be around for a few more days."

"Oh, that's great! But that means I really need to get to work," she said pulling away.

He knew better than to try and convince her to stay in bed. Any other time, he would be doing exactly the same thing she was. But he wasn't going to let her go without making more plans to see her. "Should we try one of the other restaurants tonight?"

"Maybe we should see how room service is and stay in?" Izabelle responded, throwing him a coy look over her shoulder from where she was booting up her laptop.

"Now, that is an excellent idea." He smiled at the indication that she was just as down to stay in as he was. She padded over to him in her bare feet. He shifted up in the bed, hoping she was going to climb back in. "It's a date. Let's say 8:30." She reached for his hand. "Now, I'm sorry to do this, but you have to go so I can focus," she said, pulling him by the wrist.

He obligingly rolled out of the bed. "Are you apologizing—"

"I'm apologizing for throwing you without a shirt like a one-night stand," Izabelle said, playfully pushing him toward the door. "Not for the fact that you are sexy enough to be a work-halting distraction." She continued to shove him out of it.

"Bye, Izabelle," Jake said, looking back and giving her a leisurely up-and-down through the door opening.

"Bye, Jake," she said, shutting the door while maintaining eye contact.

As he walked away, he was completely unable to stop grinning. *Let's hope that she also forgets to put clothes on tonight.*

Fourteen

IZABELLE

It was unlike Izabelle to be unable to jump right into work. But every time she looked at her laptop, she saw a highlight reel of last night rather than the words on the screen. The hot tub. Her leaving. Him towering over her in the doorway. Her sprawled across the bed. Waking up in his arms. His goofy smile as she closed the door in his face. She was buzzing. The more she thought about it, the more distracted she got. *I really need to get something done today.*

And yet, the already unproductive part of her mind wanted to call Jake and see what activities he wanted to get up to. The only thing holding her back was she knew the second she dialed his number, she wouldn't be sitting back down at her laptop for a long while. The next best choice was to call one of the babes and recount her adventures. She was dying to fill them in on everything that had happened and get some kudos for actually going for it.

Checking the time, she realized that Sabrina was probably still asleep from her event from the night before, and Ava was teaching her morning class, leaving Charlie as the only one likely to pick up the phone. She rang her on FaceTime. It didn't even complete a full ring before the chat connected.

"Thank god you called." Charlie put her head in her hand and let her auburn ponytail flop to one side. "I needed an excuse to not go to this meeting. I do not need to waste my time with something called 'small talk, big discoveries' right now. What are you up to? Enjoying the sun?"

"Oh yeah," Izabelle responded in what she thought was her most casual of tones.

Charlie looked incredulous, leaning back into her office chair. "Really? I figured I was going to be fielding a stress-ball version of you. How are you not freaking out?" She reached for one of the fidget toys on her desk. "Don't tell me that one of those crystal vortexes Ava talked about actually worked."

"Ha! No. And I'm still extremely stressed about the presentation. I just figured I would take a small mental break. Try and shake off some things that are distracting me," Izabelle said.

"Distracting you? I thought you were impossible to distract. What in the world could possibly be distracting you?"

Izabelle couldn't help it. A small smile started at one edge of her lips and ran across her entire mouth. She tried to cover it by biting at her thumb. "You could say there are some..." That smile turned into a giggle mid-sentence. "...very intriguing distractions at this place."

"Why are you giggling in the middle of that sentence? You sound like Ava when she talks about that gym owner next to hers," Charlie said, moving her phone closer to her face and giving Izabelle a very suspicious look.

"Wellllll..." Izabelle responded.

Charlie rocketed forward in her chair and clapped a hand on her desk. "Holy shit! Izabelle Green! You tell me right now where you picked up this distraction!"

Izabelle laughed as she moved from her desk chair to the edge of the bed to sit. "Do you remember the guy I told you about in the rideshare? The one that you said must be the hottest man on Earth to make me forget about work?"

"The guy you said there was zero chance you were ever going to see again?"

Izabelle nodded. "Soooo, it turns out he is also staying here at the resort, annnddd we might have hung out."

Charlie knitted her eyebrows together. "Hung out? Are you fifteen? What does that mean exactly?"

"We ran back into each other, and then we went on a little hike-swim thing, and then I got cold, so he invited me to his hot tub and..."

"And then what?" Charlie circled her hand. "Spit it out."

"And he came back to my hotel room and stayed the night."

Charlie beamed. "Oh shit! Congrats on the sex! Was it good?"

Izabelle knew the next bit was really going to get Charlie's attention. "We actually didn't have full-on sex. He just went down on me, but—"

Charlie held up a hand to interrupt her. "I'm sorry, what? A sexy-ass man came over and then just went down on you for an evening and wanted nothing in return? Are you sure you aren't hallucinating? Are you well? Did the stress finally crack your brain?"

"I swear!" Izabelle laughed. "It's crazy, but it's true. I just passed out so hard afterward that I didn't even register I wasn't returning the favor."

"Wow," Charlie said, shaking her head in disbelief. "Where can I find one of these unicorn-man hybrids? Are you going to see him again?"

"Hell yes." Izabelle couldn't get the words out fast enough. After last night, all of her trepidations seemed so trivial. There wasn't anything to have been so scared of, at least in the Jake department. She wanted to see him as many times as she could. She had followed the good and found great.

"This is incredible. I fully support this. Anything that gets you even a little bit more relaxed is a godsend," Charlie said with a huge smile.

Izabelle couldn't help but laugh at her friend's enthusiastic support of this vacation hookup. "I figured you were going to warn me about the risks of meeting a stranger, or getting emotionally entangled, or not having my head in game-day mode or something along those lines."

"You're an adult. And honestly, if he's gotten you to come out of the mental hidey-hole that you call a presentation, he must be a very intriguing guy. Plus, on top of that, he's clearly a giver, so what is there to warn you about?" Charlie switched her voice to sound like some sort of Little League coach, talking out of the side of her mouth. "Just have safe sex, and get back out there, champ."

Izabelle laughed at the botched impression. "You are an insane person." She sighed. "God, I really should get back to the presentation."

"Noooo. I want to keep talking about this fantasy man."

Izabelle let out a combination of a sigh and a laugh. "I

know. I do too, but I really do have to get back to it. I don't have it down yet. I feel like I've ripped it apart and put it together a million times."

"You need to just do it start to finish in front of another person. You can't keep picking it apart in your own brain. Do you want to do it for me on the phone?"

"No," Izabelle responded quickly out of instinct but then thought about it. "But kind of yes?"

Charlie gestured with her hand. "Okay. Well then, stand up, hold the laptop, and do it."

Izabelle pulled back from the phone in her hand. "Now? Really? That seems super awkward."

"It will be way more awkward if you go to do it for the first time and haven't said a word of it out loud."

Izabelle thought about it. Charlie had a point. "Ugh. You're right. Okay." Izabelle stood and took a deep breath. "Just give me a minute to get set up."

"That'a girl," Charlie said.

Izabelle propped her phone against the wall, moving her laptop onto the desk next to it so she could click through the slides while Charlie watched. "Ready?" she asked Charlie.

Charlie gave her a thumbs-up. "You've got this."

Izabelle took a series of overly quick breaths and tried to shake out a full-body shiver. She counted to three before she forced herself to say, "Ladies and gentlemen, thank you for—"

"Shit. Iz, hold on," Charlie said as Izabelle watched the screen go from Charlie's face to the top of her desk. She heard a male voice.

"Are you coming to the training?"

"Yes, definitely!" Charlie responded to the voice with

uncharacteristic cheerfulness. "I just had to finish up something in here really quick. I'll be right down."

"You're probably going to miss out on the donuts unless you come right now."

"I think I'll survive." Izabelle could hear the annoyance starting to creep into Charlie's voice.

"Okay, well, don't act like I didn't warn you," the male voice continued.

"I definitely won't." Her voice was leaning fully into snark now.

After a pause, Izabelle heard a door shut. "Did you hear that?" Charlie asked, her face back in the frame again.

"I did," Izabelle said. "I'm guessing you have to go."

Charlie rubbed at her temples. "Yes. I'm sorry. Freaking Allen won't let me live for half of a second. But seriously, get someone to watch it. You have to rip the Band-Aid off. Maybe Mr. Giver can help you out with this too," she said.

"Is that his nickname now?" Izabelle asked.

"Hey. I call 'em like I see 'em," Charlie said, giving Izabelle a warm smile.

"Bye, girl. Enjoy your meeting," Izabelle said, waving.

"Bye, girl. I won't." Charlie waved back and then clicked an end to the connection.

Izabelle sat back down at her laptop and stared at the slides. Talking to Charlie about her "fantasy man" had been fun. Staring at her reality was definitely not. It was frustrating.

Charlie was right. She really needed to rip the Band-Aid off, do the pitch out loud, and collect some feedback. But the thought scared the shit out of her for all of the reasons. This had always been the pitfall of being a one-woman business. She really didn't have anyone other than her friends to reach out to when she needed advice. They were all ambitious and supportive, but they didn't know the nuts and bolts of the start-up world. She hoped through the competition, she could gain a mentor, but that didn't help her situation now.

She considered Charlie's suggestion of asking Jake. He was in business, so he was likely to be slightly more helpful than a random off the street or her friends, but she wasn't sure how she was going to pivot from "I shut down at dinner from the mere suggestion of you trying to help me" to "please let me monopolize hours of your vacation time to bore you with a presentation that I already know is crap but that I desperately need to be amazing." The real kicker was that she was not at all confident she could actually get to version two without a repeat of version one. With her stress levels about this thing running ever higher, she could feel herself fraying at the edges. She didn't want to risk another meltdown in front of Jake. Or anyone, for that matter.

She was relieved when the phone rang again, and she picked it up, glad Charlie had called her back so soon.

"You must have gotten my brain wave," Izabelle said.

"Was the brain wave that I can't stop thinking about you?" Jake asked, playfully.

"Oh! Hi. You weren't who I was expecting."

"Do you get a lot of calls on your hotel room phone?"

Izabelle looked at her cell phone on the bed to the room phone in her hand. *Lord, Iz. You are so out of it you didn't even distinguish between your cell phone and the room phone.*

"Ha. No, sorry. I'm just not as focused as I would like."

"Hmm. I was hoping to do some heavy flirting over the

phone, but I don't want to distract you. Instead, I'll just ask if you know what you want for dinner tonight? I was going to order it ahead."

Awe. It was really sweet that he would try to plan ahead for her, but she could barely figure out what to type next, much less what she would want to eat in eight hours. "It's so nice of you to ask, but I can't think about anything other than my slides right now."

"Then I won't get in your way. We can just figure it out when you get here. See you tonight, gorgeous."

Izabelle felt herself lift at the casual way he complimented her. He had a knack for helping her smooth over her stressors. Izabelle had half a mind to go to his room and see what other kinds of stress they could work out over lunch, but then she heard her computer ding with a new email and thought better of it.

Alright. Shake it off. You can have your treat tonight if you get work done now. "See you tonight, Jake." Izabelle hung up the room phone and situated herself at her desk, straightened her spine, and took two deep breaths. *Focus.* Just as she clacked the first few keys, there was a knock at the door.

Izabelle dropped her head to her forearms in frustration at yet another interruption. *You've got to be fucking kidding me.* Pulling open the door, she was greeted by one of the hotel desk clerks, holding a small bag.

"Hello, Ms. Green. A delivery for you."

"Uhhh, thanks. But I didn't order anything."

"Yes. It was a call-in order. Please let us know if there is anything else you need."

Izabelle took the white paper bag from him. "Thanks

again," she said to the man as he turned and headed back down the hallway. Izabelle shut the door and opened the bag. Condoms. And a note.

__Go get 'em tiger!__
__-Charlie__

Fifteen

JAKE

Izabelle knocked on his door just before 8:30. "Come in!" Jake shouted from the kitchen. He heard the hammered wrought iron latch clink as she swung open the door. When he turned to make eye contact, he couldn't tell what she saw first, him or the food.

"Thank god you didn't listen to me." She tossed her head back in relief as she closed the door. "I am absolutely starved. I haven't eaten anything today except an apple and a cheese stick." She crossed the Spanish-tile floor with her eyes fixed on the feast he had spread out over the table. "I was going to be super hangry if we had to wait for room service."

Jake chuckled with mild concern. "We should really consider getting you on a more consistent eating schedule. This is the second time you've been on the verge of a meal crisis in as many days." He moved around the island toward her with a glass of red wine, pressing it into her hand. "At least this time, you weren't threatening to gnaw on my limbs."

"For now," Izabelle replied, smirking at him. She turned to

survey the table in earnest. "Jesus. Did you order everything on the menu?"

Jake shrugged. "Like I said, I knew my limbs were at stake here. Therefore, I got the only logical thing—steak. Plus a bunch of other stuff."

"Sheesh. Dad pun alert," Izabelle replied, laughing as she turned back towards him. "Who knew you took my appetite to be an actual threat."

He wrapped his arms around her. "A smorgasbord worked well for me once. Why mess with a good thing?" He planted a soft kiss on her head. It was an overly familiar move, but unlike most of their early interactions, he felt no awkwardness about it. They could do this. Enjoy each other like this. They could keep the competition and their...whatever this was, separate. It would all work out. He let her go as he moved to take his seat. "How did it go today?"

Izabelle looked away from him with a frown. "Not great. It was kind of a long day. Not sure I want to talk about it." She looked back at him with a beaming smile, that didn't match her voice. "How was your day?"

Jake knew that something was off but answered her question. "After I was unceremoniously thrown out of your bed this morning—" He tossed out a gratuitous wink. "—I went for a long walk, which I followed with roughly two hours of trying to hack into my own company's network."

Her smile was more genuine now as she reached for the plate of roasted potatoes. "Oh yeah? Any luck with that?"

Jake shook his head gravely. "Absolutely none. I tried every variation of my old passwords and then just went wild with any new ones I could think of. I can affirmatively say that Cam didn't change it to 'youreonvacationyoushouldntbeattemptingthis' or 'IwouldntmakeitsomethingyoucouldguessJake' or 'hahahayoullneverguessitinamillionyears.' I even tried adding the numbers one through one hundred to the end of those one at a time, but still nothing."

Izabelle belly laughed, slicing off a hearty bite of steak. "You aren't exactly selling the wonderful portion of that statement."

"No. It was fine. Truly, I have nothing to complain about. It's just a strange feeling going from full speed, everyone needing a piece of your time, and hating it to suddenly having nothing to do and desperately wanting a project. It's weird."

She nodded in understanding as she sipped her wine. Her expression changed from casual to intentional. "I've got a project for you."

He looked at her with flirty anticipation. "Your wish is my command."

She took another sip of her wine. "I need you to watch my presentation and give me feedback."

Jake's mind screeched to a halt.

Izabelle started to gently crack her knuckles. "I don't usually ask for help, but I'm at the point where I can't deny that I need some. So, I was hoping that you could give me some feedback on my pitch."

Every single cell of Jake's body deflated at once. He had walked right into this and didn't even see it coming. Again. *Idiot.* He had been banking on her statement that she wanted to keep her personal and professional lives separate, that she didn't like any insinuation that she needed help with her business. It had been the one thing that had allowed him to ignore his guilt about entangling Izabelle in a potentially messy situation. The one excuse that let him go to Izabelle's room and give in to what he wanted. He could keep it from being messy if he just kept it separate. Watching her presentation was not keeping it separate.

He looked at her expectant face, digging furiously through his mind to come up with something to say. "I'm sure it's fantastic, Izabelle. You don't need my help."

She raised her eyebrows at him. "You haven't seen it. How do you know if it sucks or not?"

"There is no way it sucks." Jake felt himself starting to break out in a sweat. "You are an extremely competent woman. You got yourself into the best start-up investment competition in the country. I find it hard to believe that it is anything short of amazing." Not only was Jake caught off guard that she was asking him to watch it, but he was also very surprised that she felt this unsure about it.

Izabelle's eyes narrowed as she tilted her head. "As much as I appreciate the blind support, it does suck. I know because after ripping it apart for the millionth time, I haven't finished putting it back together, and it's not that many days until I have to do it in front of a bunch of people, and I don't know what I'm doing."

Shit. It was not good news that she didn't have the presentation finished. But that wasn't a huge deal. Jake was sure she could throw something together in a few hours. "I'm confident you can pull it together. I don't even know what I would be able to tell you." Which was one hundred percent true. Jake was working out on the fly what would and wouldn't be okay for him to say at this point.

"Ha. Confidence," Izabelle said dryly, not meeting his eyes. "That's the issue. I have zero confidence about this." She scratched at her head. "And I don't think you realize how much it bothers me to say that. Everyone expects that this would be no problem for me, that I could do it like I did everything else, but I..." Tears welled up in Izabelle's eyes, which made his heart pound even harder. She shook her head. "But it's fine. You're right. I'm sure I can figure this out." She tilted her head back as she blinked rapidly, avoiding his eyes.

"I—it's not that I don't want to—"

"No. I know. It's no big deal. I just thought..." She shook her head again. She looked back at him, and her eyes were glassy. "Anyway. Let's get back to whatever else we were talking about before this." The closed-lip smile she attempted was warped at the corners of her mouth.

Jake's heart was breaking looking at Izabelle's face grow splotchy with the effort not to cry. She tried faking a smile again, but her lip quivered on the way up, and it broke him. Fuck trying to keep himself away from her. He got up from the table and went to her, scooping her out of the chair and wrapping her up in his arms. The second he did, he felt her sag against him, as if the pressure of keeping it all in was the only thing holding her up. He stroked her head, squeezing her against him. "Izabelle, it's okay. It's going to be okay." She cried then.

"No, it's not! I shouldn't be crying about this. It's so embarrassing." The tears muffled her voice. "What the hell is wrong with me? It took me all afternoon to work up the courage to even ask you to watch it, and I couldn't even do that without a meltdown." Her breath hitched as he rubbed her back. "This is why I walked out of dinner the other day, and now I'm crying all over you. I'm so sorry. I should go. This is so dumb." She tried to push away from him, but he held on to her and ran his hand over her hair.

Jake's heart twisted. In that moment what he thought he wanted changed. "It's not dumb. None of it is dumb. You are incredible." He didn't know how he was going to make this work, but everything in him told him that he had to try. She meant too much to him, and this competition meant too much to her to do anything else. He kissed the top of her head. "I'm not going anywhere, and neither are you."

She sniffed and nodded against his chest. They stayed like that for a while, giving Jake time to collect his thoughts. When her breathing eventually slowed and her sniffles subsided, Jake's mind was made up. He felt her take a deep inhale, and she sat up.

"I'm so sorry. That was a lot," she said, wiping her eyes. "I swear I'm not usually this person. It's just—everything been a lot."

Jake grabbed her hands and held them. "Iz. You have nothing to apologize for. I want to help you however I can."

She looked up at him and beamed, her eyes somehow an even more vibrant green as a result of her tears. His heart soared and then immediately crashed back down. It was the next part that was going to kill him.

"Alright. Let's get you to bed. You need to get some actual rest if you're going to do the first run-through tomorrow." She nodded and stood, still holding his hand, pulling him toward the bedroom. It was a knife to the heart. "No. I meant that I'll take you back to your room."

She looked up at him, the surprise clear on her face. "Oh. You don't want to..." Her eyes flicked toward the bedroom.

Jake squeezed her hand; it was more of a brace for himself than it was a reassurance for her. "Izabelle. I want to." He squeezed just a little harder. "You have no idea how much I want to. But I think, in this case, your position on not mixing business and personal is the right one. If I'm going to help you with your presentation, we're going to have to wait on some other things."

And that was it. That was the line that Jake knew he had to draw. As much as he wanted every single part of her, they were not in a position where that was going to work right now. She needed help with her presentation. That much was clear. There were ways he could help her without undermining EtaSella or Izabelle herself. He wasn't an investor, and he hadn't spoken to any of the investors that were coming this year and wouldn't be before he left. It wasn't like he was going to be influencing their decisions. Plus, he was so far out of the loop on what the most recent years of EtaSella had been like he really couldn't give any special insider advice anyway. He clearly hadn't known who any of the participants were this year, or he would have seen this coming. Izabelle just needed someone to listen to her and help get her over whatever was eating away at her. He could do that. He could be that person for her. But that meant that they really shouldn't be sleeping together. That was blurring the lines too much. And it went against everything she said she wanted. She had said at breakfast yesterday that she didn't mix personal and professional. So he wouldn't. At least not anymore than they already had. He could do that for her.

Izabelle looked at Jake with an expression he couldn't quite place, but she nodded. "Okay. That makes sense." She moved toward the front door of the casita. "Walk me back?"

"It would be my pleasure."

They walked back mostly in silence, but for once, it wasn't an awkward one. Izabelle still hadn't let go of his hand. He had the passing thought that holding hands was a little wigglier than the straight line he had hoped to draw between them, but as long as she was okay with it, then he was more than okay with it. And she hadn't let go yet. As they walked down the hallway to her room, Izabelle slowed her pace.

"Hey, Jake?"

Jake was relieved that the tremor in her voice was gone. "Yes?"

"Thank you."

"It's nothing. Really," he said.

They reached her door, and she turned to face him. She looked up at him, eyes full. "No. It's not nothing. It means a lot." She rocked onto her tippy-toes, and Jake shut his eyes. He wanted her to kiss him, to take whatever boundary line he was trying to construct and smash it. To want him as ferociously as he wanted her. But then he felt her soft lips on his cheek, and he savored the sweetness just as much.

She whispered into his ear. "Until tomorrow."

Sixteen

JAKE

They had agreed to meet up just before ten to give Izabelle time to get herself set up. At ten o'clock on the dot, Jake knocked on Izabelle's door. She pulled it open before he had even finished his second knock. The look on her face immediately let him know he had fucked up.

"What the hell are you wearing?" she asked, eyes wide, scanning him up and down.

"A suit?" he responded.

"I can tell it's a suit. Why are you wearing a suit?"

"I thought it would help if I looked like the audience. The audience will be wearing suits, right? I thought that was the whole point."

"It is! But now I'm not wearing a suit. Should I wear a suit for this? Shit," she said, her voice ticking up at the end of the sentence, her anxiety audibly rising. "I thought this was just a casual run-through."

"No, I don't think you have to. I mean, if you want to—"

His mind was scrambling at this abrupt change in tone. He was deeply glad he hadn't worn a tie.

"How the fuck is it that I end up underdressed for my own practice pitch in my own hotel room?"

He felt awful that her nerves had set in this badly in the short time he hadn't been with her. He had no idea that she was this anxious about it. "Shit. I'm so sorry. I was trying to help. Truly."

A growling noise came from the back of her throat. More frustration than feral, but the message that she wasn't pleased was loud and clear. "I know. Maybe I should go put one on. Or maybe just the blazer." She started to crack her knuckles as she looked toward the closet in her room.

Jake knew he had to shift the tone, or this whole thing was going to go down in flames. "How about we do a first run-through, no suit, and then the second time through, we can add on to it. There is plenty of time to run it as many times as you want." He took a stab at lightening the mood. "Unless your presentation is multiple days long. In which case—"

"It's twenty-nine minutes and thirty seconds," Izabelle interrupted him. "The maximum time limit is thirty minutes."

Probably not the time to make jokes. "Okay, so you've definitely run this before if you know it down to the second."

"I said I've never done it in front of other people, not that I hadn't done it at all. Now, shush. Sit down and let me get in the headspace to do this thing. You've got me all off."

He took off his suit jacket and sat where she told him at the edge of the bed, trying to keep his expressions placid. Anything to recover from the suit debacle. But god almighty, it was difficult to keep his face still. She was pacing in the small space between the desk, the bed, and the window, taking the knuckles of her right hand and crackling them with her left. She nodded her head slightly, as if she was counting something with each step. It made him want to pull her in for a hug, stroke her hair, tell her she was amazing, and not to be so freaking nervous. It was just the first run-through, for god's sake.

Seeing as reaching out would probably only result in him getting his hands smacked away, he resolved to just watch her. Which he couldn't lie, nerves and suit mistakes aside, was pretty great. It was incredible to see this side of her, to enjoy how she moved, to see her focus and determination up close. It was hot as hell. The hardest part of paying attention to her presentation was that he was going to be paying too much attention to her.

"Okay," Izabelle said, abruptly turning on her heel to face him. She set her shoulders and took a visibly deep inhale. "Ladies and gentlemen, thank you very much for coming today. It is an honor to get to talk to you today about Me-E-O, a do-it-yourself resource for any entrepreneur to become their own CEO."

Off to a good start. Clever company name.

Izabelle clicked to the next slide on her laptop, which was precariously propped up on a makeshift podium made from books and binders from around the room. She took another breath as she looked at the slide. "Me-E-O allows fledgling businesses to call their own shots. They can manage—oh shoot, that's a typo." She bent to fix it. "Okay." She smiled a wan smile and then clicked again, maintaining eye contact with him as she did it. She read off every bullet point of the next slide. It wasn't the best audience engagement technique, but they could work on that. He gave her an encouraging thumbs-up when she finished and clicked again. The next slide had the same background as the first three but instead of bullet points read "INSERT SOMETHING THAT IS MORE INTERESTING THAN THIS LAME STOCK PHOTO HERE" in giant letters across the heading.

Jake looked from the slide to Izabelle, who was continuing on. "It lets you become a CEO on your own terms." She clocked his quizzical expression and then looked back at the screen as she went to click again. "Shit. I thought I fixed that." She bent again to start filling things in, visibly flustered. She clicked around the screen too rapidly. On one of the errant clicks, she deleted the entire slide she had been working on. "Fuck! No! Come back." She kept clicking and started pressing keys, keeping her head down as she did it.

"Hey, Iz."

She swore again, her pace of clicking increasing at a frantic rate. "Come back, come back, please come back.

"Izabelle. Woah. Take a minute."

She didn't look up but had a huge sniff. "No. I'm okay. I just need a minute. I can fix it really quick." Her voice was shaking just like it had last night.

He couldn't take it anymore. He got up from his assigned place on the bed and went to her. She turned away from him to face the wall.

"Just give me a second. I have to do this. I have to..."

He moved next to her to put his arm around her, and she wriggled away. "No." Her voice was sharp. "Don't. I'm not having a repeat of last night."

Jake backed up to the bed again. "It's just me, so don't

worry if it's not perfect." He resumed his seat, hating the distance between them.

Izabelle remained facing the wall, clutching her laptop, for an uncomfortable amount of time until she winged herself around and immediately launched back into where she had left off. She made it through one slide before she came to a dead stop. "I can't do this." Her face was icily serious.

"What? Of course you can do this. What's wrong?"

That was the wrong thing to say.

"Everything is wrong!" She was full-on shouting as she pointed to the laptop. "My presentation is a mess! I'm a mess! It's my company, for christ's sake. I should be able to talk about it like a normal person, but I can't! I am racking my brain all day, every day for months on how to make my presentation to a bunch of investors 'pop' or 'wow' or 'sparkle' or whatever the hell cliché adjective you want to use. I am just so fucking frustrated at this point I can barely see straight!" Jake was paralyzed as he watched Izabelle's anger boiling over into despair. "But none of that is going to matter because I am too fucking scared to actually give the presentation in the first place!" It was then that all the steam inside of her condensed into tears. Her voice lost its power and went small. "No. Not again. I don't want to cry."

Jake got up from the bed and wrapped her in his arms. She didn't bat him away this time.

Hearing her doubt herself and be this upset was turning him inside out. He hugged her tighter. "You thought you could do this because you can."

"I can't." She cried into his chest. "I can't do it all by myself anymore. It's too much. I'm just—I'm just scared all the time."

He held her head, his fingers continuing to brush through her hair. "Why are you scared?" She shook her head against his chest. "Izabelle, I want to know."

She shook her head again but then let out a laugh mixed with her cry. "That's the problem. I know you do, and I still don't want to tell you."

"I want to hear everything you have to tell me. Is it the public speaking part? Lots of people are scared of that. We can work on it."

She sounded morose as she mumbled into his chest. "No." She sniffed. "Well, yes. But that's not all of it."

"Okay." Jake tried to sound as sunny as possible. "See, that's great. You know what it is."

"It's just... it's mostly—I'm just scared that if I do this, everything will get taken away from me, and I'm scared that if I don't, it will all go away anyway." Jake didn't want to interrupt her, but he made a mental note to circle back on what she was talking about. It didn't really make sense, and he needed more information. "And I feel like such a dumbass for crying and for coming to a competition without a perfect pitch deck when the whole point of the competition is the presentation of the pitch deck."

"Well, that we can fix."

She laughed dejectedly. "Which part?"

"Let's start with the pitch deck and then work backward from there." He felt her laugh more fully this time. "Let's get the slides the way you want them, one at a time. Then we can worry about the presentation part." She nodded against his chest, squeezed him, and then went to get her laptop as he retook his place on the edge of the bed.

She sat next to him and went back through the first few slides she had covered, filling in the graphic that was missing and adjusting the spacing. She clicked through to the next slide.

"This one is fine. It's just the numbers for the next three slides." She clicked through them quickly.

"Wait, go back," Jake said. *These numbers can't be real.*

She clicked back to the profit and loss chart and then again to the balance sheets. "Is there something wrong with them?"

"No. Not at all. I just wanted to take a look at them closer." He studied the screen. "These are real and not projected figures?"

"Yep." She eyed him nervously. "Do you think they're bad?"

"The opposite, actually. Sorry, you can keep going." As she continued to click through the slides, tweaking things here and there, Jake was increasingly impressed by the numbers and soundness of her business plan. He should have guessed Izabelle's company would be just as amazing as she was. But what she had here wasn't just amazing. It was rock star level. It was one of the best companies he had ever seen come through EtaSella. He was dying to dig through her written materials and really get into the numbers but knew he would have to wait. The numbers wouldn't mean anything if she couldn't get through her pitch. That and digging through her competition application was another line he shouldn't be crossing.

Over the next couple of hours, they ran through the entire deck of slides three more times, making sure to catch each comma splice and placeholder. Each time they ran through it, Jake could feel Izabelle relax a bit more, and he did too. She didn't need help with the company; the numbers would entice any investor worth their salt. It was just getting those numbers out into the world that she needed help with. All he had to do was help her overcome a bit of stage fright and steer her toward a bit of polishing, maybe center her pitch around a theme, find a hook. And that was help he could give. He could still be here for her without interfering in the competition directly. A small glimmer of hope that this entire thing wasn't doomed allowed itself to shine.

Seventeen

IZABELLE

"Ready to run it now?" Jake looked over at her expectantly. After three editing passes on the slides, they were now error-free. It was a natural question.

"Is it bad if I say no?" Between the events of last night and this morning, Izabelle felt wiped out. She had never intended to cry like that. Either time. It felt weirdly like when you fall and hurt yourself, and you would be totally fine until someone asks you, "Oh my gosh, are you okay?" and then in that moment, you start crying like a baby. When Jake looked at her and asked her how she was, she crumbled into a million tear-soaked pieces. Which was not the bad-ass CEO persona that she was trying to project. Attempting to run the slides when she was this tired and raw put her at risk of losing it a third time and really shattering her image. It was a risk she didn't want to accept.

"We can take a lunch break and then come back to it," Jake said.

"I'm not sure I want to. I'm tired. I think I might need to step away from it for a little bit. Start fresh tomorrow. I feel better that we actually got everything together, but saying it all out loud is still a little daunting."

Jake nodded, his eyes calm. "I get it. We've still got plenty of time, so no need to push yourself. What would you like to do, then?"

Now that her mind was transitioning off the angst of the slides and her various slide-related meltdowns, she became more cognizant of the entire left side of her body pressed up against Jake as they sat there on her bed. The bed where they had... The thought of what they had gotten into on this bed made her clench her thighs in an effort not to drape them over him. It was her own rules Jake was following. She was the one who had said she didn't mix personal and professional. He was just trying to give her what she wanted. But that was what made it so hot. She was seriously starting to think any rules she had about keeping things strictly business were stupid. She scooched away from him on the bed in order to give herself some space. "I'm game for anything as long as it isn't screen-based."

"Alright, how about golf?"

"Golf?" she asked incredulously.

"I recall you saying that you're game for anything. Golf is a game."

"That is very literal, but no golf. I'm not eighty."

He frowned at her. "I said golf, not shuffleboard. Golf is not played by only old people. Have you never heard of the PGA?"

Izabelle gave his frown right back to him. "Still a no to golf."

"Okay, how about pickleball?"

"What? I'm not eighty or twenty. Do people in their thirties even play pickleball?"

He chuckled deeply. "Alright. I'm going to need a little bit more guidance, then, Ms. Anything."

Izabelle set her shoulders. "Let me rephrase—I am not game for anything, and I don't really want anything game-based. I am stressed as hell, and I want to take my mind off of it, but I don't want to learn anything new, and I don't want to move that much because I'm freaking exhausted." Izabelle felt the same tension winding up in her again. "Do you have any ideas that are lying down based?"

Jake wrapped his arm around her shoulders, and that tension quickly made itself scarce. "Now, that I can work with. I need to make a quick call. Go in the bathroom, take your clothes off, and put a robe on."

The same force that had been clenching her thighs closed immediately transitioned to propelling her toward the bathroom to follow orders. She damn near sprinted from the room. Rules be damned. She wanted this and was beyond glad Jake had given up on trying to keep things separate. She whipped her top over her head without giving a shit about how it affected her hair. She then started stripping off her jeans, hopping to pull off the tight fabric where it was bunched up around her ankles.

Izabelle paused for a moment once she got the pants off. She looked in the mirror. The jeans had definitely left those weird red marks around her stomach from sitting too long, but fuck it, he wasn't going to care. She reached behind her for her bra clasp, then hesitated. Was it hotter if she had it on or didn't have it on? Stupid thing wasn't comfy—might as well get it off too. She flicked open the clasp, wigged out of it, and then yanked down her panties. She took a deep breath as she reached for the robe, sliding into it with the hope that he ripped it off like last time. *You can do this, girl. You deserve this.*

Izabelle strode out of the bathroom, light-headed with anticipation.

Jake bit his lip as his eyes raked over her. "Are you ready to go?"

Izabelle's heart was hammering. "Definitely."

Jake took her by the hand. "Good. Don't forget your room key."

∽

"The spa?" She could see through the clear doors of the spa, a serene space of creams and tans. The lighting was warm and low, and there was a faint gurgle of a water feature slipping out from behind the plate glass. The robe made sense now. She really should have put that together. She thought the room key line had been weird but was hoping he was just taking her back to his room. She hadn't known why they had to make that transition naked in robes, but she wasn't opposed to it. Now that they were standing in front of the doors, everything that had just happened had a much less sexy feel, which was disappointing.

"Have you never been to one?" he asked from her side.

"No." Her answer was flat, but that was because she was still trying to get her heart rate to come down to a normal not-about-to-have-penetrative-sex-for-the-first-time-in-a-long-time level.

Jake wrapped his arm around her shoulders and squeezed.

"I hope you like it. This is a good one, and you deserve it." He opened the door for her. "After you."

The scent of lavender and eucalyptus ushered her into the lobby, where a woman stood behind a pale marble counter with a tray holding glasses of water infused with cucumber and mint.

"Hi, you must be Charise. I'm Jake, the one who just gave you a call."

"Yes, of course. We hope that you very much enjoy your journey with us this afternoon. We have you set up to start your experience with your couple's massage in Suite 3." She gestured gracefully down the hall.

"I'm sure we will." Jake retook Izabelle's hand and started off down the hallway indicated.

"Couple's massage?" Izabelle asked. Maybe this did still have a sexy bent after all.

"It was easier than explaining all the details." He gave her a wink, turning the handle of the suite door.

The room was just as tranquil as the reception area. Two massage tables were centered in the room, and the addition of a white adobe fireplace added a sensual heat and crackling energy. But as she watched Jake slide off his robe and onto the table, it may not have been just the fireplace that was making her feel the way she did.

A full sixty minutes of massage later, she fully understood why people raved about spa days. As she lay facedown on the table, the knots in her shoulders were gone, replaced by hot stones, keeping any habitual tension at bay. The attendants had left them to "absorb the energy" of the room before their next treatment.

Izabelle groaned, vocalizing the languid feeling in her

muscles. "I really should have gotten a massage sooner. It's heavenly."

"I am so glad you enjoyed it. But if you keep groaning like that, I'm certainly not going to walk out of this room any less tense than I walked in."

She raised her head to look at him. His back dwarfed the stones that ran down his spine, the full curve of it blocked by the towel covering his lower half. Izabelle couldn't help but let out an appreciative "mmmmm."

The noise caused him to stir, raising his head up to meet her gaze, pure heat in his eyes. "What did I say about those?"

She opened her mouth to answer, liking where this was going. The movement caused his eyes to flicker toward her lips and then abruptly to the door as the masseurs came in with the next treatment.

"You made an excellent choice by choosing to follow up with the prickly pear wrap," the woman said, wheeling in a cart full of jars and warm towels.

"I'm not so sure I would make the same one if you asked me in this moment," Jake replied under his breath, shooting Izabelle a knowing look.

What followed was a very interesting process of being scrubbed, brushed, and wrapped tightly into warm towels and a layer of space blanket that allowed the prickly-pear concoction to work its magic, allegedly.

Once they had been fully wrapped and left to stew, Izabelle couldn't help but giggle. "I feel like a sausage."

She heard Jake's deep rumbling chuckle beside her. "It's weird the first time, but trust me, it's magic for your skin. Makes it so soft."

Izabelle shuddered, thinking about Jake running his hands over her skin, the way he had covered every inch of her with his palms. It caused a rush of heat to burn through her that had nothing to do with the tinfoil she was wrapped in. "How did you get to be such an expert on spa treatments?"

Jake was silent, long enough to make her think he hadn't heard her, but then he let out a hollow chuckle, his voice heavy. "My mom, actually."

Izabelle could tell there was something Jake wasn't saying. It hung in the air. Then she realized what it was, and she knew the feeling well. "What was she like?"

"Hm." The pensiveness was clear in his voice, and the silence followed again.

"You don't have to talk about her if you don't want to."

"No, it's not that. It's just... People rarely ask me, and when they do, I'm never sure what to say because I don't know if what I remember is what I actually remember or just what I've seen in photographs."

She let the silence linger a moment before she continued. She had to collect herself. She hadn't anticipated him saying what she had felt for so long. "How old were you when she died?"

"Seven. Wait. How did you know she died?"

"I could hear it in your voice. I was five when my parents died."

"Oh, Iz. I'm so sorry, I didn't... I shouldn't be so caught up in my own stuff. I didn't even think about how you figured out what I meant so quickly."

"Please don't apologize. It's actually kind of nice to talk to someone who gets it. Usually, people just pity me when they hear about it. It was worse when it happened because it was in the news."

"The news?"

"Drunk driver."

"Jesus."

"You?"

"Cancer. I didn't even put it together until I was older. The way I remember it, she was fine one day and gone the next. My dad never talked about it then or after."

"Jesus." Izabelle let the silence linger this time. It was a certain type of irony that this kind of emotional moment would happen while she was swaddled like a baby wrapped in cactus goo, arms wrapped up tightly against her while her heart was reaching for him. She settled for rolling over on her side to look at him, wriggling like a caterpillar to do it. "So, tell me how she got you going to the spa."

Jake continued to stare straight up at the ceiling, but she saw the upturn of a smile on his face. "I don't have any siblings, so I spent all of my time with my parents. My parents worked together, so they would always take me to meetings and the office, but sometimes my mom would slip away somewhere and not say where she was going. When she was gone, I would cry and cry. So eventually, she took me with her, and we went to the spa." He paused and gave a small laugh. "God help the poor masseuse who had to massage a toddler, but I thought it was just the best. I wanted the cucumbers on my eyes so bad and the towel wrapped around my head. I didn't even know what it was for but I thought it looked cool. After that first time, we went together a lot. It was special just the two of us time. After she died..." He paused again, not breaking eye contact with the ceiling. "I just felt like it was a place where I felt close to her."

"See, you remember more than you think." She looked at him and the overly controlled rise and fall of his chest. She thought she heard him sniff.

When Jake spoke again, his voice was thick. "I'm sorry. I don't know why I'm putting all of this on you. I never talk about this kind of stuff. And now I'm over here acting like I'm the only person who has ever lost their parents. When you—"

"Jake, it's fine." She paused, the twist in her gut that always came when she talked about this wringing her again. Old hurts that she had learned to live with. "Well, it's not fine, actually. But I've worked through it. I remember their laughs, and our house, and how they read me *Goodnight Moon*, and that they loved me."

"Iz."

He rolled toward her, the look in his eyes matching hers. An understanding, deep and raw. Longing and loneliness. He made a move toward her, entirely forgetting that he was a human burrito, and took a tumble off the table, hitting the ground with a thud.

"Jake!" Izabelle reacted by reaching out to catch him, which resulted in her also flopping to the ground. The impact hadn't been hard, thanks to the layers of fluff around her. But it was jarring enough for her hands to break free. Jake must have had the same experience because he reached out and scooped her up, pulling her into him with a force that was nearly as great as her hitting the floor.

"Are you hurt?" He was patting her like he was checking for broken bones. "Why the hell did you do that?"

"I was going to catch you!" A nervous laugh shook itself loose once she realized they were both okay. "This is why I was never allowed to sleep in the top bunk as a kid."

His look of concern eased as he dropped his forehead onto hers. He drew away as his own giggles started to erupt. "I feel like a Crunchwrap Supreme that got dropped out of the Taco Bell drive-through window."

"I've felt like a pig in a blanket this whole time."

Jake started tearing off the remaining layers of his wrap. "How about we get out of here? We can head into town and grab something to eat."

"Sushi?" She looked up at him as she started tearing herself free.

"I don't think I could recommend sushi this far from the ocean..." He caught her eye and understood her joke. "Spring rolls?"

"Chicken wraps?"

"Burritos?"

"Definitely burritos." She grabbed Jake's outstretched hand.

"Let's just promise that from now on, we both do a little less falling," he said as he gave her hand a squeeze.

Her heart zinged. *Not falling might be a problem.*

Eighteen

IZABELLE

Izabelle carefully backed through the swinging door to the patio, focusing on balancing the red plastic tray of food in her hands. Successfully navigating the door with only a tiny wobble from her margarita, she scanned the patio, looking for Jake. He waved to her from the table where he was sitting near the wrought iron railing. She beamed at him in response. He looked too perfect, leaning back in his chair with the sun on his face. "I finally get to be the one triumphantly arriving with a tray of food!" Izabelle said as she crossed the patio. She reached the table and set the tray down with a thunk. "I feel like I have provided."

"And I get to be the one who let themselves get way too hungry. Thank you. It looks incredible." He reached for his burrito and Corona and immediately went in for a bite.

Izabelle took in the sight of him as he moaned in appreciation of his carne asada. "I know you were trying to get me to take my mind off things with the spa today, but I gotta say I think it might have worked more on you. You are looking awfully relaxed and happy for someone who said they were being forced on this trip against their will."

Jake laughed, holding up a finger to her to wait as he finished chewing his bite. "Can I call Cam so she can hear you say that? Because I don't think she will believe it if I tell her."

"Oh, come on. That can't be true," Izabelle responded.

"Oh, it certainly is. I..." He looked away from her toward the mountains in the distance, his jaw tightening as the ease in his face was replaced with a tension that made Izabelle wish she hadn't said anything. "I'm not known for being a particularly happy or relaxed person at work." He looked back to her hesitantly. "I'm pretty sure most people would describe me as angry."

Izabelle was shocked by that. "Really? That honestly surprises me." She tilted her head, trying to wrap her mind around the idea of an angry Jake. She understood the not relaxed part, but angry? That was hard to square with the Jake that she knew. "Why?"

Jake picked up his beer and took a long sip, shifting uncomfortably in his chair.

Izabelle realized she might be digging a bit too much. It wasn't really fair for her to be holding back so much of herself and then be asking Jake these super-personal questions about the core of who he was. Especially if they were trying to keep some distance. Her mind flicked back to the way they had connected in the spa. Not that they had been particularly successful in keeping that distance so far, but still. "Sorry. I see now that's rather personal. You don't have to answer."

He furrowed his brow. "No. It's a good question. It's just..." He dragged the bottom of the bottle around the table in small circles. "I guess I just haven't had to justify or explain why."

Izabelle sat with that for a minute, not sure what to say next. But after a pause, Jake took in a deep breath and started in again.

"I think I said before that my dad was much better with people than I am. He always knew what to say and how to connect with anyone. It was really something to watch. People joke that he never met a stranger because he would talk to anyone like an old friend, and it was true. I think it's why he was able to build the company and be as successful as he was." Jake sighed. "But as much as I tried, I was never the natural that he was. He always said I knew the business better than he did, was better at numbers, the forecasts, the technologies. But I was never able to do what he could." Jake circled his hand. "Just talk to people. People would fall over themselves to do what he asked. He had such an easy command of the room."

Izabelle could see a storm cloud start to roll across Jake's face. She wanted desperately to bring the light back to it. "But that's okay. You don't have to be just like him to be successful."

"Yeah, but the problem is I always wanted to be just like him. And then after he died, everyone else wanted me to be just like him too. And I couldn't. And it made me mad. I just felt like I was disappointing everyone all the time. They were looking to me to give them something that I never had. Which made me surly towards everyone, and eventually, I realized that people would fall over themselves to do what I asked, but it wasn't because they liked me; it was because they were afraid of upsetting me. Which just made me angrier because that's not who I am." Jake sighed and dropped his head into his hand, pinching the bridge of his nose with his fingers. "And all of that sucks to admit."

Izabelle wanted to launch herself across the table at Jake and wrap him in a hug. The thought of Jake struggling to be what he wanted to be and what everyone else thought he should be shredded her. He was perfect. He was kind and thoughtful and occasionally awkward, and that was incredible. She wanted to kiss him and tell him with every ounce of her body that he was wonderful and enough. He was unlike any man she had ever met, and that made her want to say fuck you to every single rule she had ever put in place about mixing business and relationships. Just when she was about to get up from the table and crawl into his lap, Jake took his head out of his hand.

"God. Iz. I'm so sorry. You said you didn't want to mix personal and professional, and yet here I am, trampling all over that for the second time today. I don't mean to keep dumping all of this on you when you have so much else on your mind. Let's just forget all of that, please."

Izabelle's heart clenched. The reminder of the boundaries kept her in her seat. "No. Thank you for sharing all of that with me. I'm sorry that you didn't feel like you could say that to anyone before."

He nodded. "I'm sure I could have if I really wanted to. And I think Cam could tell. She was always making sure my surliness didn't cross over into asshole-ness. But I think she saw it was getting harder and harder to do, and that's why she pushed me so hard to take this trip." Jake's shoulders slumped. "Soooo, yeah." Jake's lips twitched to the side as he looked over the patio rail. "I hope that doesn't change how you think about me."

Izabelle's response was automatic. "I would never judge you for being honest. But if you're worried, it doesn't change how I feel about you at all."

Jake's eyes met hers, a different kind of intensity mixing with the sadness. "Feel?"

Jake's highlighting of the word made her breath catch. "Er, I mean, I would never think ill of a...of a friend for something like that."

"Thank you for listening." Jake smiled wanly, despite the intensity still in his gaze. "Friend."

Izabelle knew that they had to move away from this topic of conversation, or else she was going to crack and give a big middle finger to this "just friends" rule they had been following. She blew out a deep breath. "It's been a rather intense day, hasn't it? I'm sorry I started it off with such a meltdown."

Jake must have sensed what she was trying to do because he shook his head slightly as if trying to clear a thought before putting on a less intense expression. "I've told you that you don't need to apologize, for anything, but especially not for shouldering so much. If anyone should be apologizing, it's me. By my count, I've put you through not one but two emotional breakdowns today over shit that I shouldn't be dumping on you." Jake chuckled darkly. "Or anyone, really."

Izabelle raised her glass. "Well, what are friends for if not dumping all your shit on and hoping they'll help you clean it up?"

Jake raised his eyebrows in surprise but grabbed his glass in a cheers. "To friends."

They spent the rest of the meal in an easy but tenuous state of banter. Izabelle didn't dare risk getting into anything heavier.

She was very certain that if they talked much more about feelings or if Jake looked at her with any kind of desire she was going to cross some lines. Which was ironic because they were her own lines. Her own rules. But her reasons for drawing them seemed less and less distinct the more she was around Jake. She sipped the dregs of her margarita with the thought that she should have gotten another one.

Jake watched her as she set her glass down. "Well? Should we get you back to the hotel? I figure you want to get some good sleep before we get back to it tomorrow."

Yep. She definitely should have gotten the second drink. It would have been a good way to stall. Everything Jake said was correct. She should get a good night's rest, and they should jump right into the presentation tomorrow, which meant they should leave now, but she just didn't want to. She wanted to linger a bit. Izabelle had never been this much of a procrastinator, but sitting here in the warm, setting sun was much more appealing than sliding back into the office chair of anxiety and ass aches in her room. "Let's walk around a bit. I'm not ready to go back yet."

Jake gathered up the tray containing the remains of dinner with one hand while he gestured with the other. "After you."

As they exited the patio onto the sidewalk, they turned toward the row of stores that lined the main drag of town. Izabelle instinctively reached for Jake's hand but stopped herself. She really couldn't justify cutting herself off from Jake at dinner for fear that she would want much, much more and then suddenly go for his hand here. All of this was beginning to seem really stupid. She dawdled behind Jake, store windows a blur to her left as she stared at the cracks in the sidewalk, deep in thought, trying to tease out what she actually wanted from what her rules dictated. She wanted to hold his hand. She didn't want to be holding herself back. She wanted to talk about feelings and emotions and all of the very real things that Jake had shared with her. She wanted to be as open with him as he had been with her. And what she really wanted was to tumble back into bed with him. Now. Here. At the resort. Not when she was done with her presentation or some random, may-never-happen date in the future when they were home and re-absorbed into their hectic lives. So why wasn't she going for what she wanted?

"Sorry most of the stores are closed. I didn't realize how early town rolled up." Jake looked back at her with an apologetic expression.

Izabelle looked up into his eyes and then quickly turned toward the window next to them. "It's really fine. I just wasn't ready to go back yet, and the windows are all so full of things that it's fun to just look." She stepped closer to the window full of Kokopelli statues, turquoise, and crystals. The sun had set behind the ridge, but it left enough straggling rays for the pane of glass to reflect the planes of Jake's face behind her. Her eyes flicked up, and she caught him staring at her. The glare of the glass didn't transmit the details of his gaze, but she knew it would have the intensity that she craved, that she was trying not to cave to. She bent to take in the intricacies of a silver necklace, avoiding turning around and confirming what she already knew.

"Izabelle."

She flicked her eyes up again, heart beating faster, and he was still staring at her. She didn't trust herself to do anything other than continue to stare at the shining silver necklace in the window.

"I know this will put me a risk of saying yet another thing I shouldn't today, but I have to." Izabelle straightened slightly but didn't turn. Jake stepped closer to her as he continued. "When you said I looked relaxed earlier." He paused, and she held her breath. "You should know that has nothing to do with the spa and everything to do with you. I want to thank you for spending this time with me. It's only because of you that I look relaxed and happy. That I *am* relaxed and happy. I hope that I can give some of that back to you because you're amazing, and you deserve that."

Fuck the stupid rules. Izabelle turned and closed the gap between her and Jake. She rose onto her tiptoes as she circled her hand around the back of his neck, pulling him down to her. She caught his lips, parted in surprise. His surprise lasted only a second until he tumbled headfirst in her kiss. His hands immediately encircled her waist, giving her the contact she'd been craving. She pulled him, walking backward until she was pinned against the adobe wall of the store, delighting in the feel of his weight on top of her again. This wasn't holding hands; this wasn't sitting next to each other on the bed. Izabelle was trying to make this perfectly clear that this wasn't just as friends. She ran her hands through his hair, pulling at the nape of it.

"What are you trying to do to me?" he asked, his voice rasping as Izabelle started to work down his neck.

Izabelle chuckled against Jake's neck. "I'm trying to get you into bed. I'd hoped it was obvious."

She felt the groan reverberate through Jake's entire body. He grabbed her by the hips, fingers gripping her firmly as he pushed her away slightly. "Just so we're clear, does this mean you don't want to wait until after the presentation is over? You're okay to mix this?" Jake asked, searching her expression.

Izabelle met his question with fire in her eyes. "I'm done waiting for what I want. Are you?"

"I don't know why I ever thought I could."

Nineteen

JAKE

He yanked the car door shut with force and latched his seat belt in the next second. "Just so you know, I am not going to speed, but good god do I want to."

Izabelle laughed, delighted, as he threw the car into drive. Tearing up the mountain road, he couldn't help but glance over as Izabelle crossed and uncrossed her thighs.

"Izabelle, I swear to god, if you keep doing that with your legs, I cannot guarantee that I don't run us off the road." He was being hyperbolic, but god damn, it was distracting.

"Doing what?" Izabelle asked, her voice pitching higher in a way that said she knew exactly what she was doing.

He could see out of the corner of his eye she was leaning toward him in her seat. She reached up and raked her fingers into the hair at the back of his head. As she meandered in delicate circles around his scalp, he couldn't help but groan. It was the sweetest torture. By the time he turned into the hotel parking lot, every inch of him was pressing against his zipper. "Izabelle, the second I put this car in park, I'm going to need you to sprint to the casita, or else I swear on my life I'm going to take you wherever it is I catch you."

Izabelle took her hand away from his hair to unclick her seat belt. "Roger that," she said as she placed her hand on the door latch with a laugh.

And sure enough, as soon as he got the car into park, she was running full tilt across the terracotta-colored pavers toward the door of the casita. Something primal bubbled up within him as he took off after her. They got to the door at the same time, his body reaching over hers for the latch on the door. Having her body pressed up against his was intoxicating. He was certain she could feel how hard he was as she pressed her hips back against his with a wanting groan. He opened the door and pushed her through, slamming it shut and immediately grabbing for her hips, pulling her ass back against him.

He snaked one hand upward into her shirt, and the other he slid down, finding the warmth and softness of her belly as he went. She rolled her head back onto his shoulder with a delicious moan. "Do you want this?" he asked, so close to her ear that his lips brushed against it.

"Jesus, Jake. Haven't I made that obvious?"

"I wanted you the moment I saw you in that car," he said as his fingers began to circle her nipple and her clit at the same time. "I wanted you when I saw you lying by the pool." He continued his circling as he began to punctuate his words with kisses against her neck, her choppy breaths driving him wild. "I wanted you when you walked into the restaurant, wearing that slinky dress. I wanted you when I came to your hotel room. When you came for me. When you kissed me. And I want you right now."

Her hips ground against him as he continued sliding his lips over the pulse of her neck, never relenting the circles of his fingers. "I want you too," she whispered through ragged breaths.

It was what he wanted to hear. He curled his fingers into her, feeling without a doubt that she wanted him, that she was ready for him. He felt the moan she let out reverberate throughout her entire luscious body.

He was able to growl out, "Bedroom. Now," but just barely. They both sprinted to the bedroom. He leapt over her shirt as it hit the floor. As she reached the bed, she spun around and sat on the edge of it. As if she could read his thoughts, she got to work unbuttoning his jeans while he unclasped her bra. The sight of Izabelle staring up at him with those perfect, sexy eyes while undressing him made his head spin.

He brought himself down on her, dragging her up the bed. He had to kiss her. Have her. Now. As soon as their lips touched, her mouth opened, and her tongue sought his. She ran her hands over his back, nails grazing his skin in long, intentional strokes. *Jesus Christ.* His body ached for her.

He wasn't sure that he was going to keep it together much longer when she hooked her fingers into his boxer briefs, pulling them past the ridge of his hips, freeing him. He immediately returned the favor by stripping her panties down her thighs.

"More," Izabelle groaned against his mouth. She pulled him on top of her. When she reached between them to grasp his length, it was his turn to have a sharp intake of breath. "Just—" She paused, looking up at him. "Take it easy at first. You aren't the only one who's a little rusty at this."

He bent to kiss her. "Any way you want it." He slowly

thrust his hips into her, inch by inch, relishing the feeling of her slick muscles taking him in, enveloping him. His head spun with the pleasure of it. "Holy shit, Izabelle, you are amazing. I won't move until you tell me to."

She met his gaze with the same level of intensity and heat. "More."

Fuck. He didn't think he had ever seen a sight as wonderful as her head rolling back in waves of pleasure that matched each of his thrusts. He wanted all of her. He felt the compulsion to touch her everywhere at once. His hands roamed over her ribs, breasts, hips, would flick over her clit and then run the cycle again. She met each of his strokes by raising and grinding her hips. Every time she moaned, it echoed through him, a primal rumble, and their synchronicity pushed him higher and higher.

"Don't stop. Keep touching me. Right there. I want to come with you," Izabelle gasped. He coupled his deep strokes with light circles. The feel of her writhing beneath him drove him wild. He wanted it to last forever but knew he wasn't going to last long.

"Oh fuck! Yes, Jake!" Izabelle shouted, and he could feel her body spasming from its core. She brought her hand up to her mouth to cover her shout.

"Don't you ever hide from me." He tore her hand away from her mouth, pinning it down on the bed beside her. "I want to hear everything you feel." He covered her mouth with his. The second their lips connected, he was overcome. *Fuuuck.* He felt everything at once in a way that wiped his mind. The room spun around them while her face stayed centered. As he spiraled down, he felt the heaving of Izabelle's chest matching his own.

They lay there for quite a while, catching their breath. Izabelle laughed once and then absolutely cracked up laughing in between pants.

"What?" Jake asked. Izabelle didn't answer but continued to laugh, pressing her forehead into his chest. "Seriously, what?"

"You're telling me you fuck like that and you've still had women leave you?"

Jake laughed with relief. "I'm pretty sure it's the only reason they stayed as long as they did."

"Jesus."

"I know. Bleak but true."

She continued laughing, alternating chuckles and pants. "I'm pretty sure that if you keep laying it down like that, I wouldn't go anywhere, much less get out of this bed."

Jake joined in her laughter. "Well, give me a few minutes, and I can hold you to that promise." All jokes aside, Jake was more than happy to oblige. He wanted to give Izabelle whatever she wanted, and if what she wanted was him, then he could give that to her again and again. He would gladly give himself to her forever.

Twenty

IZABELLE

Izabelle woke feeling warm, safe, and slightly sore in all the right places. She languished in the feeling of being tucked in the hollow created by Jake's shoulders wrapped around her. She savored the gentle rocking she felt as his chest moved in and out with each slow, sleepy breath. She knew she had slept in later than normal again. The sun wasn't just peeking through the window shades but was fully asserting itself in its midmorning glory. But unlike their first morning together, she didn't feel the compulsion to launch herself out of the bed toward her laptop.

She didn't even really want to be awake. After the events of last night, she wanted nothing more than to remain in this peaceful place, wrapped in a blanket of bicep. She knew mixing up Jake, her presentation, all of her baggage, and stress was a risk. Yet, there was some small part of her that also knew it was inevitable. And after last night, she knew it was worth it. But she had to check back in with the reality that the presentation was inching ever closer, and it wasn't going to polish itself. She sighed and pressed her cheek against his warm arm one last time, savoring the moment, then started to wiggle free. *Maybe I wore him out and he won't wake up.*

"Please tell me you're just getting up to pee and you're coming right back," he said sleepily into her shoulder.

Damn. "I mean, I do have to pee, but it is the time of the morning in which responsible adults wake up." She made a move toward the edge of the bed, but he hauled her back into his chest. "Trust me, as much as I would like to lie around in bed all day, we've got slides to run and presentations to perfect."

He shifted slightly. "We?"

Izabelle's stomach sank. The we was probably an overstep. "If you don't want to anymore, it's—"

Jake gave her a squeeze as he interrupted her. "I very much do want to. I want to watch you do anything and everything. I was only asking to make sure you were okay with me still being involved in the presentation. I don't want you to feel you have to do something you're uncomfortable with. If anything has changed since last night, then just say the word and I will leave you be for the day. But just the day, I'm still going to claim your nights."

Izabelle relaxed into him, relieved. "Yes. I still need the help. So, if you're willing to kill another day of vacation with me, then that would be amazing. Can't say it's going to be as sexy as last night, but..."

"I very much beg to differ. Watching you talk business—" He growled into her neck. "—it very much works for me." Nipping at her shoulder he pulled her in tighter against him. "But seriously. Thank you for trusting me with this. I know how big of a deal this is, and I'm honored."

Trusting me. She dwelled on those two words. She did trust him. Well, kind of. Mostly. Clearly, she trusted him with her body. He had more than earned that trust. And he seemed to trust her. He had shared memories and places that were clearly special to him. It was that vulnerability that made her feel like she could share her presentation and her fears surrounding it with him. She was trusting him with the information and the work that consumed all of her waking hours. Trusting he wouldn't run away with it. Trusting him with her nerves, and her stress, and her slides, and her emotions. Trusting he was different than every other guy she had ever known. It was a lot. She felt like she was split in two. There was the half of her that felt that it was too soon, and too weird, to keep trusting a semi-stranger with all of this. But the other half of her felt like this hug she was wrapped in. It felt right.

He rubbed her back gently. "Hey, you okay?"

She nodded into his chest. "Yeah, I'm just a bit freaked-out even thinking about it."

"It's just me. There's no pressure."

"I mean, there is. A shit ton," she replied.

"Fair. But let's just take this one step at a time."

She nodded again. "I won't bail on doing it this time." She said it just as much to him as to herself. The knots in her stomach and shoulders were reforming at the thought of going through with it.

He kissed her shoulder gently. "You can do this."

I have to.

There was no question. She was definitely wearing a suit this time; she was not about to be upstaged by Jake looking overly dapper again. After Jake's pep talk this morning, they had agreed that they would each get cleaned up and then reconvene at noon. Izabelle figured that would give her enough time to shower, change, eat something, freak out in private, stare at her computer, freak out again, feel like she should pack it all up and go home, and then finally get it together enough to do the run-through for the first time. Out loud. For real.

She already had her laptop set up on its ramshackle stack of phone books and bibles from the nightstand drawers. She had also run through a few breathing techniques so she didn't have to do her embarrassing psych-up routine in front of him again. The good news was that it really couldn't get much worse than yesterday. And even if it did all go to shit again, history suggested Jake would just sit calmly next to her until it was right.

He knocked on the door five minutes early and let himself in. She turned to greet him. His presence bringing an involuntary smile to her face. *Lord, he looks good in everything.* His short-sleeve cotton button-down wasn't a look many men could pull off without looking like they were wearing a bowling shirt. But here he was, looking like a model for some sort of Italian cologne.

"Thank god you didn't wear a suit this time."

"I'm not that big of an idiot," he said, bending to kiss her. "Are you ready to go?"

"Yep. Come on in. I've got everything set up in here."

"Well, pack it back up because we're taking a field trip."

"Jake," she said, turning around with her hands planted on

her hips. "I really can't go anywhere. It's getting down to crunch time."

"Agreed. But we're going to do this run-through somewhere other than here. I think it would be better to practice on a fresh slate."

This really isn't the time to be tossing more distractions my way. One is more than enough. They stood staring at each other, neither of them indicating they were going to cave.

"I promise this is going to be good. Trust me."

She narrowed her eyes, considering him. *Trust me.* There it was again. But he hadn't given her a reason to doubt him yet. "Ugh. Fine. I'll pack up."

As she trotted along next to him through the hotel, she wondered why they weren't making the turn toward his casita.

"Where are we—" Their arrival in front of the ballroom doors interrupted her question.

He smiled. "It's always best to practice on the actual stage, right?"

"How did you get—"

"Just had to ask. They have it set up exactly like it will be on the pitch day. You have use of the big screen and the podium and everything."

Izabelle looked at him while experiencing what she could only describe as a full-body awe. No one had ever set up a gesture like this. It was thoughtful, helpful, sweet. It was quintessential Jake. *This is why I love you.* She smiled at him, radiating the affection she felt. *Wait, what? Love him? What the hell?* How in the world did her brain come up with that? Why in the world did an "I love you" just pop into her brain like it was a completely casual thought? Jake must have fucked a few screws loose last night. It couldn't be that she had fallen for a stranger during the most important week of her life. That was insanity. There was absolutely no way.

Her gaze turned from Jake's face toward the empty room as he opened the door. Her stomach plummeted. Her complicated feelings about Jake were consumed by much more stressful ones. *Holy shit, this is a bigger room than I thought it would be.*

Rows and rows of chairs stretched back from the raised stage constructed in front of the windows. A glossy podium sat to one side of the platform, so there was an unobstructed view of the projector screen behind it. She moved timidly into the room, her feet propelling her to keep up with Jake as he quick-stepped to the stage. Walking past the rows of chairs, it set in that each of those chairs equaled a person. A person with eyes. Eyes that would be boring into her like little anxiety-inducing laser beams in a few days' time.

"Are you okay? You aren't saying anything," Jake asked, taking in her demeanor.

She was definitively not okay. *I just went from wondering why the hell my brain thinks I love you to how the hell am I supposed to do this?* Knowing she couldn't say any of that aloud, she tried to arrange her features into something resembling a brave face. "Yeah. Definitely. I was just running the pitch deck through my head."

"Oh, that was your game face. Got it. Well, I'm ready when you are," he said, taking a seat in the front row.

She carefully climbed the stairs to the podium. She wanted to avoid face-planting at all costs. Gripping the podium, she attempted to plug in her laptop.

Thank god he can't see my hands. They were quivering as if she was back in the frigid water at Slide Rock. Any confidence she had corralled when she finished the presentation was quickly running away from her. The USB cable must have felt pity for her and her shaking hand because it slid into its receiver without her having to do the usual routine of flipping it over and over. Her presentation loaded onto the screen behind her. She looked at the slides behind her and then at Jake's expectant face in the front row. He gave her a thumbs-up. *I guess that's my cue.* She took a deep breath, trying to remember all of the public speaking tips and only remembering one. *Make sure to project so the people in the back can hear.* "Ladies and gentlemen, thank you—"

"Are you going to use the mic?" Jake asked from his seat.

"The what?"

"There's a mic that you can clip to your shirt so you can walk around and not have to shout."

"Oh." She didn't even know that was an option. She went back to the podium to look for it. She found it, clipped it on, and restarted the presentation. She got through the introduction and then went back to the podium to click the next slide.

"Do you know that there's a clicker to change the slides?"

"Oh. Yeah. I'll grab it." *Fuck. I didn't realize there was a clicker either.* After getting the clicker, she went back to the center of the stage to continue, making an effort to move about the stage and keep it "dynamic" like all the public speaking instructional videos she had watched blabbed on about.

"Do you know that each time you walk back and forth, you end up blocking the words on the screen?"

"No! I didn't know that! I don't know what I'm doing! And my hands are shaking so bad that I can barely hang on to this stupid clicker!" She could feel the boiling frustration inside of her starting to condense into tears. She avoided his eyes because if he had anything resembling a caring expression, he was going to send her over the cry cliff. *Pull it together for christ's sake.* Never in her life had her emotions been on this kind of hair trigger.

"Iz, breathe. It's just me, and we have all day to practice. It doesn't have to be perfect right now. You haven't ever been in this room before. Don't beat yourself up for not knowing all of the ins and outs."

"Well, you haven't been here before, and you seem to know a hell of a lot about it."

Jake ran his hand through his hair. "Eh. This isn't about me. It's about you. Is it okay if I come up there and give you some pointers?"

Izabelle nodded in thankful defeat, hating that she needed this much help. It wasn't like her to be both this unprepared and this flustered.

Jake vaulted onto the stage with ease. *Bastard. I would have knocked myself out doing that.* He dug around under the podium and in a matter of minutes had the sound, screen, and lighting of the room adjusted.

"You're going to have to show me how you did that."

Jake moved away from the podium. "I'll just write down the settings, and then the sound guy can replicate them for you."

"How do you know if there even is a sound guy?" He snapped his head around at her question. "I'm not about to rely on some mysterious sound guy. So teach me what you did." Her voice was too sharp, the anxious tension still puling at her insides. She took a short breath. "Please."

"You're right. Here." He gestured for her to come over and spent the next few minutes explaining what each of the buttons and switches on the control panel did. Learning the minutiae of the soundboard made her feel back in control. It had broken the problem into smaller pieces and put her back in charge of something.

"Let's do each of the slides one at a time. Smaller chunks would probably help me not get overwhelmed."

"Totally fine," Jake said, taking his place in the front row again.

And that was what they did for the next hour. Just like yesterday, they went slide by slide, blocking out where she would stand and when she would click. Jake reminded her not to just read from the slides but to speak to the audience. She felt like she was learning the choreography to a very plodding dance. At the end of two very slow cycles of practice, she finally felt like she could do it in real time.

She walked to the podium and then took a few steps to the left, just like they had practiced. She looked out into the sea of chairs and immediately got nervous all over again. *Shit.* "Why can't I shake this stage fright?"

"Just imagine the audience in their underwear. I've heard that works."

"If the entire audience looks like you, then god help me because that would really be something to see." She smirked at him. If she had learned anything over the past few days, it was that there was one surefire way to get her confidence up. *Time to flirt.* "I just don't think I can picture it."

He caught her look and mirrored her smirk. "Can you not?

You can't picture what an audience full of me would look like shirtless?"

"Gosh. Can't say that it rings a bell. Do you have, like, a chart or a diagram or something?" Izabelle said, raising the intonation of her voice at the end of each sentence in her best impression of a valley girl.

He moved his hands up to the collar of his shirt, working slowly at the buttons as he spoke. The way his fingers moved over the tiny mother-of-pearl circles brought to mind what else his fingers could do. "I think I could pull something together to show you." He undid another button. "Maybe give you something to think about..." Another button. "Instead of the rest of the people in the audience." Another and another. "Actually, now that we're talking about it, I think it would really help your nerves if you interacted with the audience." Another. "It would show you they aren't as scary as your mind makes them out to be."

Izabelle could feel her heart rate creeping up for a reason entirely separate from her nerves. "Should this interaction with the audience be a hands-on demonstrative, or is it just a show-and-tell?"

"Definitely a hands-on situation," he said as he finished the row of buttons.

"Do I have a volunteer?" Izabelle asked, looking past Jake toward the array of empty chairs. Jake casually lifted his hand. His shirt fell open, exposing his chest. "Anybody... Anybody?" She stepped down off the stage toward him. As she got closer, Jake started waving his hand and extending it higher. "I mean, if no one wants to volunteer, I'm going to have to pick someone at random." As she stopped in front of Jake, he scooped her into his lap. Laughing, she continued. "Ah. Yes. You will do just fine. Thank you for agreeing to be a part of this demonstration."

"Anything for you," Jake replied, planting a kiss on her. She moved to straddle his waist as he strung a row of kisses down her neck. She ran her hands down his exposed chest, nails lightly skimming the muscle as he gripped her hips. She shifted her weight into him, closing the gap between them, only for him to stand up abruptly, dumping her out of his lap, at the sound of the door.

"Hello, Mr.—"

"Yes, we're fine, thank you," Jake responded gruffly, cutting the guy off before he had even said anything.

"I just wanted to make sure that everything was to your liking regarding the setup."

"Yes. It's great. Thanks. In fact, we need to reserve the room again tomorrow. We have some other business that we need to attend to."

"Yes. Of course, Mr.—"

"Great. Thank you. I'll talk to you tomorrow," Jake called toward the door. He turned back to her with a mischievous grin, "Now, let's really get down to business."

Twenty-One

JAKE

"That has to be our last distraction," Izabelle said, stepping out of her shower.

"Pity," Jake said, stepping out after her. "The distractions are my favorite part."

"I'll give you credit, you've gotten me the closest to actually doing it the whole way through," she said as she walked into the room to pick out clothes. "But I don't think close is going to be good enough."

I wish you weren't right. Jake plunked down on the edge of the bed, resting his forearms on his knees and letting his head hang. Close would not be good enough, and after this morning, he knew Izabelle's presentation was at risk of falling into that category.

Seeing her up there today, so nervous, had been brutal to watch. Her company was just as special as she was. But her instincts that the presentation lacked something were correct. He had felt hope yesterday when she had gone through her numbers. He had let himself relax thinking that once they combed over the slides and put them in her own words, it would be just as amazing as she was.

He didn't doubt for a second that her company was worth every single one of the potential investors' dollars. And he didn't doubt Izabelle herself for a second. She could do this. With a few more practices, she could work through her nerves. In his mind, she could do anything. But she still clearly doubted herself, and it was preventing her from connecting with her presentation. If she couldn't connect to the presentation, then there was no way the audience of investors could connect with her.

It was killing him that he couldn't just call in his teams and have them consult with her. *I mean, I could, but there are so many damn reasons why that's a horrible idea.* He knew they could whip up slick graphics and handouts—hell, they would present the entire thing if he asked them to. But not only was that not helpful, it also didn't seem likely to solve the problem.

Taking over her presentation would undermine the incredible achievement she had attained in getting herself here. Plus, he was so far down in this mess he'd made he couldn't even fathom trying to explain who he was, how he could help, and why he hadn't told her earlier. That was excluding the fact that fraternizing with a company was an unwritten no-no. And yet here he was, agonizing over Izabelle's presentation, having done a serious amount of fraternizing over the last couple of days.

Aside from the personal reasons, he was equally mad he had to have this debate at all. It shouldn't matter if he knew her or not, cared for her or not, helped her or not, and it really shouldn't matter if someone slickly produced her slides. It should be enough that she had the most realistic and sound business plan, with all the actualized numbers to back it up. That was the point of EtaSella. She shouldn't need bells and whistles to get people's attention to how amazing she was. It was obvious. Looking at her now, it was all he could think. *You are amazing.*

"Hey. You. Earth to Jake." He looked up to see Izabelle waving her hand in a giant arc. "Are you there? I was asking, do you really think that they will let us use the ballroom tomorrow too?"

"Oh yeah. It won't be a problem."

"I don't know who you bribed to let us in there early, but I can't thank you enough. At least I got the initial shock out of my system."

It isn't a bribe when your company is paying for the whole thing. That was the other thing that was chewing him up. He should have been honest with her from the jump. This had gone on for too long. He had been so caught up in his plan to keep them separate and then so wrapped up in how he felt when they were together that the logistics of this mess had faded from his mind. Now that they were only a few days out from the opening rounds of the presentations, Jake knew he had to find a way to make this all work out. Otherwise, he was risking not only Izabelle's shot at getting investors but also his relationship with Izabelle herself. It was way too near a miss today in the ballroom when the resort's event coordinator almost addressed him by name. How he had avoided telling Izabelle the truth of who he was and why he was here for this long was mind-boggling, and the pressure between his temples was only getting worse. He massaged them with slow circles as he tried to think. *I've got to tell her tonight at dinner.*

"Hello? Did you hear what I said?" Izabelle asked. "Are you okay? Did that shower romp take away your ability to think clearly?" She came over and sat on his lap. The warmth from her body washed over the anxiety within him. He dropped his head onto her shoulder.

"I'm fine. Just tired. Want to grab an early dinner at the restaurant we haven't been to yet and then spend the night in?"

"The usual, then?" Izabelle responded with a wink. "Are you going to go like this?" Her eyes raked over this naked torso towards the towel at his waist.

"Nah. Only you get to see me like this, gorgeous." He kissed a lingering droplet of water from her shoulder. "How about I go throw some clean clothes on while you finish getting dressed, and I'll meet you there in a few."

"Sounds good," Izabelle said, rising to walk back into the bathroom. "As long as you promise to miss me while you're gone."

"I'll miss you like crazy." *And that's the problem.*

～

Izabelle was waiting for him outside the doors of the restaurant when he walked up. "I love that you're always early," she said, rising up on her tiptoes to give him a kiss. The brief touch of her lips was enough to make him forget what he had been so distraught by moments before.

"After you." He pulled the door of the restaurant open and let her pass through. The host gave Izabelle an appreciative up-down. *Watch yourself, junior.* Jake made note of the name tag affixed to his vest. *Peter.* Peter walked them to their table by the windows, as Jake had requested. "I've got it," Jake said, stepping in front of Peter's attempt to pull Izabelle's chair out for her. He more than understood the impulse, but that didn't mean he wasn't going to let Peter know who she was on this date with.

Izabelle eyed him humorously as he took a seat across from her. "I'm not running off with the poor host anytime soon." *Shit.* She had caught that possessiveness. His anxiety about the giant mess they were in was allowing his surlier side to creep back in. Not what he wanted. Izabelle leaned over the table to grab his hand, maintaining eye contact. "I seriously doubt he fucks half as well as you do."

Jake guffawed. She had done exactly what he needed to shake himself out of his negative head space. He ran his eyes over her, all heat and admiration.

She blushed. "Why are you looking at me like that? Don't make me feel weird by being all puritanical about it."

"I..." Jake continued to stare at her with an expression of awe.

"You what?"

"I'm not even sure what to say other than you are the most incredible person I have ever met."

"You are being a flatterer, but I'll take it." She sipped her water. "I need the ego boost today."

Jake shook his head. "You don't need anything. You've done so much on your own, and there are a million top CEOs who have never even done a tenth of the things that you have in building a business. Trust me, I know."

"Keep talking, keep talking," Izabelle said, jokingly circling her hand.

"I'm being serious. How did you get so good?"

She tilted her head at him. "I'm hardly good at this. Thus far, I've broken down crying over slides—*multiple times*—and haven't gotten through an entire pitch without stopping."

"I mean with business in general. The presentation is marketing—that's a different thing."

"Well, it seems that marketing is the only thing that matters these days," she said with a shrug.

The waiter came to take their orders. Izabelle's expression was one of relief. "I'm not letting you off the hook, Izabelle. I'm going to get to the bottom of this."

She grimaced in response.

After their orders were placed, he picked up where he had left off. "Come on. Start with your first lemonade stand, and then go from there."

Izabelle chuckled. "I never had a single lemonade stand."

"Seriously? Pretty much everyone I know who eventually got into entrepreneurship has a lemonade stand story."

"Ha. No. That had too much overhead."

He laughed at the joke, but then her expression made him second-guess. "Too much overhead? What can sugar and lemons possibly cost?"

Izabelle sighed as she took a sip of her drink. "A whole bunch that we didn't have if you were raised the way I was."

"What?"

"After my parents died, my grandmother took me in. She was in her late sixties at that point and living on social security. She used their life insurance money to move to the best school district in our area. But that meant there wasn't any extra room in the budget, especially to be wasting on things like lemonade."

I had no idea. Jake felt like an ass. He hadn't ever stopped to think that Izabelle's life would be so different from his own. "I'm sorry. I—"

Izabelle waved off his apology. "Don't apologize. Truly. It sounds sadder than it was. Me and Gram had a lot of fun times. I just don't have a lemonade stand story." They each sat there in silence for a while, clearly unsure what to say next. Izabelle nervously cracked her knuckles. "I did have some other things I tried though."

Jake was so relieved she had the wherewithal to keep going after he had completely stuck his foot in his mouth that he nearly upset his water glass reaching for her hand. "I would love to hear about them."

She gave his hand a squeeze and then started her story. "So, I started a bunch of small little businesses here and there, but nothing really worked out. Lawn mowing tanked because everyone wanted to hire the boys, and getting gas was difficult. Selling makeup was a nonstarter because I wasn't girly enough —plus, it was a pyramid scheme. Babysitting didn't work out because apparently kids didn't want a bunch of math lessons on Saturday nights. Dog training didn't work because I didn't have dogs growing up, so I had no idea what I was doing, and they all ended up worse behaved than when I started. But I knew that I had something with the dog part. Everyone had one, but they didn't really want to seem to do all the work of caring for them. There were already a million dog walkers, so I didn't want to compete in that way, but I eventually"—she smirked—"walked right into the idea for Pooper Scoopers."

"What now?"

"Pooper Scoopers. It was the one market where I had no competitors, no overhead, and unlimited demand."

"I think I know where this is going, but what exactly were you doing?" He smirked at her.

"I'll tell you, but you have to promise not to laugh. Everyone laughed about it."

He wiped the smirk off his face so fast it was like he smacked it off. "I'm not, and I won't."

Izabelle nodded as she took a sip of her wine and continued. "Well, near where I grew up, there were a lot of what I thought were super-rich people but, looking back, were just upper-middle-class people with big yards. Basically, everyone had a dog, hence why I thought that dog training would be a good idea originally. But walking home one day, I was cutting through some yard and stepped in a pile of dog poop. The owner of the house had seen me do it and apologized and said something to the effect of 'I'm just so busy I can never seem to have time to pick it all up.' So, I got a shovel and a bucket, printed some flyers at the library, and that's how Pooper Scoopers was born. I'd go around and pick up all the dog poop from people's yards that they didn't want to pick up themselves."

Jake raised both of his eyebrows and had to curl his lips into his mouth. He wasn't fighting the urge to laugh because it was funny but because it was genius. And also a little funny. *You have to ask a question before you lose it.* He desperately did not want her to think he was laughing at her. "How did you get to all of these yards?"

"Great question." She tipped her wineglass at him in acknowledgment. "At first, I walked to the rich neighborhood. Then once I got the business going, I was able to buy a bike, which allowed me to get everywhere twice as fast and to expand to two more neighborhoods. Those neighborhoods gave me enough revenue to start saving for a car. So, once I was old enough to get my permit, I bought one, which in turn gave me the means to go to even more neighborhoods."

"When did you start this?"

"When I was eleven."

"This was a years-long thing?"

"Oh yeah. It actually got pretty big. After I got the car, I realized that this was going to be my best, and only, shot to save up for college, so I just kept it going. I could have even hired employees, but it's hard to get people into it. So in lieu of more people, I just woke up earlier and earlier as I took on more clients."

"I have heard people pitch a lot of things, but I have never in my life ever heard of this. It is honestly genius."

"Yeah. The teasing was merciless though. Going through elementary, middle, and high school as the 'dog shit girl' really does a number on you. Coming from where I did, people knew I was the poor kid and found it funny to say, 'Makes sense that all you will ever be good at is shoveling shit.'"

"Holy shit, that's awful."

"That's your response? Holy shit?"

Oh no. Please don't take that the wrong way. "No, no, I'm not making fun, I swear. I—"

Izabelle smiled, pointing a finger at him. "Gotcha there."

Oh, thank god. "I just—I'm just in awe of you. How can someone with that much wherewithal doubt themselves for a single second?"

"Because that was the last thing that worked out." She

didn't elaborate, taking another bite of her steak instead of continuing.

"What do you mean?" he asked. She took another bite before responding, clearly stalling for time. "I don't want to push, but I don't understand."

"No, no. It's fine. I just haven't sat down and told people this entire saga in one go before. But you've always been honest and reflective with me, so I should be too." Her assertion that he had been honest with her stung a bit. He really needed to tell her, but he didn't want to interrupt.

She took a sip of her wine and continued. "I had saved up enough to get a good start on college expenses, and then scholarships got me most of the rest of the way. But then Gram died just after high school graduation." Izabelle paused, pushing some food around her plate before settling on taking a sip of wine instead. "She said she was going to hold on and see me walk come hell or high water, and she did. But after she was gone, the last thing I wanted was to stay in town, so I went to school as far away from home as I could get. But the late switch meant I was back to square one in terms of money—my scholarships didn't transfer. I tried to start some other ideas, but I ran into a lot of dead ends. I looked around my program and just felt like I was way out of my league. The other kids had trust funds, and networks, and famous parents, and day-traded as hobbies. They could take internships that didn't pay anything just for the experience. That was straight up not an option for me." She sighed. "So, I just started working for other people. Which was fine. It paid the bills, and there were way fewer dog shit jokes, but it was frustrating to not do what you are passionate about. Not that I was passionate about dog shit, but at least I was the CEO of my own business."

Jake had thought at points in the last week that a freight train of feelings had hit him. He had talked about both of his parents with Izabelle and his anger and thought that he would crack open from the experience, but hearing her story had fully split his heart. He reached out and grabbed her hand to steady himself, gently enveloping the soft warmth of her hand in his. He had never expected she'd ever had to struggle like she had. He understood now why she was holding herself back. "So that's why you started your company?"

"Partly. I just didn't want people to feel like I did. That they needed something or someone fancy and couldn't do it themselves."

"And you've been working on it all this time?"

"Ha. No. I only started Me-E-O five years ago," she said. "There were some things that tripped me up in the meantime." Izabelle twisted her lips to the side. "But that isn't worth rehashing. It's old news at this point. I'm here, and that's all that matters." She clinked her glass against his on the table in a cheers.

Jake was stunned by her, his heart wrenched by all she had been through and bursting with pride for how she had overcome it. She didn't just deserve an investor; she deserved the world, and he wanted her to have it. His head was buzzing with ideas on how they could work this backstory into the presentation. Make the investors understand that this was where they should be putting their money because she cared, she was talented, and she had worked her ass off her entire life. This was the kind of thing that would make them sit up and take notice. Make them understand that she was a smart investment.

"Anyway." Izabelle blew her hair out of her face. "That is more than enough about me for one evening."

"I will never get sick of hearing anything about you, trust me."

She smiled at him in return. He knew she was going to have to trust him in order to listen to his ideas about changes she could make to her presentation. Which meant he really couldn't be dropping the truth about who he was in this moment. A part of him knew he had let this go on too long for there to ever be a good time, but that time certainly wasn't now. Jake deeply wished it didn't have to be ever.

Twenty-Two
IZABELLE

"As you can see from these charts, Me-E-O has had growth year over year." Izabelle pointed to the screen on the ballroom stage behind her.

Jake cleared his throat behind her. "I know I said I wouldn't interrupt, but..."

She turned and threw him an agitated glare. She actually wanted, for once, to get through the entire presentation without stopping or having a nervous breakdown. After two false starts this morning, she had actually made it to the midpoint of this one with just being nervous, no breakdown, and now Jake was interrupting and breaking her streak. "But what?"

"You can't see the numbers because your shadow is blocking the center of your graph. You just have to take a few steps to the side."

"Oh." She shuffled to the left.

"Better."

"Hm." She tossed her hair. "Now, where was I?" She looked

back to the screen and clicked to the next slide to continue running through the numbers. When she got to the slide covering the profit and loss statements, she looked out into the audience like they had practiced. What she saw was Jake's face twisted up like he was thinking about how to solve the world's problems all at once. "What?"

"No, don't stop. I can hold my comments until the end."

Izabelle put her hand on her hip. "This is hard enough without having to look at—" She waved an irritated hand around in a chaotic swish. "—whatever face you're making right now. I've already stopped; I might as well hear what you have to say."

"I've just been thinking about ways we can improve this. Make the presentation really connect more. Infuse it with the 'pop' and 'sparkle' you are worried about missing."

"We?" Izabelle generally liked when Jake referred to them as a "we," but she had a bad feeling about where he was taking this.

Jake seemed not to hear her question and continued on. "I've been thinking about this for a while. Do you have any case studies about how small businesses have applied or used Me-E-O and grown as a result?"

"Yes, of course."

"Okay." He looked at her quizzically. "But they aren't in the presentation."

"The original test case was my friend Ava's fitness studio, and it didn't seem very professional to talk about how my earliest success case was one of my best friends."

"Okay. I disagree; people do that all the time. But I understand where you're coming from. So, what about people you don't know personally?"

This was really not what she wanted to be getting into right now. "I've interacted with some businesses via the app and helped them work through beta versions of the service."

"That's great. What kinds of businesses?"

Izabelle put her hand on her hip. "Everything from social justice bakeries to a group of sisters that flip old houses."

"So why don't you talk about them?" Jake asked.

Izabelle started counting on her fingers. "First, I didn't ask them permission, and I'm not going to break their trust in me, and second, because it feels too personal. I don't want to seem so connected or entwined with everything. I want this business to be separate from me." Izabelle now knew for sure she didn't like where this conversation was going.

"No, see, that's where you're wrong." Izabelle bristled at the word *wrong* as Jake charged ahead. "You have to seem invested in these things and talk about yourself. I've been thinking about this constantly since last night and even before that. People need to know how great you are. You need to talk about Pooper Scoopers. Talk about your parents. Your perseverance through failed endeavors. Those are the reasons you're so good at business, why you've never given up, why and how this business came to be. That's the kind of thing investors want to know. That you aren't going to just piddle their money away because you know the value of a dollar."

She could not believe he would actually suggest such a thing. Had he not been listening to her at all? "I am not about to get on a stage and tell a room full of strangers any part of that story. Definitely not to strangers who are big-time professionals. Hell no."

"Why not?"

"Why not? I am not about to be laughed out of another room and get branded as either the dog shit girl, or the sad girl with the dead parents, or the one who couldn't make it work, all over again. I literally moved across the country for college to a place where literally no one knew me in order to get away from all of that. I am not going to volunteer that information at this stage of my life to a giant group of investors just so they can either use it against me or pity me." Izabelle could feel what was already a high level of anxiety and frustration rising. She had trusted Jake with her stories, and now he wanted to turn them into a sales pitch.

"Then talk about it generally, how your own entrepreneurship paid for your college and that after one business failed, you learned and rebuilt."

Failed and rebuilt. He had no fucking clue how hard she had failed and how she'd had to fight to rebuild. If he did, he wouldn't dare say any of this to her. Izabelle had to clench her jaw as she spoke to keep from shouting. "You don't understand how much I *really* don't want to revisit either of those life events. I just want this to be professional and impersonal. I have the numbers up there, I have the business plan up there, and that's what I want to be judged on. Nothing else. I've had enough of other people's judgement on the rest of it." She turned back toward the screen. She wanted to wrap this conversation up and move on before she lost her grip on her emotions. Which was about to be soon.

"But it takes more than numbers to get investors. You have to sell them on *why* they should give you their money."

She snapped her head around to look at him squarely. "Do you actually think that I don't know that? Have you been checked out of all the conversations we've had where I'm freaking out because I'm a numbers person and not a salesperson? Do you really think I would be struggling with all of this if I could just magically come up with ways to"—she raised her fingers in scare quotes—"sell them on it?"

"Yeah, but to be a successful businessperson, you have to be both."

Izabelle could feel tears welling up behind her eyes. "Oh, that's rich from you. Do you really think you can say that to me? After everything you said about how you run your business, I thought we were actually connecting on not being people-people. At least I own that about myself and don't go around pissed off, pretending to be something I'm not."

Jake's head snapped to the side so fast it was like she had slapped him. *Fuck.* She shouldn't have said that.

She expected him to yell at her but his voice was measured. "I was just trying—"

She was relieved he hadn't flown off the handle at her, but she was too keyed up at this point to ratchet back down. "Trying to what exactly? Make me feel like shit? Swoop in and tell me that your ideas are better about *my* company when you just saw the numbers a few days ago?"

"I was only trying to suggest—"

"Well, you know what? I'm going to suggest that you haven't been the least bit helpful. I built this company all by myself for a very good reason, Jake."

"I promised I would give my honest feedback, and I really think that if you consider including a bit more of you that it wouldn't be as bad as you think. People couldn't help but love you."

Love. There it was again, except this time, it felt like a punch instead of a flutter. "Love and business don't go together. I learned that the hard way. And so I made that rule for a reason. Don't make me regret breaking it."

Jake looked at her with genuine compassion, which only pissed her off more. "I know. And it's a good rule, but you have to consider that your business is just one person, and it's built from your life experiences. The goal is to help other people build their life experiences into businesses as well. There is no way that you can make this solely about business and tell a compelling story."

"You don't know what you're talking about, and you don't understand what you're asking me to do." She could feel herself icing over, trying to cool a red-hot rage that was bubbling up. Izabelle crossed her arms over her chest, physically trying to hold herself together.

He stood up and walked toward her onstage, arms out for a hug. "I know how much you've struggled, and I want to help you. I want to make this easier. We can do this. We can work through the nerves."

The "we" was just too much. It broke her. She never wanted to hear the word "we" from a man meddling in her business ever again. She had sworn she wouldn't get here again, and yet she had walked right into it. She was such an idiot to think that it would be different this time, that the rules didn't apply to Jake. Any hope she had had of not screaming in frustration went right out the window. "*No!*"

Jake stopped in his tracks, clearly taken aback by the venom in her shout. "You *do not* understand. You *do not* know everything. I *will not* be told how to run my business, by you or anyone else."

"I'm not trying to—"

She cut him off. "Yes you are! You just spent the last ten minutes *trying* to do a whole bunch of things. Trying to make it whatever you think it should be! I don't want your suggestions!"

He stepped towards her again. "I would never—"

She turned away from him. She couldn't take his look of pity or empathy or whatever the hell it was. She didn't want him or his feelings anywhere near her. "Leave. You've done more than enough."

"I—"

"Leave!"

He stopped again, and she heard him let out a small sigh. "I'm very sorry." And he turned and walked out of the ballroom.

Twenty-Three

IZABELLE

Not. Again. No fucking way. As soon as she heard the click of the door closing, her anger boiled over into hot tears of frustration. Izabelle paced around the stage, hiccupping breaths matching her choppy thoughts. *I should have never asked him to watch it in the first place.* She crunched her knuckles in her hand. *Why in the world, after everything you've been through, would you ever think that mixing Jake up in this would be a good idea? You knew it was a bad idea, and you did it anyway. You should have just waited for one of the girls to be free. He was so freaking arrogant about it.*

Speaking of the girls, she felt the need to yell at something other than the echo chamber of her own thoughts. She reached for her phone and dialed up her favorite sounding board for all things shitty men.

She tried to lengthen her breaths to match the length of the rings coming from the other end of the earpiece. She was just starting to get a hold of herself when Sabrina's voice came through the line.

"Hello, you've reached Sabrina. Sorry I can't come to the phone right now. But leave—"

Izabelle smacked at the red End button on the screen. "Goddamnit." Her tears welled up again. "Where are you?" *I really need to vent.* She immediately rang Charlie, trying to catch her on a lunch break. A voice that she didn't recognize took over the line.

"You've reached the voicemail box of three, zero, one—"

"Oh, for shit's sake, she really has to change that." Izabelle dialed Ava. She continued to stalk back and forth, expecting to get another voicemail.

Riiiiiing. "Iz, hi! How's it—"

"Not. Good," Izabelle said, her words clipped as they forced themselves between clenched teeth.

"Oh no. Are you okay? What happened?"

"Fucking. Men. And their dumbass opinions."

"What do you mean? I thought you weren't giving the presentation until Saturday. What went wrong?" The dulcet tones of Ava's caring voice clashed with her twitching nerves. She needed a bit more vitriol for her vent. Her phone started to vibrate in her hand. It was Charlie calling back. "Hold on, I'm going to merge in Charlie."

"Hi, girl! You calling to give me some more steamy updates about that fine-ass man?" Charlie asked.

"Wrong bandwagon, Char," Ava responded before Izabelle had the chance to.

"Oh shit. Are you okay?"

"No," Izabelle said. Which wasn't exactly true. "I mean, I'm physically fine. But all of this is just way too much, and now the thing that was supposed to be relieving my stress just got really fucking stressful."

"Alright, start from the beginning," Charlie said. "Get us up to speed."

Izabelle then launched into updating her friends about everything that had happened, starting with dinner and running through to the events of the morning. "...and then he had the nerve to come in here and tell me how I should be presenting my own company. How I needed to work in more stories about myself. He even said that I should detail Ava's business in the presentation as a kind of case study."

Ava piped in, "I'm happy for you to talk about how your model helped my studio if it's going to help you. I always said that you could."

"What?" Izabelle's rage was starting to mutate. Was the point about the examples in her presentation the only thing Ava had heard in the story she'd just told? "I mean—thank you, but that isn't really the point. He was acting like he was some kind of expert on EtaSella and marketing, and it was just *infuriating*. Why do men always have to act like their idea is better than yours? I'm not putting up with this shit again."

Ava and Charlie remained quiet. Which was just about the worst thing they could do. "Hello? What the hell is with the silence? I need a little more burn-him-at-the-stake energy right now."

"Ava, you go first," Charlie said.

"Gee. Thanks so much," Ava responded.

"Seriously? What is your guys' deal right now?" Izabelle demanded.

Ava let out a soft sigh before she began. "I can't tell what you're actually mad at. Are you actually mad at Jake, or are you mad that he has a point, or are you really just mad at Simon still?"

"I second that," Charlie chimed in.

I cannot believe these two right now. "What's that supposed to mean?" Izabelle could feel her anger simmering, and she was getting more heated by the second.

"Iz. Come on. You know what she means. From everything you just told us, Jake isn't like Simon. He sounds like a genuinely solid guy who was trying to help. The suggestion he had is a good one. You're super impressive, and you've experienced a lot. You should consider hyping yourself up more."

"We know your other businesses not working out is a sore spot, but—"

"Sore spot! It's *way* more than just a sore spot." Izabelle was starting to boil over.

Ava continued. "You're right. That's fair. I can understand why you haven't wanted to talk about them. But maybe it's time to embrace what happened."

"How is that helpful?" Izabelle replied in utter disbelief that her friends were not backing her in her anger.

Charlie took over. "Iz. You have very valid reasons for wanting to be pissed off until the end of time, but you do have to recognize at a certain point that you may need to involve the ideas of other people. And to me, it sounds like Jake was just trying to help."

"Yeah, but this is different," Izabelle insisted.

"Exactly. This is different. You can't keep treating it like the past," Charlie said. "Nothing suggests Jake is trying to royally screw you over like Simon did." Charlie made a noise like she was spitting. "May he burn in hell."

"Charlie's right, Iz. Jake seems really great from everything that you've told us. You deserve to have things go well, and it sounds like they actually are. You shouldn't fight so hard against it."

Izabelle's phone buzzed in her hand. Sabrina was ringing back in. She hung up on her. "Why are you guys taking his side in this?" The pitch of her voice rose as she spoke.

"We aren't taking his side," they said, nearly in unison.

"We're on your side always—that's why we want you to do well. And we don't want you to go through life miserable because your ex was a piece of shit. Oh, wait. Hold on," Charlie said. "Sabs called. I patched her in."

"Hey, guys! Is everyone on this call? Iz, I tried to call you back. What did I miss?" Sabrina asked.

Izabelle couldn't handle the thought of having to explain everything over again just to have another one of her friends act like she was the unreasonable one. It was too much. "You didn't miss a damn thing," Izabelle said as she smacked the End Call button. She stuffed her phone into her pocket and headed for the glass exit doors of the conference room. She needed somewhere to direct her rage, and she definitely needed to get the hell out of this room.

∽

Izabelle was charging in a straight line up the hiking path at the back of the hotel, but her thoughts were running in a constant loop. *I swore I wouldn't let someone dictate my business again—I lost everything before—I made a vow that I wouldn't ever mix my business and personal life again—I knew this would happen—Why didn't I just leave it alone—I am not going to be embarrassed—Why don't my friends get it—I am so tired of men thinking they know more than me—I know I'm not a salesperson, so why does everyone feel the need to point it out to me—I worked so hard to get here—I am not going to have someone take it from me again.*

Nothing was right. The slight crunch of the dirt under her feet had been relaxing on every other walk. Now, it grated at her nerves with each footfall. The sun had transformed from a relaxing-embrace warmth to a smothering heat. Her once breezy tank was lacquered to her back with a layer of sweat. She shoved her hands into her back pockets only to take them out and shove them into her front pockets and then put them back on her hips.

Having Jake tell her what he thought of the presentation and his ideas on how "we" could fix it had immediately triggered everything she had been pushing down for the last five years, which upset her. Which made her even more mad that something she so desperately wanted to be over was affecting her like this. Mad that her skin hadn't gotten any thicker in the intervening years. Much less in the few days since she had walked out of dinner on Jake. *You rebuilt it all yourself, and you built it better. They don't understand. They will never know what it felt like.* And yet here she was, blazing up a hiking path because a few suggestions had sent her spiraling.

It was just an extra shitty cherry on top of a pissed-off cake that her friends had said exactly the wrong things over the phone. *I know that everyone is trying to look out for me, but they don't even know this guy. How can they act like this is no big deal?*

"Oomph." Her casual tennis shoes slipped on the loose, aggravating, crunchy dirt, and she went down on her hands and knees. Hard. The famous red sandstone ground the skin off her knees instantly. "*Ow!*" She rolled over onto her butt to survey the damage. *Yowch.* She looked like a little kid who had hit the deck after running too fast. Blood was already rising to the surface of the abrasions. She tried to wipe it off but instead just turned her knees into bad impressions of a Jackson Pollock painting when the blood mixed with the dirt. *I can't even do angry hiking right today.* It was all just too much. And her knees really fucking hurt.

Her breathing, already strained from the exertion of her impulsive hike, immediately went ragged with sobs. It was like all the years of all the bullshit got together and decided to rampage through her tear ducts in this very moment. She bawled. She let herself cry in a way she hadn't cried since Simon ambushed her with their breakup in his stupid car and walked away with everything they had built together. They had been a "we"—they had built their business together, and then he'd stolen it from her. She had told herself all these years that she was too strong to cry over him, that she was too busy to cry over what he did. But goddamnit, it had hurt. Simon had hurt her, and so had that fall.

She thought she was past all his manipulations. Yet, here she was, bawling, alone, her head resting on top of two scraped knees because Simon was a fucking jerk who had tried to ruin her life. *It seems like he's still doing a pretty good job of ruining it, honestly.* His years of making her feel small had made her so insecure, so ready to assume that someone was trying to own her hard work, that the littlest comment by an entirely different man had made her spiral on him, snap on her friends, and then jog up a hill in her cute tennis shoes only to eat shit because she had been so triggered by the memory of his condescension. A few small suggestions by Jake had sent her right back to that place where she felt so unworthy. So angry. So embarrassed. Even when she knew in her heart, he hadn't meant to. It made her remember all the times Simon had convinced her that her ideas weren't good enough. That she wasn't good enough. That she was the numbers girl, so she shouldn't try with the people-facing parts, she wasn't going to ever be good at it, so she should just let him do it.

He had always acted like everything she said was ridiculous, only to turn around, use them all, and act as if they were his all along. The irony of that sentiment was deep, considering it was on her ideas that Simon was continuing to make a living for himself.

"God, you fucking sucked," she said as she flopped onto her back in the middle of the trail. "You still fucking suck." She let her arms splay out next to her in the red dirt. Since she was already covered in dust and sweat, she decided she might as well go full wallow. So she kept crying.

She cried about all of it. Her parents, her grandmother, the kids who made fun of her, the business she started with Simon, the trust she had put in him and he had broken without another thought. She cried for all the times she'd had to start over and for all of the times that it hadn't worked out. She cried about what she'd loved and lost, what could have been and what never was.

When she had let every tear loose to run down her face onto the dirt beneath her, she opened her clenched eyes and stared up at the perfect blue dome above her. *Stupid sky. Why can't you be cloudy?* It was very difficult to wallow in your emotional low point when the sun was insistent on being relentlessly cheery. In a moment this profound and moody, it would have been nice if the weather had been slightly more accommodating.

As her breathing slowed, so did her thoughts. Now that her blood wasn't pounding in her ears, she could actually hear what everyone was trying to tell her this morning.

In a vacuum, no one had said anything wrong. But in a world still dominated by her feelings and fears about Simon, everything was wrong. As much as she had told herself she was over it, she clearly wasn't. Today had proven that. But it had also proven that it was holding her back. "You can't keep treating it like the past," Charlie had said. *Shit. I hate that she's right.*

She sat up and brushed herself off, looking down the trail to the hotel below. The past had gotten her here, but she would be damned if it kept informing her present.

Twenty-Four
JAKE

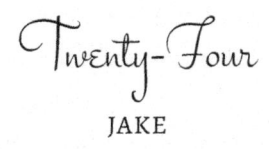

"Cam, I fucked up," Jake blurted out as soon as Cam picked up the phone.

"How? I specifically routed all the Stevenson deal calls around you so that you couldn't piss anybody off," Cam said. "How did you even guess the password to the network?"

"Wait, what?" Jake was clearly missing something here. "I haven't been able to get on the network since you locked me out."

Cam paused. "Oh. You haven't?"

"No. I haven't talked to anybody. What's going on with the Stevenson—"

Cam cut him off. "I thought this call was about how you fucked up? Why are you suddenly making it about the Stevenson deal?"

He knew this was some black-belt-level mental jujitsu on Cam's part, but he wasn't in the mood to care. "It isn't about any of the deals. I need some advice."

Cam laughed in her usual way. "You're the one with the

fancy business degree, but I'm happy to provide feedback on whatever issue you're having."

"No, I need some personal advice."

"Uh. Yeah." The hesitation in Cam's voice was clear. "I'd be happy to patch you through to one of your guy friends... Not sure why you called me to do that instead of calling them directly, but hey."

She does have a point. Why did I call her? "I can call them directly if I want. I'm not that helpless. I just figured you would be a better sounding board for this particular problem."

"Considering I'm the best at all things, you probably aren't wrong," Cam said.

"I'm starting to regret the choice," Jake replied.

"Alright, you actually sound miserable. I'll be serious for a second."

"I fucked up with a girl that I met while I was down here."

"Yeesh. Are you sure you don't want me to patch you through to one of your guy friends? Reid likes to pretend he isn't reachable on that boat, but I know he has a satellite phone with him at all times."

"No. Come on. You know Reid wouldn't get it. We don't really talk about relationships or our *feelings*."

"Two things. One, I think you're underestimating the emotional capacity of the modern man. Two, you and I haven't ever talked specifics about relationships or feelings, and yet here we are, standing on the precipice of doing so."

"I'm sorry. You're right. I didn't mean to make you uncomfortable."

"Jake, it's fine. What's going on?" Cam asked.

"I said I would give someone my opinion on something

because I was trying to make something better, and then she got mad at me when I did."

"That is almost certainly *not* what happened."

"No, I swear that's what happened."

"I'm not saying that isn't what literally happened. I'm saying that people don't just get pissed off because of an opinion. They get pissed off because of what that opinion means in the greater scheme of things. Also, did you give this opinion unsolicited? Because in that case, they might be pissed off on the opinion alone."

"No," Jake said, irritated. "She asked for my help, and I said I would give it. And then I tried to give her some advice."

"Okay. I'm going to be a stickler here. Did she ask for your feedback or for your help? Those are two very different things."

Shit. Were they? Jake didn't answer her.

Cam continued. "I'm going to take a stab in the dark here and say that when she said feedback, she meant positive support, not negative criticism. Or advice."

Goddamnit. How did Cam see that over the phone and I missed it in real life? "Hm."

"I am going to take that harumph as a 'Cam! You genius! You figured it out! What a value add you are to my life!'"

"Hm."

"Just go apologize. I'm sure you can figure that one out on your own."

"Bye, Cam."

"Excuse me? I think you missed something in that last sentence."

"Thank you." He hung up the phone and headed out of his room. He had some apologies to make.

Jake uncrumpled another piece of hotel stationery in his hands. *Maybe I should have gone with this one. It's more in line with how I feel.*

Izabelle,
I am a fucking idiot who doesn't know anything. Please forgive me for what I said. You are perfect. Can we please have dinner? I will lose my mind if I lose you.
-Jake

He had labored over what to say in his apology. He didn't want to pressure her by sulking around her door and seeing if she wanted to see him again, so he figured a note would be better. But trying to write everything he had felt and wanted to say ended up taking two hours and two pads of paper to get right. Now that he was back from taping the dumb note on the door, he didn't feel like it was right at all. He looked at another rejected draft.

Izabelle,
I am a liar who doesn't deserve you.
-Jake

That one had been rejected because he didn't want to admit he was a fraud in writing. It was bad enough he hadn't come clean yet. It would have been even worse to do it in a nameless, faceless note. He had eventually settled with an overly bland, not at all descriptive version of:

Izabelle,
I sincerely apologize for overstepping this morning. Please give me the chance to make it up to you. I promise we won't talk business.
-Jake

Now that he was back in his own room, he realized he should have added "no pressure" or "I will just sit there silently if that is what you want" or "I would never in a million years do anything other than love and support you if I could," but those were all crumpled in paper balls next to him. Seeing as it was now early evening, he knew his chances of anything he had said actually being accepted as an apology were dwindling. It had been hours since he had knocked and left the note. She was within her rights to ghost him, but he continued to stare at the hotel phone just in case.

When it rang, he didn't even let it make it halfway through the first chime before he picked it up.

"Izabelle?"

She laughed. It was the first time he had heard her genuinely laugh today, and the sound ran through him as relief incarnate. "What if it wasn't me?" she asked.

"It wasn't you earlier, but the guy at the front desk didn't seem offended. I'm glad you called. Did you get the note? I taped it to your door. I knocked, but I wasn't sure if you were in there or not."

"Yes, I got it. I wasn't there. I went for a hike. And then I had to call my friends and do some apologizing."

"Izabelle, I am so sorry—"

"It's fine, really. I took a step back from everything, and I know you were just trying to help. I want to talk to you about it over dinner if you're still offering."

"Of course. Just tell me which restaurant and what time."

"I'm getting kind of hungry, so whatever one you think will have the shortest wait."

"Yeah, about that. I called all three of them and told them to hold a table for me just in case."

"Seriously?" Izabelle asked.

"I wanted to make sure I had the opportunity to make it up to you if you called."

"Well, in that case, how about we meet in fifteen minutes at one of the ones that we haven't eaten at. Something casual though."

"Mesa Grill it is, then."

"I'll see you there." She hung up the phone, and he sprinted out of the room toward the restaurant.

~

He stood as she approached the table. He was determined not to reach for her unless she wanted to touch him first. He didn't want to step over her boundaries any more than he already had. That held firm until he saw the angry red scrapes on her knees.

"Jesus. Izabelle, are you okay?" He stepped out and scooped her into him, his stomach turning at the thought she had fallen and he hadn't been there to catch her.

"Wha—?" Her confusion was smashed into his pec.

"How did you fall? Are you hurt?" He pushed her away and grabbed for her hands. Checking them, he was relieved that there were only a few tiny scratches on her palms.

She looked up at him with a grateful expression. "I'm fine. But I think I'm going to give up on pissed-off hiking for a while." She gave him a timid smile and then slid into one of the chairs. "I want to apologize for yelling at you today. There is a reason for it—not an excuse for it, but a reason, and I want to explain to you why."

He took the seat adjacent to her, close enough to reach her and still see her face fully. "You don't have to apologize or explain anything to me. I—"

"No, I want to. It's important." She started fidgeting with her napkin and looked away, smoothing her hand over her ponytail. "When I told you about my business experience, I wasn't fully honest with you, and I left a big..." She tilted her head from side to side. "...rather informative chunk out."

Jake tensed at her mentioning honesty. "Izabelle, it's fine. There are some things that I haven't fully explained either. You don't have to tell me if you don't want to." Jake dreaded the idea of having this conversation now.

"I have to. It's been long enough." Izabelle took a sip of her water and a big inhale. "I said I only started this business five years ago. Which is true. But this business came about because of what happened before that..." She paused, looking around as if she was trying to find a word. "I had invested everything in—" She tilted her head back and scoffed. "God. I don't know why this is so hard for me to say. I had invested everything in another business partnership." Jake wasn't sure what to say, so he just stayed quiet as Izabelle continued. "But it was more than that. We were in a romantic relationship as well." She paused and scratched at her head. "I mentioned that when I went away to school, I ended up in this fancy business program, and coming from where I did, I just never felt like I fit in. I wasn't able to network on the level the other kids were because I couldn't invite classmates to daddy's yacht or mommy's beach cottage. And I certainly didn't have anyone to give me seed money to get an idea off the ground. It eventually felt like I was never going to succeed without all those other things. That my businesses or ideas were never going to be noticed. That *I* was never going to be noticed." She paused again. This was clearly difficult for her to get through. She took another sip of her drink before continuing. "Well, someone eventually did notice me, and he had all of the things that I thought you needed to succeed. He seemed like the perfect person to go into business with." Izabelle ran her tongue over her teeth as she tilted her head back. "God, it's so embarrassing I thought this." She brought her head back down and continued. "And to build a life with. At least that's what I thought we were doing. We started up a business with my idea and him filling in the gaps, using his network, building out the board, getting investment. Long story short, it went really well, or at least I thought it did, until it didn't. He ended up taking everything we built, and I got nothing." Izabelle sighed and rubbed at the corner of her eye.

Nothing Izabelle had just said was anything Jake had expected to hear. If he could reach back in time and strangle this idiot Izabelle was describing, he would. Hearing the hurt in her voice as she explained what had actually led up to today made him want to rage. No wonder she wanted to keep her professional and private lives separate. He reached out his hand to take hers. "I had no idea."

She took his hand and squeezed it. "Thanks. It definitely fucked me up and shook my confidence pretty bad. But I had to do something, or else I was going to starve. So, I took that experience, figured out how to have it never happen again, to me or anyone else, and turned it into Me-E-O." She shrugged apprehensively. "So here we are."

"But wait. I don't understand. He couldn't just walk away with everything you had worked for. As a founding member, you would have been on the board, right?"

"Oh, I was. But unbeknownst to me, so were most of his fraternity brothers and family members. When I signed off on the new bylaws for the expanded board, I didn't realize I was agreeing to a quorum number that meant I never had to be present for a decision to be made."

"Oh shit."

"Yeah." Izabelle nodded solemnly. "Shit."

"What about legal counsel?" Jake asked.

"His aunt. I just thought we were getting a great deal getting such a high-powered corporate attorney for such a good rate." Izabelle shrugged. "And to a degree, we were. Or, rather, he was."

Jake was grasping for anything where he could go back in time and make this right. He would gladly throw any number of attorneys on his legal team toward this problem if Izabelle wanted him to. "But what about your stock? They had to cash you out at the end."

Izabelle raised her eyebrows as she blew out a long breath through her pursed lips. "Yeahhhhh. That's where it gets really tragic. Did you ever see the movie *The Social Network*?"

"About the founding of Facebook?"

"Yep. That's the one." Izabelle took a sip of her water. "Remember how in the movie Mark Zuckerberg pulls a legal fast one on Eduardo Severin and dilutes Severin's stock to nothing? My ex apparently read the same books that Zuckerberg and his lawyers did." Izabelle chuckled. "If I ever meet Eduardo, I'm going to buy that guy a drink because I know exactly how he feels." She paused, tilting her head in consideration. "Except he just experienced a stock split and a firing. I got the stock split, stupidly quit, and then got dumped. So maybe he should buy me the drink," she joked darkly.

Jake felt like he had been punched in the gut. "Jesus. I—"

Izabelle waved him off. "It's tragic. But it's in the past, and nothing is going to change that. What I really hope is that this gives you an idea of why I didn't react well to you offering suggestions earlier," she said sheepishly. "Everything about that, and this"—she gestured with her hand back and forth between them—"kind of conflated into one."

"God. I truly had no idea. I feel like such an ass now. I don't even know what to say other than I'm sorry." Her hand was not enough for him. He continued to hold on to it as he got up from his chair and came around to her side of the table, pulling her up into a hug. As he gathered her in close, he said, "Please know, I would never try to take anything from you. Please believe that."

Jake felt Izabelle's head nod in agreement against his chest. "I do. Well, at least I think I do. It feels like I know that." She sighed. "I'm working on it." She pulled away slightly and scratched her head. "Is it just me, or is this entire trip not what you expected it to be?" she asked with a nervous chuckle.

The candor of her tone and abrupt shift in the conversation caused him to let out the same chuckle. "It's not just you. This is nothing like I thought it would be."

"But it's good. Right?" she said, half statement and half question, a familiar flame starting to flicker in her eyes.

"It's much more than good." Jake felt every feeling of goodness rising in him at once. He wanted to show her how good this was. How good he could be for her. How they could make each other feel.

"Would it be okay if we just went back and got dinner in your room? My appetite is suddenly not going to be satisfied by food."

Izabelle, you wonderful woman. "Let's see if I can satisfy it."

Twenty-Five
IZABELLE

As they walked hand in hand along the path back to Jake's casita, Izabelle wrapped her other hand around his bicep and dropped her head to his shoulder. The warmth of his body against hers triggered a heat that was both arousing and calming. She hadn't told anyone other than her friends the Simon saga. And even then, they had lived through a lot of it, so she had never fully had to explain it. Getting all of it out of her system left her feeling lighter but also raw and hollow.

"I hope I didn't dump too much on you at dinner," Izabelle said, looking up at him, feeling a wave of insecurity crash over her. "I know that was kind of...a lot. You just—I don't know, I just end up telling you things I didn't think I would ever share with anyone."

He stopped abruptly, grasping both of her hands so that she was facing him. "Never apologize for being honest. You are never a lot. I hate that you've been through so much. If I had the ability to go back and make it easier, I would. I never want you to feel like that again."

She felt herself melt at his words, the care in his eyes delivering on his wish to make it all easier. She wound her hands around his neck, pulling him down toward her, craving his kiss. The taste of him was intoxicating, her head swimming in the rush of it. He slid his hands down her ribs and around her waist to pull her closer. She reciprocated by letting her hands wander over the breadth of his back. He groaned when she ran her nails through the hair at the nape of his neck. As his hands roamed her curves, she deepened the kiss. He bent to pick her up, and she wrapped her legs around his waist, another groan slipping from his mouth to hers.

"Oh! Um. Sorry!" They broke their kiss as they both turned toward the voice. She immediately saw it was coming from a startled hotel guest who had come around the corner to see them going at it. The poor guy took a jerky step to the left and then to the right and then, with an awkward half wave, turned back and jogged off away from them.

She and Jake looked at each other with bashful expressions that quickly devolved into laughter. The seriousness of the evening, the tension after their fight, and all of her worries about Simon quickly evaporated in the desert night.

"We should take this somewhere more private," she said between giggles.

"Exactly what I was thinking," Jake said, bending down, grabbing Izabelle just above the knees, and easily tossing her over his shoulder.

"Jake!" she yelped. "I swear to god, if you drop me on my head!"

"What? Like this?" He bounced her slightly.

"Jake!" Izabelle said between laughing shrieks.

He gave her a light smack on the ass. "You seemed to like it when I picked you up just a few minutes ago."

"Put me down!" Izabelle said, half command, half squeal. "I can walk!"

"Oh, I'm going to put you down, but it's going to be in my bed."

∼

"Umpfh," Jake said, tossing Izabelle on the bed.

Izabelle raised herself up onto her forearms to look at him. "I gotta say, I always thought being carried to bed by a man would be more romantic. Less potato sack."

"I agree. Next time, I'll hop on your shoulder, and we can see if it goes better that way." He threw her a wink as he flopped onto the duvet next to her.

"Now that you've got me here, what are your plans?" Izabelle asked.

"Dropping you on the bed was the plan. Had no intentions past that," Jake responded, stifling a grin.

"Nothing? You don't have any interest at all in continuing what we started out there?" Izabelle said, eyeing him with playful questioning written on her face.

"Hmmm, remind me what exactly we were up to? The exertion of that fireman's carry seems to have erased it from my mind."

"God, you're a cheeseball," Izabelle said, rolling over onto his chest. "You know you don't need the corny setup, right? You can just keep making out with me. But since you seem to want a reminder..." She finished her sentence with a kiss and immediately felt a ripple of tension roll through his body underneath her. "Ringing any bells?"

"It's all coming back to me now. But keep reminding me—I'm enjoying the walk down memory lane," Jake said, his hands coming up to her hips.

She could feel the warmth of his palms through her shirt. She planted her lips on his again. He slid his hands up her waist, taking the hem of her shirt with them. The skin on her back goose-bumped in the sudden coolness of the air-conditioning. She shivered at the compounding sensations. As he deepened the kiss, the softness of his mouth was in direct conflict with the hardness beneath her. She felt herself melting into the contours of his body.

She sat up, pulling back from their kiss. "How in god's name are you so good at this?"

"Mmmmm." Jake made a noise somewhere between a hum and a growl that sent a wave of vibration from his chest straight to where she was straddling him. "Don't stop. I want to keep proving what else I'm good at."

"Suddenly in such a rush. Seems like your memory is back," Izabelle quipped.

"You could say I'm experiencing a bit of muscle memory," Jake said, pulling her more firmly down onto his hips, making his point very clearly.

"Let's see if we can't make some new memories." She pulled up the hem of his shirt, granting herself access to his torso. Jake raised his eyebrow, but his expression lasted only a brief second. As soon as she ran her fingernails over the skin just above his waistband, his entire body jolted.

"Shit, Iz." He grabbed her wrists. "That is both very sexy and very tickly."

"Tickly?" Izabelle laughed. "Quite the word to use in a moment like this."

"Tell me I'm wrong," Jake said just before he swiftly sat up, grabbed her, and rolled her under him in one swift move. Now on top of her, he pulled her shirt up, softly running his fingers against the ridges of her hip bones, skimming them down the soft valleys that ran toward her center.

"Ack! Jake!" She yelped as she tried to squirm away.

"Is it not tickly?" he asked, repeating the move with an even softer touch.

"Yes!" she exclaimed, her body jerking involuntarily.

"No, no, you have to say it's tickly." He replaced his fingers with his face, lightly running his stubble over the same spot. The roughness on her skin produced the same jolt.

"Yes! I yield!" Izabelle squealed. "It's tickly."

"But also sexy, right?" Jake asked. She felt the warmth of his breath ripple across the surface of her skin.

"Not if you keep torturing me via tickles!" Izabelle said through her laughter. This entire setup was ridiculous and fun and exactly what she needed.

"I can make it sexier," Jake said, replacing the stubble of his cheek with a languid stroke of his tongue.

Oh. Hello. Her laughter shifted immediately to something much more primal. "Much better." The heady feeling from earlier returned.

He continued lapping up her body, stringing a line of grazes and licks up her stomach and ribs. He stopped the parade of kisses at the underwire of her bra.

"You don't need this anymore," he rumbled into her chest. He slid his hands around the lower edge of the lacy band toward the back and unclasped it with ease. Izabelle moved to pull her T-shirt over her head so that he could pull it all the way off, but he stopped her. "I will not have you accuse me of being in a rush." He pulled her shirt back down to where it had started.

"Wha—" Izabelle tried to protest, but Jake cut her off with a kiss.

He reached through the arm hole of her shirt, hooking his fingers around her bra strap and pulling it down her arm. He repeated on the other side, moving slowly, deliberately. Once her arms were free, he skimmed his hand over her stomach again. She arched into his touch with a whine, but he kept her shirt down, pulling her bra free and tossing it into the expanse of the room. He then lightly ran his thumbs over her nipples through the fabric of her shirt. "I haven't given these the attention they deserve." He circled them with his fingers, the fabric diluting and diffusing the sensation across her breasts. He incrementally increased the pressure, exactly in tune with the pressure building in her body. He lowered his mouth to her nipples, nipping at one, then the other.

"Jake, please," she gasped. She didn't even know what she was asking for. She just knew she needed more.

She didn't have to specify; he knew exactly what she meant. He pulled up her shirt again, lowering his mouth to tease at one nipple and then the next. She groaned when his mouth left her and began to move down her stomach. When he reached the waistband of her shorts, she could feel the rumbling of his voice again.

"You don't need these anymore either."

Jake undid the button on the denim, and she lifted her hips. He wasted no time yanking her shorts down her thighs.

"I think you forgot something," Izabelle said, looking down to where Jake had left her panties intact.

"Like I said, I'm not in a rush."

He proceeded to tease her clit over top of the lacy fabric in the same way that he had her nipples. Her body felt like a live wire, popping and sparking along with his ministrations. "Jesus," she panted. "I don't know how much longer I can take this."

"Now, that's what I like to hear." In two quick motions, Jake stripped off the rest of the fabric covering her body. Shedding his with equal ease. He crashed back down to her with a hunger that she easily met. She arched into him, signaling exactly what she wanted.

Goddd. Yessss. He entered her, and her mind wiped everything but him. They fell into each other, giving and taking, in a rhythm they implicitly understood. They worked each other higher and higher until everything hit at once. She gasped his name, reveling in the full force of her pleasure. She heard Jake echo hers in return.

They lay there panting for a long, leisurely while, and she let herself drift slowly down.

Somewhere along the line, Jake moved from on top of her to snuggling behind her. She settled into his arms, their usual position. She couldn't say when she fell asleep, only that she felt she was exactly where she needed to be.

Twenty-Six

IZABELLE

Izabelle woke up feeling like everything had clicked into place. She shimmied toward the side of the bed, trying her best not to wake Jake up beside her. But the second she lifted her head from his arm, she heard his voice in the hazy dark.

"Hey, you okay?"

She rolled over and kissed his head. "Yeah. I'm fine. I just need to make a few calls. Go back to sleep. I'll be back in a bit."

Jake gave an understanding rumble and settled back into the sheets. Izabelle padded out of the room, grabbing her phone and heading for the back patio of Jake's casita.

Settling into a sunny chair, she dialed Sabrina's number. She had called each of the girls yesterday when she had gotten back to her room to apologize for how she had acted on their call. They had all assured her that one stressed-out snap wasn't going to break them up. They were here for her, even when things were rough. But each one in turn had made it a point that if she needed help, they were more than willing to help, and she didn't have to be doing this all alone. She was about to take Sabrina up on that offer.

"Morning, sunshine. How are those banged-up knees?" Sabrina answered on the second ring.

Izabelle laughed softly. "They're alright. Not quite as bad as the banged-up ego for acting like such a jerk to everyone yesterday, but I deserve it."

"Thank you for apologizing, but it's fine, Iz. You're forgiven. It wasn't as bad as you're making it out to be."

"Thank god for that because if not, I would feel even worse for what I'm about to ask."

"And that is?"

Izabelle took a breath and then blew it out slowly. "Sooo, you remember how you said you would help me if I needed it? Well, I've decided I need it."

"Really?" Sabrina asked with an uncharacteristic amount of shock. "Don't get me wrong. I am more than happy to help. I'm just surprised. You haven't asked for help in all the time I've known you. And especially after yesterday… Are you okay?"

Izabelle paused before answering, tucking her knees up and snuggling into the corner of the chair. "You know, I think for the first time in a while, I actually am okay."

"Wow. That's quite the turnaround from yesterday."

"I told Jake about Simon."

"That he exists or…"

"No. About everything."

"Everything?" Sabrina asked incredulously.

"Everything. Started at the college and business school insecurities and ran all the way through how he stole all my fucking ideas and company."

"Woah."

"Yeah." Izabelle nodded. "Woah."

"How did he take it?"

Izabelle smiled up at the red sandstone around her; it was coming into its full color in the morning sun. "He took it like he does everything. He was super supportive and kind, and I think he has become a fully pledged member of the wants-to-strangle-Simon-on-sight club. But he certainly wasn't fazed by it in any kind of negative way."

"And how do you feel?"

Izabelle rolled the question around in her mind, considering it. "I feel good. Really good, actually." Her voice gained certainty as she went on. "That's why I said I think I'm going to be okay. That I am okay."

"That's amazing! I'm so happy for you!"

Izabelle's smile broke fully across her face now. "Well, stay in that headspace because I'm about to ask you for a rather large favor." Even though Sabrina couldn't see her face, Izabelle still winced as she asked, "Do you think you could take my slides and... pretty them up a bit?"

"Pretty them up?" Sabrina repeated.

"It's just, you're really great with presentations and making things aesthetically appealing. I've seen what you do with your client pitches and it's way better than anything I've come up with. I was hoping I could send you my slides and you could design them a bit better, make them more coordinated. I know it's a lot to ask, but—"

"That's it? Seriously?"

Izabelle's face and voice remained sheepish. "Yes?"

Sabrina laughed. "Iz, that's nothing. Of course I'll do it for you! I was really hoping you would ask. I worked something up months ago in case this exact scenario played out."

Now it was Izabelle's turn to laugh. "You're kidding."

"Not in the least! I just didn't want to step on your toes and insist that I do it for you."

Izabelle dropped her head back, shaking it in disbelief. "I envy your ability to always have a plan. Actually, it's more than that, you always have a plan and then numerous backup plans—which you're actually able to execute. I'm jealous of that. That's the level of got-my-shit-together I want to be when I grow up."

"Ha!" Sabrina laughed. "Plans are my job. But you've more than got your shit together. It's just in a different way. Let us not forget that I famously nearly burnt my kitchen down trying to cook you guys dinner last year."

Izabelle laughed at the memory. Sabrina was not the most domestic of the four of them; she had left a pizza box in her oven and then forgot about it, so when she went to preheat it to make them all some food before their *Bachelor* premiere watch party, things went a bit awry. "You know, that does make me feel better."

"As it should. You can at least fix yourself dinner without risking property damage. But I can at least get these slides looking pretty in a couple of hours."

Izabelle slumped in her seat, relief washing over her. "I can't thank you enough, Sabs. You have no idea how much this is going to help."

"I only wish you would have asked me earlier."

"Me too," Izabelle responded.

"Well, better late than never," Sabrina said.

"You're damn right about that." Izabelle caught a bit of movement out of the corner of her eyes. She turned her head toward the casita door. She saw Jake giving her a wave through the door. Shirtless with tousled hair, he was really something to see.

"Now, speaking of better late than never. Since I'm going to be in possession of your pride and joy for the next couple of hours, you need to go do something fun. Don't fight me on this."

"You know I normally would. But now I can think of a few things that qualify as fun." Her eyes flicked back to Jake. His back was to her as he poured two cups of coffee, the mugs sitting next to each other on the stone countertop.

"And Iz?" Sabrina interrupted her thought. "I think Jake is a good egg."

Izabelle felt herself warm at her friend's words, perfectly timed with a beaming smile from Jake as he approached with her coffee. "I do too."

"Good. I'll email you in a couple of hours when I'm done with them. Bye, girl, love you."

"Love you too! Bye!" Izabelle said as she hung up the phone. She dropped it in her lap just as Jake approached, handing her a mug. Izabelle raised her chin and received a light kiss on her forehead.

"Morning, gorgeous. Everything okay?"

Izabelle chuckled. That really was the question of the morning. "Yes. Everything's fine." She raised her coffee cup in a cheers as he took the seat catty-corner from hers. "Better than fine with this. Thank you."

"Of course. So, when would you like to get started on the presentation this morning?"

Izabelle nodded as she took a sip. "Actually, I don't." Jake furrowed his eyebrows in confusion. "At least not this morning. That's what I was on the phone about. I'm sending my pitch deck to my friend Sabrina for a few hours. She's going to get it looking a lot more interesting than the default PowerPoint background I've got going at the moment."

Jake stopped mid-sip, obviously stunned. "Wow. That's—that's great."

Izabelle shrugged bashfully. "Yeah. I took some advice, and the advice was that I should be open to taking advice. And some help. Here and there."

Jake's lips twitched in a stifled smirk as he sipped his coffee, but he didn't say anything.

"I know it's been a lot—that *I've* been a lot—but I can't thank you enough for sticking by me."

Jake sighed softly. "Izabelle. You should never apologize for being you, especially to me. You are incredible, and you continue to be incredible. Don't say you're sorry for that."

Jake was looking at her in the way she had always wanted, like she was more than enough, like she would always be enough. It made her feel like she was the incredible person he was gushing about. She got up and moved to snuggle into his lap. He nestled her into his chest with a squeeze. "Well, I'm certainly not sorry I met you."

"Let's hope to god that sticks," Jake said with a chuckle that vibrated against her cheek.

Izabelle didn't think there was a single thing Jake could do at this point that would throw her off how she felt. Because all of this felt exactly right. "I was thinking since we have some time to kill this morning…"

"That we could go back to bed?" Jake asked, scooping up her knees and making a move to stand up and carry her back to the bedroom.

Izabelle squealed as he picked her up. "I was thinking more breakfast than bedroom!"

Jake looked down at her, eyes mischievous as he sidestepped through the open french doors to the casita, taking extra care not to hit her head. "There is more than enough time for both."

~

Izabelle rested her hand on her stomach. Standing on this stage, in this ballroom, was never going to feel anything other than sucky. Which was a real shame because it was overshadowing what an excellent day this had been so far. The sex this morning had rocked her world. The plate of bacon and perfectly fluffy waffles she had taken down at breakfast, divine. The slides she got back from Sabrina, so aesthetically pleasing you would have thought it was a corporate version of a West Elm catalog. The hype email Sabrina had sent along with them made her feel like the presentation finally had a chance. But the moment she stepped up on this cursed stage, all of those warm, fuzzy feelings evaporated, and she was back to feeling so nervous she could throw up. Which would be such a waste of waffles.

Jake called up from where he sat in the front row. "You've got this. You've practiced, and you are perfect."

Izabelle dry swallowed. The lump in her throat didn't move. "I don't want you to say anything or do anything, or even move, until I get to the end of it. If you can keep your face neutral, that would help too. I'm probably just going to look over your head the whole time so I don't make eye contact, okay?"

Jake gave her a smile, a nod, and a thumbs-up.

"Good. Thank you for following directions." She turned back to the podium and sucked in the biggest rib cage–expanding breath that she could muster. "Ladies and gentlemen, I am Izabelle Green, and I am delighted to share my business with you." She worked through the familiar slides one at a time. She walked to the places on the stage where they had practiced. She had the clicker in her hand, and she didn't drop it. Izabelle couldn't say she felt easy-breezy doing it, but she also didn't feel like she was going to pass out. But when she got through the slides explaining her numbers, she felt her blood pressure ratchet up a bit. This was going to diverge from the plan, but it felt right. It was the advice she knew she should take. *You can do this.*

"But numbers only tell so much of the story, because the rest of the story is my own. I started this business so that others didn't have to feel the crushing defeat of failed ventures or not knowing where to start. I wanted to reach out to others like me and give them the guide to starting a business and the connections and resources I wish I had when I was starting out." She clicked to the next slide. "I had the dreams of my businesses mocked, stifled, and even stolen, but I never gave up. I wanted fledgling CEOs to feel like they didn't have to give up on their dreams either. That if they persevered, through whatever it was that was holding them back, they could build themselves and their companies into something more. So, just like I have invested in them, in their dreams, I'm asking you to invest in me and my dream, Me-E-O. Thank you." She looked down at Jake, full of apprehension.

His face was blotchy, and his body was under visible strain. The bottom of Izabelle's stomach fell out. "Oh god. Is it that bad? I can take all the stuff out at the end. I knew it was schmaltzy."

"Am I allowed to talk now?"

"Yes. Give it to me straight."

Jake let out a breath that he had clearly been holding for a while and hopped out of his chair. "It was wonderful! I am so proud of you! Do not take out the stuff at the end. It was amazing." He gathered her up in a hug. "*You* are amazing. Sitting there quietly while you went through it damn near killed me. Trying not to cheer as you nailed all of the slides and your marks nearly gave me a stroke." Jake grabbed her on each side of her face and kissed her deeply. Izabelle felt her whole body relax.

"Okay. But are you sure you aren't just saying that? I swear I can take a critique this time."

"Izabelle. It's really good. You get across what you need to, you made it personal, the slides look very professional. As long as you do it exactly like that, you won't have any trouble come presentation day."

Izabelle believed him, and more importantly, she believed in herself. She believed that she could do this. She blew a long breath out between her lips. "Alright. Let's do it a few more times and make sure I've got it super dialed in."

"Absolutely. As long as I can cheer this time."

Izabelle gave Jake a squeeze. "Okay, just a little."

Twenty-Seven

JAKE

They were halfway through their entrées when Izabelle looked up. "I know I shouldn't say this out loud for fear of a jinx, but today was the first day I actually felt like things might work out." She punctuated the thought with a smile so jubilant it lifted her entire face.

Jake felt like he was floating up with the corners of her lips. She looked so perfect when she smiled. He reached out for her hand, stroking her knuckles with his thumb. "I totally get it."

Izabelle tilted her head. "You do? Why?"

Shit. He did get it. On two levels. Both his anxiety about helping her with the presentation and his and Izabelle's fledgling relationship. If he didn't explain what he meant, it would sound like he had doubted her from the beginning, when in fact, what he meant was that he finally felt like he hadn't helped her in any inappropriate way. He didn't want to risk shaking the confidence she had built and all the progress she had made. The presentation was the best it had ever been. She had added some key personal anecdotes, and her friend Sabrina had made the slides light-years more cohesive than they'd been before. After watching it this afternoon, he finally felt she had a good shot at this, and he hadn't directly intervened, just supported.

But if he did say something, he was going to have to explain everything. Because otherwise, it wouldn't make much sense why he was anxious about helping her with her presentation at all. He was caught between saying everything and saying nothing because both were going to hurt her. But everything had gone so right today he hoped like hell this would go right too. "There is something that I've been wanting to say for a long time. I know I should have said something way sooner than now, but—"

"Well, I'll be damned! If it isn't the man himself!"

Izabelle pulled her hand back out of his, looking from Jake to the man who had shouted across the dining room at them.

Fuck. Things had definitely just gone wrong. What were the odds that goddamn Barry Brockenheimer was in this restaurant? Jake crashed down to reality all at once. *Pretty fucking high, dumbass, considering the event starts in three days.* Now Barry was shoving through tables on his way over to him. Sheer panic set in. It was too late to leave, and he didn't have enough time to explain. Before he had time to even think of a plan or even stand up, Barry was forcing a meaty hand into his for an aggressive handshake, paired with a jarring clap on the back.

"Aren't you looking fine!" Barry said, clearly as a statement rather than a question. "So good to see you. How have you been?" In his typical style, Barry didn't bother to wait for a response before charging ahead with his next statement. "Hope business is as good for you as it's been for me. Really booming. How's the golf game? Really would love to hit the links with you sometime. Did you see the write-up in *Forbes* about me? Ahh, of course you did, of course you did. So great to talk with ya, chief. Let's do this again soon. I'm sure someone in that big ol' building of yours has my number. I'll let you get back to it."

Releasing Jake's hand after continuously shaking it during his monologue, Barry turned on his heel and sauntered back in the direction he came. Jake was stunned. First, that he had seen Barry at all, or rather that Barry had spotted him, and second, that he had scraped by, yet again, without someone he knew blowing his cover. He turned back to look at Izabelle.

"God, that guy sucks. He didn't even acknowledge that I exist, much less let you get a word in edgewise. Who is he, and how the hell do you know him?"

Jake never thought it before and would never think it after, but in this one moment, he was eternally grateful that Barry was a chauvinistic pig. His complete disregard for Izabelle was the only reason that Jake's lies were not going to blow up in his face in the middle of this restaurant. "His name is Barry Brockenheimer. He's a guy that did business with my dad back in the day and now fancies himself as king of the world."

"Bleh. That's the exact type of person I try to avoid doing business with."

Bleh was one word for it. Jake had certainly lost any appetite to continue sitting at this table, knowing that Blowhard Barry could circle back at any moment. "Yeah. Let's get out of here."

"Oh. Uh. Okay." She rose from the table with an uncertain look. "Are you okay?"

Jake grabbed Izabelle by the hand and started to gently pull her out of the restaurant in a hurry. *That remains to be seen.*

Barry barging into their dinner had completely thrown him off. One minute, he was completely immersed in how perfect Izabelle was and how wonderful they were together. How everything was going to work out. But then Barry had shown up and ripped off his rose-colored glasses. Things weren't perfect. He was still wrapped up in a lie. His mind was straining so hard to logic a way out of this that he was just blindly dragging Izabelle behind him in the direction of his casita.

"Jake, are you okay? Is something going on with that guy?"

"No, I'm fine. It has nothing to do with him. I just want to wait until we're back at the casita to tell you." It was a stall, a sloppy punt downfield that was intended to give him more time. Time to think of all the right words to say and how to say them in the perfect order.

"Hey." She pulled at his arm to slow him down. "You can tell me if something's going on."

He stopped and turned to look at her, and he thought his heart would break into two. She was clearly worried. And now that he was manically stalling, she was starting to have a look of panic. He knew then he couldn't lie. "I have to leave." *Fuck.* That hadn't been what he meant to say. It was also still a lie. He had no plans to leave tomorrow, but it was the first, and easiest, way he could think of to physically get himself out of this situation.

The look of concern on her face deepened, and she started to pull her hand away. "What?"

The rambling took over, just like it always did when he was flustered. "This has all been incredible, and I didn't expect it, and I didn't think I needed it, but I wanted it when I knew I shouldn't."

"Jake, what the hell are you saying?"

He knew this was all coming out wrong, but he couldn't stop. "I just want you to know that you're amazing, and you don't need me, and—"

"And what?" she asked, her eyes shimmery with tears.

"And now work is in the way, like it's always in the way, and I should have told you sooner, but I didn't, and I'm so sorry. But I have to go back to San Francisco tomorrow. There is no other way."

"So—are you—" She tipped her head back and crunched her knuckles. "I guess this isn't the right words for this—we didn't define anything—but...are you breaking up with me?'

He pulled her into him. Damnit. Why did he always say the wrong thing? "God no. No, no. I don't want that at all. I want to be with you. I just can't right now. I have to go back to the city."

"For work?"

Jake couldn't bring himself to say anything. The indecision on what to say came out as a groan.

"Is that what you wanted to say at dinner?" Izabelle asked. "That you had to go back to the city?"

Jake groaned again, aphasia setting in as he died slowly from the inside out.

She lightly smacked his chest and pulled away from him. "Jesus. You scared the shit out of me. It's fine if you have to go back to work. I get it. I can see you when I get back." She took his hand again and started pulling him toward the casita again. "Lord. Just say something came up. That speech had me going in a completely other direction." She continued to chuckle the rest of the walk about how all he needed to say was that his flight got moved or a project needed him. "Save me the drama next time. My nerves can't take it with everything else I've got going on."

Jake followed behind in a daze. How in the hell had that just happened? He had tried to run, and she had just taken it in stride. A huge part of him was relieved he hadn't hurt her until he processed that the only reason she wasn't hurt was because he hadn't told her the *actual* reason he had to leave, only that he needed to. A throbbing was setting in between his temples. Each step toward the casita ricocheted tension. He had to do this. He had to find the words.

They walked into the casita, and she turned on the fireplace. Snuggling up into a corner of the couch, she reached out for him to join her. Saying nothing, Jake sat down on the couch next to her. She instinctively moved to lean against his shoulder. "Look, I'm sorry about tonight at dinner and—"

"You don't have to apologize for that guy."

"No, I don't mean him," Jake said, turning slightly so that he could look into her eyes. "I'm talking about what I said. I'm sorry I worried you." He paused and exhaled a long, slow breath. "I just want you to know that this has been one of the most incredible weeks of my life and I meant every word about wanting to see you again. No matter what happens, I will always be glad that you're sitting here with your beautiful head on my undeserving shoulder."

She turned her head up, finding his lips. He met them with a yearning hunger. He kissed her like he wouldn't get the chance again. She sighed her desire into him, moving to deepen the kiss.

He broke away from her but kept his face near hers. "I need you to know that this isn't about sex. That I'm serious about you, about us."

"Can it at least be about kissing?" she laughed. "Because I was enjoying that moment." She drew back from his shoulder with a teasing look on her face but silenced her next smart-aleck remark when she saw the seriousness on his face.

"Not that you aren't incredible—you are goddamn mind-blowing, angel—I just don't want you to think that is the only reason I want to see you again. I really care about you. More than I thought I could care about anything. I need you to know that." He felt himself regressing towards being the awkward man she has met in the car but he couldn't stop.

Izabelle looked over both of her shoulders in quick succession. "Jesus, you would think that an asteroid was about to hit the earth with a speech like that. What has gotten into you tonight?" She was clearly trying to keep the mood light, but her facial expression was growing increasingly concerned.

"I'm being serious," Jake continued, his eyes boring into hers. "I just..." He squeezed her hand. "I just—I'm sorry I have to leave tomorrow."

"Me too." She leaned into him.

"And I promise you everything I feel about you is true."

"Jake, I can confidently say you haven't given me a reason to think otherwise. It's why I've been able to share so much with you." She reciprocally squeezed his hand. "Now, if I assure you that I don't think this is all about sex and that I fully believe you think I'm wonderful, can we get back to it? If this is my last night for a while, I'm not in a mood to go without," she said as her hand snaked down his arm.

He couldn't resist her. The moment to come clean had come and gone, and he had bungled it. He kissed her again slowly. It hurt to know he'd had his chance to come clean and still hadn't had the words. That this was likely the only time he had to salvage this, the best thing he had ever found. And now because of his own stupidity he could lose it all. He let her every breath and whimper burn itself into his memory. Ensured that every curve of her body was seared into his hands. That her fire and desire burnt him from within. Because the best thing that had ever happened to him was very likely to go up in flames, and it was all his fault.

Twenty-Eight
JAKE

"Morning, handsome," Izabelle said, flopping over onto his chest, hovering her face over his with an eager look in her eye.

Someone had clearly been up for a minute. "Are you waking me up for a quickie before I have to head out?" He tried to keep his tone convivial, but he wasn't sure he was successful. Waking up with her this morning was both magical and miserable. No matter how much he wanted to be here—supporting her, cheering for her—all he could do at this point was slink away in shame and hope this wouldn't seem like such a big deal after the competition. After she had triumphed, maybe she would give him the chance to grovel at her feet and apologize for not telling her, explain that the only reason he did it was to try and protect her and her company. He hoped he got that chance.

"Sadly, no. I was hoping we could run the presentation one last time before you go. Maaaybe also hoping you could work your magic and get the ballroom one last time?" Anticipatory hopefulness had infused itself in her question.

Jake sighed and shut his eyes again. He had hoped to make a quick exit this morning before anyone else spotted him.

"I think it would really help with my nerves. I felt so much better after yesterday's run-throughs." She paused for a half second. "But if you don't have time, I totally understand. I don't want you to miss your flight."

He couldn't tell her no. Just thinking about her anxious on that stage and knowing he could do this one last thing to help had him caving immediately. He couldn't in good conscience blame leaving on a flight he didn't even have arranged yet. "Of course. Let's get up and go now so you have more time to practice afterward." *And hope to god that no one else is awake yet.* "Go change, and I'll meet you in the ballroom."

Her eyes lit up. "Thank you!" They softened as she continued to look at him. "You are amazing." She planted a kiss on him and hopped out of bed.

Jake squeezed his eyes shut and flopped his head back into the pillow, hard. *No. I am an idiot.*

Izabelle ran her presentation flawlessly, all the way through. He could tell she was still nervous, but she was able to keep her voice and hands from shaking once she got going. Watching her up there was the purest sense of pride, anger, and anxiety Jake had ever felt. He was so proud of her for getting here, for building such an incredible business, for pushing through her stage fright and owning the things that had hurt her in the past. He was so mad he had to leave, that he couldn't openly support her, that he hadn't told her why.

He was so anxious for her to do well, for no one to see them in here, to get out of this resort and this town before anyone did.

"I am asking you to invest in me and my dream, Me-E-O. Thank you." She looked down at him and let out a huge breath. A smile broke out across her face. "Shoof, actually felt like that one was decent. Any notes?"

"Only that they would be fools not to invest in you."

"They're investing in the company, Jake, but I'll let that one slide." She bounded down the stairs to him, leaping into his arms for a hug. He squeezed her tightly until she begged for him to let her go. It was the last thing he wanted to do.

"A late breakfast before you leave?"

Jake ran his hand over the back of his neck. "I really shouldn't." The lightness on her face was killing him. She drew him in with such ease. He didn't want to leave her, now or ever, but knew that he was flirting with disaster the longer he stayed.

"Come on, you do have to eat."

He knew it was a bad idea before the words even left his mouth. "You're right. I do have to eat."

"Cliffside, then?" she asked.

Fuck no. That was truly asking for someone to run into them. "Uhh. How about grabbing something quick on the pool deck." He crossed his fingers that the pool was far enough out of the way.

"Aw, that's sweet. Good idea," Izabelle said, smiling.

"What is?" Jake was shocked that any of his decisions this morning would register as "good ideas."

"It's where we first ran back into each other. That would be a nice bookend." She squeezed his hand, and it ran straight to his heart, which contracted with an alarming force. His desire for her and his desire not to lose her gripped his chest at once.

"Definitely." Jake knew he needed to stall for a few minutes. He had to get himself together, and he knew walking hand in hand across the entire resort was a step too far. Lunch could look like a business meeting. Strolling with intertwined knuckles and a moonstruck look on his face was not able to be played off as an acquaintance. "Hey, uh. I'm going to check my flight details really quick. Grab us a table in the far corner. I'll meet you there in a few."

~

Walking separately proved to be a good idea. Jake had seen one of the investors as he was walking to the pool deck and had been forced to give him a wave when they made eye contact. But so far, he and Izabelle had gotten seated and ordered without him seeing anyone else or, more importantly, anyone else seeing him. He was starting to relax just a touch. They were tucked out of the way, and he would be out of here before the actual lunch rush hit. *This might actually work out.* Not that it stopped his knee from bouncing anxiously.

"Are you okay? It seems like you're looking for someone," Izabelle asked with obvious concern on her face.

Shit. He had hoped he wasn't being that obvious, but he couldn't stop scanning the grounds for anyone he might know. "I'm fine. Just taking it all in before I go." *Another fucking lie.* He hated himself for each one he told. These were going to be a mess to untangle once they were both back in San Francisco. He instinctively grabbed her hand to steady himself, running his thumb over her knuckles. He desperately hoped Izabelle would understand all of this once they were back home. Once he had time to properly think about and articulate all the reasons he had kept who he actually was from her. He heard the footsteps of the waiter coming up behind him and watched the smile and then the color run off Izabelle's face.

"Well, well, well. I didn't think you had it in you, Izabelle."

A thin man with a pinched face, dark eyes, and overly shiny, slicked-back hair walked up to Izabelle, standing way too close in her personal space. She flinched away from the human ferret, yanking her hand out of Jake's.

He stood up from his chair to put himself between this guy and Izabelle. "Do you know this guy, babe?" Izabelle's eyes widened at the word "babe." He hadn't ever called her that, but Jake wanted this rat-guy to know she was with him. Her mouth was slightly open, but she wasn't saying anything. He didn't like this. Something was wrong. Jake reached for her again. "Are you okay?"

"Sleeping your way into this thing got you too tired to respond...*babe*?" the weasel said.

"Who the fuck are you?" Jake asked, turning on this guy as Izabelle stood up.

"Makes sense she wouldn't mention the ex to the new guy, especially when it's you." He stuck out his hand for a handshake. "Simon Reeves." He paused before continuing. "I didn't think the great Jacoby Masterson Jr. and I would have so much in common," he said, giving Izabelle a lascivious up-and-down.

"Jacoby Masterson?" Izabelle said from behind him. Both he and Simon looked at her. "Jake, why is he calling you Jacoby Masterson?"

"Oh, please. There's no need to pretend you've also become an actress in the last five years. Clearly, you know who he is. *Intimately*," Simon said.

"Jacoby Masterson Jr. as in the CEO of Masterson Holdings?" The questioning was written plain as day across her face. "Wha..." Jake could hear the confusion starting to mix with a tremble in her voice. "Why didn't you..."

He took a step toward her, which she countered with a step back. *No. No. This is not how this was supposed to go down.* "Izabelle, let's go. I'll explain—"

"Explain why you lied to me?" There was a red flush creeping up her neck into her face.

"Oh. Now, this is interesting. You actually didn't know. Did you?" Simon waved his hand dismissively. "Typical Belle trusting without verifying."

"Don't call me Belle," Izabelle snapped, pulling her gaze off Jake and onto Simon. "Why are you even here?"

"As a former investment recipient, I have a standing invite to come back every year if I wish."

Izabelle stood stone-still. The flush that had been creeping up her neck had now fully engulfed her face. "You got our business into EtaSella?"

"The day I got the notice that I was in, I gave you the notice that I was out."

Izabelle's breath caught at that news. "But you already had so much. You already had investors—you didn't need—" Jake could hear Izabelle fighting through her voice catching. "You already had everything. Why would you take more?"

"Because more is more. Why would these investors bother with giving out seed money when they could give it to companies that already have proven success?" Simon looked at Izabelle like she was a small, stupid child. "Anyway, I saw your name on the participant roster and figured I would come see what you had made of yourself. But turns out, you still can't do it alone. You only seem able to get it together with a man backing you, or rather under you...over you? I don't want to assume what your preference is these days."

The tears welling up at the corners of her eyes killed him. He rounded on Simon, hoping to say anything to prevent a single one of those tears from falling. "You don't have a single fucking clue about what she's achieved to get here. You have no idea how hard she's worked. I didn't do a goddamn thing. If you say a single word out of line or even hint at suggesting otherwise, I will ensure that you regret it."

Simon looked past him, back at Izabelle. "Still have stage fright, then? Still have to get a man to speak for you?"

Izabelle looked at them both and ran. Jake leaned into Simon. "Not a word." He didn't wait for a response before he took off after her.

Twenty-Nine
IZABELLE

This goddamn fucking gate. She had hoped to get away from them before she started crying. She made it all of three steps before tears blurred her vision. At least she had her back to them. It was just this idiotic pool gate keeping her from making a break for it. It was like she was looking at the lock through a rainy windshield. "Open, you piece of shit!" She rattled it in frustration. A grown-ass woman derailed by this childproof lock. *I seriously hope they're over there so busy out-assholing each other that they don't notice me. I think an ounce more humiliation would kill me.*

"Iz, stop. Here, let me help," Jake said as he came up behind her.

I'm dead. "No," she said, swatting Jake's hand away. She was going to do this herself. "I've got it."

"I know you do," he responded as he reached over the gate and pulled the correct lever, causing the gate to swing open with ease.

It was infuriating. She couldn't think of a more perfect

summation of this past week with Jake. He had hyped her up, told her she could do anything, but meanwhile was pulling levers behind the scenes, making all of her actions seem foolish. She hauled ass through the gate, toward the back end of the property.

"Iz, please." Jake's voice was close behind her. "Izabelle, stop!" He put a hand on her shoulder. She whipped around to smack it away, glaring at him through her tears. Her chest heaving with each breath. Everything inside her felt like it was compressing into an emotional neutron bomb. "Aw, come here. Don't let that asshole make you cry," he said, reaching his arms out to hug her.

His statement set her off, and *boom*, she exploded. "That asshole! What about this asshole!" she shouted, jabbing her finger at him. "Simon has always been a lying dickhead, but I actually let myself believe that you weren't! Him showing up out of nowhere was a nasty surprise, but you're the one who actually blindsided me!"

"I'm sorry. I know I should have—"

"Told me who you were? Told me why you were here? Told me anything that wasn't a goddamn lie?"

Jake's shoulders slumped as he looked down. "I should have said something. I should have told you way earlier; it just got out of hand, and you never asked—"

"You can't possibly be saying because I never asked that I didn't deserve to know. Were you just waiting for someone to show up and make a fool out of me? See how long you could get away with it?"

"No. I swear, I was super careful to make sure that we didn't see people I knew—"

"That you knew! You were so worried about people *you* knew that you didn't even for a second think that maybe *I* should know? Because news flash! We saw plenty of people that know you, and they didn't say a word. They ignored my existence! And it turns out that it was someone *I know* who was the reason you got caught in your lying bullshit."

It was all coming to her in crashing waves, each one a miserable tsunami of understanding. He had always been vague about why he was here. Hadn't ever been fully direct about how he knew the resort so well, how he knew things about the competition. *How could I have not caught on earlier?* She felt like the world's most naive idiot. She had let herself wander so far down the garden path that she hadn't bothered to see a single red flag. "Everything makes so much sense now. Last night makes so much sense now. You saw that guy and freaked out. You thought he was going to out you at dinner and blow your cover. That's why you were being so weird. You literally said, 'no matter what happens' because you knew this was bound to happen!"

"Izabelle. I swear to you I didn't want this to happen like this. I wasn't trying to lie to you. I had hoped that when we got back to the city, I could explain myself and that nothing would come of it."

She stared back at him. "That nothing would come of it. *Wow*. Congratulations, Jake. Or rather, Jacoby. You got your wish. Nothing is going to come of this. Literally nothing. This competition is all I had. For half a second this week, I thought I had you, and now I have neither. Between you and Simon, you've certainly made it certain *nothing* good is going to come out of this."

"Iz. Please. I swear I didn't do any of this to hurt you. You have to believe that. And I don't think he's going to say anything. I told him if he did, he would regret it."

She scoffed, her mind flashing back to five years ago when Simon calmly informed her that he was taking everything with him and kicked her out of his car.

"That's a fucking joke. He was with me for years. We built a company and a life together, and then one day, out of the blue, he left me. Took everything I had worked so hard for, our company, our relationship, my whole life. And you know what he said to me when he left? 'Strictly a business decision, dear. I'm sure you'll get it one day.' So take my word for it. He doesn't give a single flying fuck about you and whatever you said to him, and he *certainly* doesn't give a fuck about me. He only cares about himself."

"It doesn't matter what he said. I still feel the same way about you. We can get over what everyone says. It doesn't change anything."

"It changes everything! How am I supposed to feel the same way about you? I can't get over the lies. I can't get over people thinking I slept my way into EtaSella. That *you* are the reason I'm here." She ran her hands over her hair, trying to push back frizzy baby hairs and fraying nerves in one go. "Furthermore, I *really* can't get over my own idiocy. I promised myself that this would never happen again. That I wouldn't let someone steal what I had worked for. I already had one boyfriend steal everything, and now you're here doing it again."

"I have a company. I'm not trying to take anything of yours. I was—"

"No shit you have a company! You have a billion-dollar

corporation. At the end of the day, this is, *at most*, just a little bit embarrassing for you. But for me, it's everything, and now, because you couldn't possibly be honest with me, I have nothing. You've taken it away."

"I swear to you I was trying to help. I wasn't trying to take anything away from you and what you've accomplished."

"And yet you have. If a single person listens to the rumors Simon is inevitably about to spread, then all of my hard work and getting here by myself is immediately delegitimized. I swore I was never going to mix business and personal again for this exact reason. I *told* you that. I told you so much about myself, and you didn't even bother to tell me who you really are." The truth of what she had just said crashed down on her, and her knees nearly buckled from the weight of it. Every vulnerability she had shared, every painfully honest moment of the last week, had been shared with someone who wasn't even honest about who they were.

"Izabe—"

"No. No more." She turned and ran. She had wanted to say "Goodbye" as a marking of finality but wasn't able to get it out before she started sobbing.

Thirty

JAKE

"World's greatest assistant speaking."

"Cam, I need a flight out of here. Now."

"You do know that EtaSella doesn't even start for two more days, right?"

"I'm the sponsor of the goddamn thing. I'm very much aware, Cam! Get me a fucking flight. Now!"

"Jesus, Jake. Do not swear at me, and do not shout at me."

Jake had to take a deep breath. "Shit." He hissed out the curse between clenched teeth. "Cam, I'm sorry. But things have gone sideways here, and I need to get the hell out before I lose it completely."

"Okay. There was still swearing in that sentence, but it wasn't directed at me, so I will help you now. Is it something with the vendors or the location because I'll just call them and—"

"No!" He slammed a fist on his thigh. He took a moment to try and compose himself as he continued to bounce his fist against his thigh. "No. The competition is fine. It doesn't need anything, but I fucked up some personal shit and need to leave ASAP."

"Okaaaay. Just so I know…is this like a you're going to need legal counsel and some bail money situation or…like a media fixer…or—"

"No," Jake responded.

"Can I get a clue here so I know how I can assist you? Tough to be an assistant when you don't really know the category of assistance needed."

"I told you I need a flight. That's it. Get me the flight, and please stop asking me to explain my personal dating life to you right now."

"I didn't ask you about your—ohhh. This is about the girl you called me about, isn't it?"

Jake remained silent; he couldn't even think about explaining what this was all about right now. All the ways that he had fucked this up.

"Alright. Say no more. I'll book your flight," Cam continued. "Where are you now?"

Jake ground his teeth. "The parking lot."

"Of the hotel or the airport?"

"Neither. I pulled over in town to call you."

"Someone packed in a hurry," Cam quipped.

"Fuck." Jake brought his palm up to his face with an audible smack.

Now Cam sounded like she was starting to get pissed. "Jake. Don't make me repeat myself about the swearing."

She had a point, but this was frustrating as all fuck. "I'm not swearing at you; I'm swearing at me. I didn't pack my shit. I just left. Can you get someone to get my stuff out of the room and ship it? I'm not going back in there."

"Wow. Okay then. Shit really did go sideways." He heard her typing and clicking rapidly. "I'm on it. Your ticket will be in your inbox by the time you get to the airport. You leave in four hours. I'll figure out your stuff and the car."

Jake sighed heavily. "Thank you. And Cam?"

"Yes?"

"I never want to talk about this again." Jake threw the phone onto the rental car seat next to him. He crossed his arms over the steering wheel and wished like hell this hadn't happened.

Thirty-One
IZABELLE

How fucking dumb do you have to be to sleep with someone and not even bother to ask specifics? The red-hot fury that had gripped her when she was yelling at Jake had dissipated as she ran away. Her rage tears evaporated in the desert heat before she got back to her room. Now lying on her crisply made hotel bed, she felt nothing but a full-body numbness, underscored by the stone-cold fact that she was an idiot.

She rolled off the bed to trudge to the bathroom. *How can I ever show my face tomorrow?* The thought of a single person thinking she had somehow used her wiles to seduce Jake in order to get a spot in the competition made her want to be swallowed up by the earth. The idea of an entire ballroom thinking that...unbearable.

She squinted as she flipped on the harsh blue-white lighting of the bathroom. *Eeesh. I really can't show this face tomorrow.* She was sporting the classic "I've been crying my eyes out" face: splotchy, puffy, eyes weirdly glassy. It was not a good look. Nor was it a good starting point to try to psych herself up. *Back to the bed it is.*

She flopped back down, the air in the fluffy comforter poofing out in an exasperated sigh for her. She made the decision to stare at a spot on the wall instead of a spot on the ceiling. *Why the hell couldn't he just tell me who he was? Why didn't I figure it out?*

It was an exceptional level of stupidity that she hadn't realized how little she knew about Jake. She knew he worked vaguely in business with his dad's company, was at the same hotel as her, had a really nice hotel casita, knew his way around the hotel and Sedona exceptionally well, had a very well-kept body, was great in bed, could book hotel ballrooms on a moment's notice, cut people off before they said his name, that his real name wasn't Jake, and that he *knew* he shouldn't have been doing any of this or else he wouldn't have bothered to lie about it.

She had taken him at his word that he had been here before and that he had just gotten some nice perks. She wanted to blame it on the fact that she was so distracted by the good sex and the pretty face that she'd never bothered to worry if Jake was telling the truth or not. The reality was she was so busy doubting herself that she never bothered to doubt him.

This is why I swore to myself I wouldn't trust anyone with my business. She had broken a promise to herself, and now she had to pay the price. She just hadn't expected the price to be her company. Again.

She had lived for so long as the girl without a social life, who spent all her time either on spreadsheets or in her sheets. Sleeping. Alone. And yet she had thrown all of her cautions away because an attractive man said he was attracted to her ambition and her body. It sounded absolutely pathetic when she summed it up: "Insecure loner girl doesn't learn lesson. Repeats the past with deeply ironic accuracy."

Although it wasn't even all that accurate a reproduction. At least before, when Simon imploded her life, she could rightfully claim the mantle of a sympathetic victim. Now she was going to be perceived as a talentless hussy who had tricked someone else into getting her to the top.

What made it all hurt so much more was she had actually thought Jake was different. She had fallen for the fantasy. The perfect man you meet on vacation. He hadn't seemed like all of the alpha-holes who had surrounded her in her business world before. He had been awkward, caring, intuitive, thoughtful, supportive. He hadn't made her feel small for a single minute. He had never doubted she had made her business what it was. He had made her feel valued. Their time together felt special, and so she never adequately questioned the feeling. She had let herself trust.

She flopped over with a groan. *It's honestly pathetic how little that took.*

Looking at the clock, she realized that the girls would probably be at dinner right now. *Might as well update them that I'll be coming home early.*

She rang Ava's number, knowing she would be the only one to have her phone on. She picked up on the second ring.

"Iz! Hi! How are—"

"Are you all together?" Izabelle asked.

"Yeah. Why? What's—"

"Are you in a spot where you all can hear me?"

"Yeah, we're outside just waiting for a table because Charlie forgot to make a reservation."

"I said I was sorry! You know that we should have put Sabrina in charge of it!" she heard Charlie shout through the phone. "Is that Iz? Hi, Iz!"

"Put me on speaker, and nobody say anything until I get through this."

She started with a healthy dose of self-loathing that she should have caught onto this before, the vagaries about work, the always going by Jake, the way that the people at the hotel bent over backward for him, and then recapped how of all fucking people, it was Simon who had shown up and informed her that it was all a lie. That she had actually been sleeping with the sponsor of EtaSella the whole time. "And now Simon is going to spread the rumor that I got here only because Jake and I are in a relationship and therefore he bought my way into the competition. No one is going to invest in me, or even if they did, it would just be to kiss Jake's ass and not because they give a damn about anything I've worked so hard for. Sooo. Yeah. That's how I'm doing," Izabelle concluded. Once she finished, there was nothing but muffled street noise on the other end. "Someone please say something because I'm on the very edge of a breakdown, and I've had way too many of those this trip."

"So, if I followed that summary correctly, the ex from your past is going to ruin your future because he knows about the man from your current who is also going to ruin your future because you didn't know about his past," Charlie said.

"Yep. That's pretty much it," Izabelle responded.

"Holy shit. It would be poetic if it wasn't so fucked-up."

Izabelle laughed for the first time today. "God, it really is such a helpless mess, isn't it?"

"Is it truly though? This all assumes that Simon is going to spread rumors, right? Maybe he won't," Ava said.

"That would be assuming he's capable of doing one decent thing in his life. We all know that isn't happening," Izabelle said, disdain dripping from her voice.

"Yeah. But there has to be something she can do," Sabrina chirped in.

"If you need me to fly out there, I'm not above resorting to violence," Charlie offered.

"I think you could kick him square in the nuts, and he wouldn't care as long as he could make money from it. There is seriously nothing he responds to other than threats to his business," Izabelle said.

"Well then, as much as I would like to kick him in the nuts or watch you kick him in the nuts, I think you have your answer," Charlie said.

"What?" the other women said in unison.

"That's your answer. Threaten his business. It's really your business anyway. Therefore, if he's threatening to take down your new business, you then have to threaten him with the old one that he stole."

"Oooo, I like it," Sabrina said.

"Ugghh, No. I don't," Izabelle responded. "That plan involves me talking to him. I really don't think I can do that."

"You slept with that heinous douche for five years. You can manage a conversation. Especially with the stakes being this high."

"Wow. Okay. That is a touch too intense of a pep talk right

now, Char," Ava said. "But she does have a point, Iz. Of course you can do this. You have to. It's a five-minute phone call that could impact the rest of your life."

"And you're going to have to do it soon. Before he has a chance to run his mouth," Sabrina said.

"Just harness all the wrath you've built up over the past five years and let it rip. You can do this. We know you can," Ava said in an uncharacteristic approval of angry confrontation.

"I hate you guys. You suck for suggesting this. But I love you," Izabelle said, feeling just a little bit less shitty than when she had called them.

"We know. And we really suck because we're going to hang up now so that you don't have an excuse not to call him."

"Wait, don't—" Izabelle heard the call end before she could beg them not to go. She slumped back down on the bed. She abandoned staring at her trusty spot on the wall to reunite with the blank spot on the ceiling, rolling onto her back with a deep sigh. "Man, I really don't want to do this." *I'll just count down from ten and then dial the phone.*

∽

It was only after she got to negative one hundred and forty-two that she dialed his number. "Hello? Who is this?"

Of course he didn't have her number saved in his phone. *Guess it's just me that thought he might want to call and apologize someday.* "It's Izabelle. I need you to promise you aren't going to say anything to anyone about today. It isn't what you think, and you don't know what you're talking about."

"And why would I do that, Belle?"

She cringed at the nickname. His "special name for his special girl." She hated it then and hated having to get over it now. But she had to, because unless she could throw Simon into a dumpster and keep him locked in there forever, she was going to need him to be quiet in another way. "Because you've broken a lot of promises to me, and I need you to keep one for once. You owe me that much." She said it with the faintest of hopes that appealing to his kinder sense would work. That she could trade on their years together for something other than the jack-all she had to show for it.

"Breaking promises has gotten me pretty far in life. I don't really see much point in changing at this point."

Fucking unrepentant asshole. When she had dialed the phone, she thought she would only have a few minutes until her nerve cracked. With everything that had happened today, she didn't trust she could make it through speaking to him without either breaking down crying or resorting to begging. But hearing his voice through the phone now made her mad. Mad was progress. Mad was what she was, and mad was what she needed to be.

She wasn't the person he had known and manipulated for all those years anymore. She wasn't the insecure girl that had taken all of his shit lying down. Let herself believe he knew more because he was born with more. Let him trample her self-confidence just to walk away with her work in the end. No. Not anymore. He'd taken everything she had once. He wasn't taking it again.

"Fine. If you don't like promises, let's make a deal. We both know you stole my company and my hard work. I have the notes and drafts time-stamped on hard drives to prove it. You have two options. You can either shut the hell up about whatever it is you think you know and leave me alone, or you can spread rumors. At which point I will then spread the truth of exactly how 'your' business came to be." She heard nothing but silence from the other end. "Deal?"

"You've changed, Belle."

"I'll take that as a yes." And she hung up the phone.

Thirty-Two
IZABELLE

Deep breaths, Izabelle. You can do this. You practiced this. It isn't new. But staring out into the packed ballroom proved that last portion to be a lie. She ducked her head back behind the waiting screen. This definitely wasn't like she had practiced with Jake. *Jake.* She really didn't have time to be thinking about him. She had been able to push the thought of him out of her head for the last forty-eight hours until now. Well, mostly.

After hanging up on Simon, falling asleep had been easier than she thought. Amazing how spending the morning crying, the afternoon moping, and the evening threatening an ex could really take it out of you. She had woken the next morning with a sense of existential dread large enough to push everything but her pitch deck out of her mind. She pored over her slides, taking out the pieces Jake had encouraged her to put in. She wasn't going to talk about her personal life; she wasn't making that mistake for a third time. She wasn't that much of an idiot.

After exorcising all traces of Jake's influence out of the presentation, she spent the day rememorizing each detail, burning into her brain exactly what she was going to say. She didn't have time to do anything else. The only moments she wasn't glued to her screen were when she rushed out to pick up her registration packet from the front desk and to drag in the room service cart when they dropped it off for dinner. She ironed her suit, laid out her laptop, triple-checked that the presentation was loaded onto her USB drive, and said the presentation in her head until she fell asleep, each slide passing through her head like she was counting sheep.

It was only this morning, in the hazy moment before she became a part of the waking world, that she wriggled backward in bed, searching for his warmth and finding nothing but the coolness of crisp cotton sheets. *That nothing would come of it* echoed through her thoughts. Too freaking true. But all the same, she had put her makeup on, shimmed into her clothes, and gotten herself here.

She peeped out at the audience again, her stomach dropping like it did every time she took in the faceless crowd. *Izabelle. Focus. He isn't thinking about you. Don't waste time thinking about him.*

"Do you have your list of presets?" In front of her stood a man in all black, with a headset and a clipboard.

"What?" Izabelle asked. His arrival had thrown off her train of thought.

"Your presets. For the lights and the sound? Do you have any other projectors or anything that needs plugged in?"

"Um. No."

"Thank god. Between the confetti cannon making a mess

and the smoke machine setting off the fire alarm earlier, I'm about to throttle someone."

"I'm sorry, who are you?" Izabelle asked.

"Head of A/V tech."

"You're the sound guy?" *Goddamnit. Jake was right.* There was a sound guy she could have handed the settings to. It was then that she realized. Of course he had been right about the sound guy. It was his event. He would know about every detail that was supposed to happen. Despite her lack of focus, the sound guy had continued speaking to her.

"...I don't really prefer that title. The job is a lot more complicated than people think, and it's not just sound. I have a degree in this, but sure, I'm the sound guy."

"Oh. I'm so sorry. I-I, um, am a little new to this."

"Mm-hm." The tech rolled his eyes. "Any other questions before you go?"

Izabelle knew this man did not have time to answer all the existential questions that were running through her mind, such as *What the hell am I doing here?* She kept it to the oh-so-eloquent "Uh, when do I go?"

He impatiently scanned his clipboard. "You're in the hole."

"So, I'm next?"

He huffed. The exasperation on his face made it clear she was taking up too much of his time. "Next would be on deck. You're next after next." He looked at her face, which was clearly broadcasting that she had no idea what the words he was saying meant in this context. "Just listen for your name. They'll say it when they introduce you."

"Okay, thanks." *I guess I'll just sit here clutching my USB drive until they call my name, then.* Against her better judgment, she peeped back out at the crowd. She scanned the audience. Nothing had changed. It was a room packed shoulder to shoulder with hundreds of faces she didn't know. A fact that was both deeply intimidating and deeply disappointing.

You can't feel disappointed that a person you never really knew isn't here.

Bang! She jumped back as a fireworks flash went off onstage. The very agitated A/V tech pushed past her. "Are they fucking kidding me with this?" He threw his clipboard to pick up a fire extinguisher. He worked behind the emcee, who was back on the stage.

"Looks like they went out with a bang *and* a blaze of glory!" the emcee joked, all shining white teeth and hair gel. The crowd laughed in response.

These presentations were nothing like she had expected. As pretty as her slides were, it was still a basic PowerPoint. Which looked like a kindergartener's stick figure drawing in comparison to these productions. But there was nothing she could do about it at this point. She started into her psych-up routine. It lasted the entire length of the next presentation. She was just starting to rehearse her presentation when she heard the emcee again.

"Now, let's welcome to the table a scrappy upstart, a one-woman operation, Izabelle Green, the founder of Me-E-Ooooo!"

Shit. Shit. Shit. She willed her feet to walk toward the podium, praying that her slow movements came off as confidence and not paralyzing fear.

She made it to the podium without tripping. *Thank god.* She plugged in her USB, her hands shaking just as much as they had in practice, but she got it connected. She was infinitely glad she'd had the foresight to put a dot of nail polish on the right side so she wouldn't have to fumble flipping it over. *So far, so good. Now you just have to show them what you've got.* She searched the crowd for a familiar face one last time.

And there he was. Right in the front row. She stopped. Her weight shifted as if her body was preparing itself to bolt. She saw the slow, smug smile unfurl across his face. *Simon. You. Fucking. Unrepentant. Asshole. How dare you think that you can throw me off.* She took another deep breath. A steady one. Stepped a few feet to the left like she had practiced. Planted her feet. *Time to show them all what you've got.*

"Ladies and gentlemen, I'm Izabelle Green."

Thirty-Three
JAKE

"Mr. Masterson, hi! I, um, I mean— Hello. I didn't think you would be in today."

Jake flinched at the sound of his name. *Damn.* He had really wanted to make it to his office without anyone speaking to him. He was not in the mood for talking. That mood certainly extended to the intern standing between him and the solitude of his closed office door.

"This is so great. Are you going to join everyone for the watch party?" the intern asked hopefully.

"What?" The word came out so clipped with frustration that it was barely a question.

"The-the watch party? For EtaSella? It was a company-wide email. I thought everyone was invited to it. So I was going to go —But uh, maybe I had it wrong. Sorry to bother you."

The look on the poor kid's face told him he was being the exact kind of corporate asshole he hated. It wasn't his employee's fault he was miserable. "It's Kai, right?"

"Yes, sir." His face brightened a bit with the recognition.

"I forgot that we call it a watch party now. We used to just call it a screening when we couldn't stream it live. Anyway, you're certainly welcome at the watch party. My father used to say it was the can't-miss event of the year. Please be there. Ask tons of questions. Learn as much as you can. Thank you for your hard work and enthusiasm." He turned, hoping to make a break for his office without getting stopped by anyone else.

"Thank you, Mr. Masterson, I definitely will. I'll see you there!" Kai called after him.

"Mmm." He threw his hand up as an over-the-shoulder wave as he walked away. He really did not have the patience today. He was regretting the choice to even come in at all.

Yesterday hadn't seemed so bad. After taking the red-eye, he was exhausted and hungry. He kept himself busy with post-trip tasks around his house, sorting the mail, doing the laundry, until he crashed into bed. But waking up this morning alone had been a nasty dose of reality. A reality he didn't want to engage with. His plan was to come in early, barricade himself in his office, talk to no one, and then work until he couldn't think about anything else.

Jake made it to his office without any other run-ins. He powered on his computer, ready to be sucked into a world of minutia. He got to work sorting the most labor-intensive parts of his financials, the ticky-tacky stuff he usually outsourced to accounting. He hadn't even had an hour of peace when he heard his door swing open.

"I wasn't expecting to see you in today."

"People seem to have a lot of expectations about where I'm supposed to be today." Jake looked up from his desk to where Cam had just opened the door and waltzed through. "Are you ever going to knock?" he asked, his gaze turning from the door to the row of sleek monitors on his desk.

Cam gave him an arch look. "I never have. Today would be a weird day to start."

"Mmm," Jake harrumphed, looking back to his spreadsheet. He didn't bother to look at her again as she sidled up to the side of his desk.

"I really didn't expect you to commit to attending the screening of the presentations either."

"I'm not," Jake said, picking a paper clip out of the shallow dish on his desk and unbending it slowly, focusing on straightening one U-shape at a time. "Why would you say I'm going?"

Cam laid a hand dramatically on her chest. "Oh, I'm not the one who's saying you are. Your new best friend, Kai the intern, is doing all of the saying. More like raving, actually." Cam started into a decent impression of the kid he had met in the hallway earlier. "He knew my name and everything. Said that the watch party was a must-see. Said he would be there."

"I did not tell him I would be there," Jake growled.

"Did you actively say you would not be there, or did you do that thing where you're trying to get out of a conversation, so you just grunt, and people take that as a yes, and then I have to field phone calls of people insisting that you agreed to something when really you weren't paying attention at all?"

"Mmm," Jake replied.

Cam pointed at him with a snap, eyebrows raised. "Exactly that."

"I'm busy today. I can't make it," he said, staring directly into the screen.

"You can't seriously be telling the person who schedules

your calendar that you're busy today. The only thing you've been busy with today is laying waste to that pile of paper clips." She looked from the unbent paper clip in his hand to the pile of straight metal rods lined up on a corner of his desk. She pulled up a chair next to his desk, a look of concern on her face. "Do you want to talk about it?"

Jake kept his gaze straight ahead. "There's nothing to talk about."

"Excellent. In that case, there is no reason you can't go watch the pitch decks today. Right?"

"I'm not going to watch them."

"And why is that?" Cam asked.

"No reason."

Cam slid into her most chipper tone of voice. "Perfect! So, you'll watch them, then."

Jake was starting to get frustrated at his friend's insistence. He reached for another paper clip. "Cam, you know why I don't want to watch them."

"False. I've taken a guess as to why you don't want to watch them. And I am a most excellent guesser. But seeing as I was asked not to talk about it by you, and you just confirmed there is quote 'nothing to talk about,' and again quote, 'there is no reason' you don't want to watch them, I have no idea why you aren't going to the watch party."

Jake sighed. This was yet another no-win situation that he had backed himself into. "If I go, can we stop talking?"

"For now."

"Then I'll go."

"Then I will too." Cam stood up and strode back toward

the door. She pulled the door shut and said, "See you at 11:30," just before it latched.

He got the notification on his desktop seconds later.

Event added to Calendar:
Name: Watch party
Location: 12th floor conference room
Time: 11:30-3:30
Notes: You'll be giving the opening remarks before we cue up the livestream. Don't be late.

"Fuck." He grabbed another paper clip.

∽

"And now I'll cede the floor to our CEO for some opening remarks." Cam smiled at him and gestured for him to take her place at the front of the room. He knew she had only come to make sure that he came. He strode to take her place in front of the projector.

"Thank you all for coming." He gave a nod and a smile and then walked back to the rear of the room.

Cam caught his eye and mouthed, "Seriously?" at him. She may have made him come, but she didn't say how many remarks he had to give. She rolled her eyes and distinctly mouthed, "Why do I even bother," to herself. She moved to turn on the livestream and gave everyone a chipper, "As they say, life should be long, and speeches should be short! Enjoy the pitches!"

As the lights at the front of the room dimmed softly, she

sidled up next to Jake. "Clearly, your small talk didn't get any better while you were away."

"You wanted me here. I'm here."

"You're something alright."

Cam left him alone as the pitches started picking up. It had been Jake's intention to just watch a few and then slink back to his office. He didn't think he could bear to watch Izabelle in front of this room full of people. But as he started to watch the presentations and his employees' reactions to them, he became increasingly more enraged. The EtaSella he was watching on the screen was nothing like the EtaSella he knew. Sure, there had always been companies that hired outside marketing firms to help, but this was on an entirely different level. Companies were up on that stage with confetti cannons and pyrotechnics and D-list celebrities. This was *not* the point of the competition. Some of the companies weren't even bothering to run through their business plan. Nearly all of the presentations were completely lacking any substance.

What made it even worse was that his employees were eating it up. Everyone's eyes were transfixed to the screen, cheering like it was a sporting event instead of a professional competition. What the hell had happened since he was last there?

The horror of witnessing this mutation of EtaSella had him staying much longer than he originally planned. He didn't even realize how much time had passed until he heard the obnoxious emcee call out Izabelle's name. While the hours before had flown by, the second he saw her step out from behind the curtain, time ground to a halt.

She was walking slowly toward the podium. He knew she was deathly afraid of tripping. His heart wanted to leap out of his chest at the sight of her calculated breaths, the way she deliberately approached the podium, clutching her USB drive. Jake leaned forward, gripping the chair in front of him to steady himself. Izabelle had joked that she hoped her legs didn't shake too bad, but now Jake's were barely able to hold him up.

He saw Cam out of the corner of his eye look at him and then his hands and then his knees in quick succession, but he didn't care. His whole body was vibrating at the sight of her, so nervous but covering it so well.

He couldn't tell if it was his imagination or reality, but the most wishful part of his heart thought he saw her eyes searching the crowd. Looking for him. He would have run through every brick wall between here and Sedona in that moment to get to her. To give her a smile and a thumbs-up from the front row if it would have helped her.

He saw her eyes widen at something in the crowd, a momentary break in her confidence, but she set her feet, tipped her chin, and started into it.

The only problem was that Jake could barely hear her over the din of the conference room. It wasn't that Izabelle wasn't speaking loud enough; it was just that no one else was paying attention. He glanced around at all of the people turned away and talking amongst themselves. Couldn't they see how amazing she was? How she deserved their undivided attention? Frustrated beyond belief, he bellowed, "Quiet!" and a hush fell over the room.

"Oooooh. It's like that," Cam said next to him.

Now that he could hear her, he turned his full focus to the image of Izabelle. Every fiber of his being willed her to do well.

Oh no. Don't block the screen. Nice. Okay. Good save. You're ahead on the slides. Don't talk too fast. We practiced this. You've got this down to the second. Slow down. You don't have to rush. Good. Good. Caught back up on the slides. Your voice isn't shaking. You're almost done. Come on, Izabelle. You can do this. Wait. What? No! Go back. Tell your story. Shit, you must have cut it. Damn. I really hope that wasn't because of me. That's okay, it's okay. The numbers are still good. Right in the center of the stage for the last bit. Deep breath.

"And that is why I'm asking you to invest in Me-E-O." He watched her walk off slowly, then sprint behind the curtain for the last few feet.

Jake exhaled for the first time since he heard them announce her company name, his chest dropping and his head following, his eyes breaking from where they were burning holes in the projector screen. He stared down at his hands, knuckles white. He let go of the chair, his fingers leaving behind distinct pressure ridges in the foam.

"That's it? It was just a PowerPoint. There weren't even slide transition effects, much less any special ones."

"She didn't even go over the time limit. Everyone else ran way over because they had so much awesome stuff."

Jake looked over to where he heard the noise. Two employees he didn't know were gesturing toward the screen, one pulling off pieces of pastry and talking with his mouth full while the other swirled their iced coffee. A third walked up to them with a plate of charcuterie. He didn't know that one either. He used to know everybody.

"How did she even get into this thing? That was the lamest one of the day."

Jake walked from his place in the back of the room to where

the trio was sitting. They immediately sat up upon his approach. The one with the pastry hastily wiped crumbs from his lap, only to replace them when he wiped his hands on his pant leg in order to reach out and attempt to shake Jake's hand.

"Mr. Masterson. Great spread you've laid out today."

"You can sit," Jake said, ignoring the outstretched hand.

The coffee one jumped up to mimic Mr. Pastry. "Really enjoying the presentations."

Charcuterie butted in with their own take. "The special effects are reaching Super Bowl level. I heard that the people who do the pyrotechnics for Coachella are there. Everyone is really bringing it this year. Except for the last one. Total waste of time, right?"

Jake clenched his fist. "You are very much *not* right," he replied in an icy, measured tone. He stood there scrutinizing them, his glare moving across them one by one. The trio blanched and didn't respond.

At this point, the chatter that had filled the rest of the room had fallen away, everyone focused on this interaction. Jake could feel their eyes on his back, whispers here and there. He could hear the insufferable emcee, another person he definitely hadn't hired, calling the next group to the stage over the speakers. Jake turned from the group and walked to the front of the room, ripping the power cord out of the projector as he went. The move brought an immediate hush over the crowded conference room. He pointed at one of the employees nearest to him.

"Susan, what was your favorite presentation of the day?"

Startled, Susan took a moment to formulate an answer. "Umm, I liked the one with the robot baristas."

"And you would invest in that if you could?" Jake questioned.

She looked sheepish as she answered. "Yes?"

Jake pointed at one of the employees toward the back of the room. "And you, Marcus. What was your favorite of the day?"

Marcus answered much more confidently. "Definitely the refrigerators that can place grocery orders for you. They get my money."

"And your least favorite?"

"The last one. It was awful."

"Mmmm." Jake surveyed the room of increasingly confused faces. Jake rolled his head from side to side, trying to dissipate the building tension in his neck. "Now, can each of you tell me what the profitability forecasts for those pitches are?"

They both looked back at him without answering, Marcus looking blankly ahead while Susan blinked rapidly, looking around the room for assistance. "How about the total available market numbers?" The silence continued. "The serviceable available market numbers?" The rest of the room started to shift uncomfortably. "Fine. How about you just tell me *anything* that shows you actually read these companies' financials before you made your opinion."

Marcus was the first to cough up an answer. "I can just tell looking at the presentation they put the time in to make it look the best. It had all kinds of things going on. It makes you confident they know what they're doing."

"And how about you, Susan?" Jake asked.

"Yeah, um, yeah—I agree. I just feel like if they have the resources to make the presentation the best, then they have the resources to make their company the best."

"I see. I'll take that as 'I didn't read a single piece of information, I just like the flashy lights' from both of you." Jake scanned the room as a whole. He registered that every single face looked taken aback, but he didn't care. "Another question for the group. Does anyone know what EtaSella means?" The question was met with silence. "What the founding purpose was?" Jake saw Kai the intern look around and then slowly raise his hand. "Well, I'm glad that the intern is both brave enough to answer and actually knows. But does anyone who is a full-time employee want to tell me what EtaSella means?"

"It's just short for companies who are in beta and want to sell. Right? Like a portmanteau?"

Jake blinked at the man who answered. He didn't know him either. "What's your name?"

"Uh, Gary?"

"Are you confused about your name or confused about my question, Gary?" Gary sat unmoving for an uncomfortable amount of time. When it became clear Gary wasn't going to follow up, Jake turned on his heel and walked stiffly to the conference room doors and opened them. "All of you can go back to your desks. Now." No one in the room moved. "*Now*," Jake commanded.

Everyone filed out of the room with haste. Not a single person other than Cam made eye contact with him as they left. When they had all filed out, Jake looked back at the darkened screen and sighed. *How did it get to this?*

Thirty-Four

IZABELLE

"Can we get another round of applause for the presenters!"

The voice came over the loudspeakers on the stage. Applause followed, along with some light whooping. Izabelle heard it from the tucked away corner of the ballroom where she had wedged herself after her presentation. The vaguely textured cream wallpaper was the correct amount of comfort. It didn't have eyes, and it didn't look back at her. She had stood there for an undetermined amount of time, trying to figure out how it had gone. The only problem was she was so nervous that she had entered some kind of fugue state where she blacked out everything between saying her name and her request to invest in Me-E-O. Her only hope was that muscle memory and pure adrenaline had carried her through.

The disembodied voice over the speaker continued. "Now, if we can get everyone into the next room, we can start the evening mixer where the real work gets done! Great job, everybody!"

Evening mixer? Already? What the hell? She turned around to see everyone cheerily strolling out of the room. Claps on the back and high fives were spreading throughout the crowd. She gathered up her bag, moving cautiously toward the next room.

"Hey! You!" She looked to her left and clutched her bag. It was the A/V guy again. "You left this in the computer after your thing." He thrust her USB drive at her. "Thanks for not being a showboat like all the others. You were the only one I didn't have to clean up after."

"Uh. Thanks." She could tell her presentation was different from the snippets of the others she had seen, but it wasn't reassuring to hear that hers had been the *only* one that was different. She took the drive and dropped it into her bag.

"Good luck over there." He jabbed a thumb in the direction of the exiting crowd. "Heard the night portion is a doozy."

Izabelle did her best impression of a genuine smile, but her confusion was warping the corners of it. "Ha. Yeah. Well, thanks again for the drive." He walked off behind the stage. *I'm definitely missing something.*

She wandered into the adjoining ballroom and was immediately confronted with what she had been missing. The "evening mixer" portion of the contest wasn't a mixer at all; it was a full-blown convention.

Tables were lined up for each of the contestants, and on them were elaborate displays full of freebies and swag emblazoned with company names and logos. Dumbstruck, she wandered down the first aisle. Screens and banners highlighted company talking points. Balloons lightly rattled in large arches. Teams of people in matching polos were handing out flyers. Overwhelmed, she paused at an empty table between the booths, trying to think how she had missed this. She didn't remember anything about this kind of convention in the registration materials. She had gone through them with a fine-tooth comb. She set her bag down on the table, which sent a small folded name card scuttling across the white tablecloth. She caught it before it went over the edge:

> **Izabelle Green**
> **Me-E-O**

Shit. Even though she had missed it, clearly the organizers had given her a table. She frantically dug in her bag and pulled out the itinerary for the weekend, scrolling down to find the line.

> **5-7pm: Evening Mixer:**
> **Opportunity for the investors to speak with the presenters in a casual setting.**

This is the furthest fucking thing from casual. No part of casual entailed having handouts and billboards to advertise yourself, much less an army of matching marketing people. Looking around the ballroom full of beautifully crafted branding and then back to her blank table made her feel about one inch tall.

Now she understood why the A/V guy had said she wasn't like all the others; it was because she was way out of her league. Why the hell in all of Jake's prepping and meddling had he not bothered to tell her about this? A bit of a heads-up would have been nice. If he wasn't going to tell her his real name, the least he could have done was warn her that she should put together a trifold board or print a flyer, for christ's sake. Jake tried to tell her all kinds of stuff she didn't want to hear. Why in the world hadn't he told her about this?

"Hey, little lady! Don't I know you?"

She was nearly toppled by a clap on the back, and she had to put a hand out on the table to keep from falling over. "Excuse you." She righted herself and turned, only to come face-to-face with the loudmouth from dinner. *Of all the people.* "No. We haven't been introduced," she said through clenched teeth.

"Name's Barry Brockenheimer." He stuck out his meaty hand.

Izabelle shook it on instinct, instantly regretting the choice as her hand was engulfed in warm sweat. "I'm aware." She took her hand back and wiped it on the side of her skirt, feeling bad for both herself and the skirt.

"Ho, ho! Glad to know the name is known far and wide! Now, where is your booth at? You look like the kind of girl I'd like to get down to business with." He gave her an overly practiced wink.

Izabelle was working so hard not to gag that she couldn't properly answer. She just gestured to the table behind her.

"Oh. Uh." Barry chuckled uncomfortably. "You guys must have sprung for one of the hospitality suites, then. Smart move. Focus the dollars where they count."

"The what?"

He looked at her with a confused expression. Then suddenly, the expression lifted. "Ah. I see what you're doing. You're right. Gotta keep that part hush-hush." He winked again. "I'll see you around tonight. I don't forget a face. Especially a pretty one. Looking forward to seeing what you have to offer." He gave her an up-down. "If you catch my drift."

Izabelle didn't have time to get a "what the fuck" out before Barry walked off, calling out to the next person he knew across the room.

She put her hands on the table to steady herself, voluntarily this time. She needed to hold herself up. She needed to not cry. Her breath was going shaky. *I should have just gone home. This is not the world I thought I was getting into.*

A champagne glass appeared beside her hand. "Here, you need this."

She looked up and saw a very elegant stranger holding her own glass of champagne. She was slightly taller than Izabelle, white hair coiffed into a perfect french twist. A crisp white shirt, cut perfectly to her frame, was unbuttoned at the collar, highlighting strings of iridescent black pearls.

"I'm sorry. I don't feel much like celebrating. But thank—"

"It isn't for celebrating. It's to cleanse your palate of Barry. Foul man. He leaves a bad taste in everyone's mouth. Or at least mine." The woman lifted her glass in a silent cheers, then took a swig, visibly swishing it in her mouth. Taking hold of the glass, Izabelle followed suit. It did help. The woman put out a hand, a delicate gold chain on her wrist and nails perfectly manicured with a nude nail polish. She was the level of put together that Izabelle aspired to be. "Helena van der Court."

Izabelle took it willingly this time. "Izabelle Green."

The woman leaned around Izabelle slightly to look at the name tag on the table. "I gathered." She took another sip of her champagne. "Your pitch deck was good. Old-school. Like they used to be."

Izabelle groaned as she finished another sip. "That isn't what I wanted to hear."

Helena tilted her head inquisitively. "Why is that?"

"I feel like such an idiot. I had no idea what this"—she gestured around the room—"whole thing was really like. I was kidding myself with my little presentation, thinking that the whole point was about the business plan. I didn't know the level of pitches I was up against, or that I was supposed to have handouts for this thing, or—" She hesitated, the queasy feeling again in her gut resurging as she recalled what Barry had said. "—that I was supposed to go to rooms with the investors? Is that really a thing? Are people sleeping with investors at this thing?"

Helena snorted into her glass. "Is that what Barry suggested? Jesus, he gets worse every year. No. People are not sleeping with the investors. This competition has gone downhill since Richard died, but not that far. Although I'm sure Barry will be at the bottom to catch whatever rolls down it." She took another sip. "Companies a few years ago started hosting after-parties in some of the suites so they could wine and dine investors on the side. It's all part of the 'spend money to make money' ethos. Same thing with all of this and the whiz-bangs from earlier." She pursed her lips in disapproval. "I'm sure that Richard would be rolling in his grave if he knew that's what was getting people term sheets now. It's against the entire ethos of why he started it."

"Richard?"

"Richard Masterson."

"Oh. Right."

"It wasn't like this when he was here, or Jacoby for that

matter. I had hoped he was going to show up this year and right the ship. Although he probably doesn't even know all this sideshow nonsense is going on."

"You know Ja—" She stopped herself before she said Jake. "Jacoby?"

"Since the day he was born."

Now, that was a twist. Izabelle didn't have a solid guess for who this woman was, but old friend of Jake's family hadn't been one of them. "Do you know why he isn't here?" Izabelle tried to word her question as neutrally as possible. This woman seemed to know everything about everyone here. If Izabelle was going to get a chance to test the waters to see if Simon had kept his mouth shut, this was it.

"No. Other than he hasn't been right since his father passed. I think it was too much for him to come here and be reminded of it all. It was Richard's favorite event. It was probably a lot on Jacoby to come without him. Not that he would ever admit it." She shrugged. "My theory anyway."

Izabelle considered that. It tracked with what Jake had said about his father and possibly why Jake hadn't warned her about this mixer. Maybe he really didn't know. "How did, or do, you know them?"

"Jacquelyn and I were old friends from grade school. When she married Richard, I had my doubts. But he turned out to be one of the few, shall we say, non-Barry's of the business world. He got me to invest in this crazy idea when he founded it. Made me quite a lot of money over the years."

Izabelle was mortified. She should have put it together. The crisp slacks, the perfectly tailored shirt. From her french twist to her Italian loafers, this woman broadcasted wealth. Of course she was an investor. "I am so sorry. I've been talking to you so casually I didn't realize that you were an investor."

"I'm not. Not anymore. Last time I invested was half a decade ago, just after Richard died. My last choice didn't take off like I thought it would. Never lived up to what I had read about it on paper. After that, I gave up on investing in nascent companies and mentoring in general. I don't need the headache anymore."

"I get it. I should have given up too."

Helena's expression was one of curiosity. "Why do you say that?"

Izabelle sighed darkly, her filter breaking down under the stress of the day. "Where do I even start? Because clearly I don't fit in with this world. I wasn't given anything from my parents. Not their fault—they died tragic and early deaths, so I literally had to shovel shit to get myself into a college program where I wasn't given the time of day until a very charming asshole decided to build a company with me and then swindle me out of it. I just found out that he actually got investments here five years ago while I was slaving away in a crappy apartment, building up a new life and a new business that people still don't want to give the time of day to." She exhaled. It felt strangely good to dump it all out like that. Inappropriate to be dumping on an investor, but at this point, she had nothing to lose. "I should have taken any one of those things as a sign and bagged it in and just been an accountant or something. I could have still been in the world of numbers without all the heartbreak."

Helena regarded her for a long minute, swirling her champagne around in its flute. Then she tilted her head back and finished her glass. "If I were you, I would get out of here. It isn't worth your time. Trust me."

The rapid tone change was jarring. *Shit. I shouldn't have said all of that.* How many times was she going to have to learn the lesson about keeping her private life out of her professional one? She had just scared off the one person who had shown her any interest today.

"Um. Okay. Do you have a card or anything? I'd like to exchange contact information." Izabelle started to dig frantically in her bag for her business cards so she could at least give out some kind of handout at this mixer and salvage something from this interaction.

"I don't. But it was very nice chatting with you, Izabelle." Helena gave her a warm smile and then turned on her heel.

"It was nice to—" Helena waved over her shoulder without looking back. Izabelle looked down at her business card she was clutching, unearthed from her bag too late. "—meet you too."

Thirty-Five

IZABELLE

I should have taken Helena's advice and just left last night. Instead, she had stuck around in the ballroom, feeling worse and worse about herself as the evening dragged on. No one else stopped to speak to her. People just gave her and her empty table a pitying once-over as they strolled by. They didn't even break stride when she tried to hand out her business cards. Meanwhile, the entire time she was being ignored, she was suffocating under the constant refrain of "Meet us at our hospitality suite tonight, we can hammer out details" that was thick in the air around her.

As the mixer went on, investors and companies partnered off one by one. Paired-off groups left the ballroom with chummy arms draped over shoulders and numbers flying back and forth. It was like prom night and a dodgeball team selection had a baby. At the end of it, she was left standing alone.

Now, she chuckled darkly in her hotel room. She had been so mad at Jake for lying and then so worried about Simon spreading lies she hadn't even considered the other option that was now staring her in the face. Her company sucked so bad that no one wanted to invest in it. Didn't even want to give her the time of day.

Why did I twist myself into knots worrying about the pitch, then Jake, then Simon...everything, when it didn't matter anyway? It had all been such a waste. She didn't have what she needed to be competitive, and it was about to become official.

She looked at her dress laid out on the bed. She had been so excited to wear it. It had been her one fashion splurge after so many years of money being tight. She had bought it thinking this would be her crowning moment. The dress she would be wearing when the last five years became worth it. The dress that would be part of the validation that her ideas were valuable, that she was worth it.

It didn't hold the same appeal anymore. It no longer seemed special. Just wasted money she didn't have. She slipped it on, struggling to pull up the zipper. Once she had wiggled herself in, she moved in front of the mirror and sighed. She had woken up early to give herself time to curl her hair. Then she only realized she wanted to do that for the photos. There wouldn't be any. She threw her hair in a bun instead. *Time to go, I guess.*

∾

The emcee from the night prior picked up another thick cream envelope from the tray next to him. "Alriiight. Reeeach Refrigeraaaation." He drew out each word to heighten the tension. "Are you ready? To find out? Who, your, new, investors are?" He looked out over the audience coyly as he cracked open the envelope, giving it a quick peek. "Oh, you're going to like this. It's...Conifer Capital!"

The table next to Izabelle erupted with cheers, everyone standing up, jumping and hugging. She swore she saw tears. *What a fucking joke.* She had seen all of them last night sitting in the lobby on the way back to her room, raising glasses and toasting to their new investment partner. They knew it was a lock before they left the mixer yesterday. Reach Refrigeration and Conifer Capital probably had term sheets nailed down before they even showed up to this brunch.

At least they won't announce me. There wasn't a point in announcing a company when there was nothing to say. Izabelle figured she was safe. She counted the tables. There were only three left. She would be able to leave soon. She was keen to pack up and be back in her own bed tonight.

"Alright, everybody! Getting down to the last few here. Who do we have next?" He grabbed another envelope. "Oh boy, or should I say girl? It's a good one. Me-E-O! Are you ready?"

The spotlight centered on her table, the wide beam highlighting the nine empty chairs around her. Her eyes blinked at the harsh change in light. *What? Really?* Did someone actually want to invest? She didn't think it was possible after the way everything had gone. No one had talked to her at the mixer. No one had pulled her aside for a private chat. Someone must have actually looked at her financial documents and business plan. They must be a numbers person like her. Not everyone needed fireworks in order to know something was good. Her heart fluttered as her stomach dropped. She watched the emcee break the seal on the envelope. She interlaced her fingers in her lap and squeezed. *I should have curled my hair.*

"Fingers crossed, Me-E-O, and here we go!" He pulled out the card. Izabelle held her breath. "Well, that doesn't happen too often." The emcee turned the card toward the audience. "It's blank!"

Izabelle felt her vision tunnel. There was no way this was happening. She couldn't fathom being any more embarrassed than she was. She willed the earth to open up and swallow her whole or set her on fire, or maybe she could spontaneously combust. Anything but this.

The emcee made a pitying noise. "That's too bad. Me-E-O clocking a big ze-e-ro. That's gotta sting."

The people who weren't already looking at her twisted around in their chairs. The murmurs started immediately. The spotlight kept blaring down on her table. *Please move on. Please move on.* She sat there enduring their stares, squeezing her hands so tight that she was starting to shake. She panned the room, catching the eyes of Simon. *Fuck.* A slow, smug smile unfurled across his face, a mirror image of his pre-presentation expression. She unclasped her hands and balled her fists as hard as she could. Her nails dug into her palms with just enough distracting pain. She jiggled her knee as she fought to keep her chin up. *You will not cry in front of him. You will not cry in front of them.* The second she sensed the light moving on from her table, she bolted.

∼

"Seems like my success has nothing to do with you after all." Simon's slithering voice crawled over her.

Fuck. I guess I'm going to have to cry in front of this bastard after all. "How did you even find me?" She thought she had found a private corner to sob in. Apparently, the three lefts and a right she took to crouch by the catering kitchen door were not enough.

"I've been watching you all morning. Dress looks great, by the way. You really didn't show off your body when we were together."

"Go away, Simon." Izabelle tried to make her voice as flat as possible and refused to turn around. He was an asshole who didn't deserve the light of day, much less her attention.

"And miss my opportunity to revel in this win? Hell no."

Now, that pissed her off, and she whipped around. "No one invested. You clearly saw that I didn't win."

Simon smiled gleefully. "I know. I'm talking about me. I won. All those years, you were probably stewing about how I stole 'your' company. Thinking how I wouldn't have gotten where I am without you." He clapped his hands together. "What a hilarious thought! This wonderful event proves *you* wrong. I didn't need you at all." He was pacing back and forth, a visible bounce in each of his steps. "It all went down just like I'd hoped. No one talking to you at the tables, no one pulling you aside to discuss terms last night, no one giving you money this morning. Perfect." He raised his fingers to his mouth in an imitation of a chef's kiss.

"*You. Bastard.*" She spat as her blood ran cold. "I actually thought you wouldn't tell anyone." She could see now why no one had bothered to talk to her. Why she felt like she was a social outcast. Because he had made her one. He had delegitimized her and her company by spreading rumors. She had thought she was in the clear when Helena didn't mention anything. Izabelle was sure she would have told her if she had heard something. But in retrospect, it was foolish to think she would know everything or that Simon hadn't put the rumor mill to work overnight. She wanted to smack the glib expression off his face.

"I didn't. Not a soul, actually."

"You're lying." For the first time in her life, she wanted Simon to be lying. If he had spread rumors, she could blame him for her failure instead of herself.

"I'm not." Simon stroked his bare chin with his fingers. "I thought about it, and I realized, why should I waste my breath saying anything about you? You couldn't do it five years ago, and there was nothing to suggest that you could do it now. You had me questioning my strategy for a moment with that mild threat of a phone call. For half a second, I thought you might have finally grown the balls for business. I even thought for another second maybe if your company was something interesting, it might be worth reaching back out to you. Do a little reinvesting myself. But after that pitch"—he waved his hand in the air dismissively—"and the *complete* lack of follow-up at the mixer, I'm glad I saved my breath."

In that moment, she knew he wasn't lying. It shattered her. Having someone to blame for this disaster had been perversely cathartic for a minute. Without Simon as a scapegoat, she was going to have to accept that all her fears had been true. She hadn't been enough. And now here was the living incarnation of her not being enough, smugly reminding her. She hadn't been enough five years ago, and she wasn't enough now.

"How can you stand here and gloat over me after what you

did?" She looked up at him through tear-blurred eyes, hating herself that she was showing any vulnerability in front of him.

"What I did? I just explained to you how I didn't do anything. Did you miss the part where I explained how you failed all on your own?" Simon asked, looking at her like she was a simpleton.

"I mean what you did five years ago. And for the years we were together before that. You waltz around like you did nothing wrong. Like you didn't just up and walk away with everything we built."

"What I did was incubate an idea, invest my own capital, hire lawyers to actually make it a corporation, submit it to this competition, hire a marketing team for it, get them to present the idea, won even more investors here, and then launched a successful business. That's what I did five years ago."

"Is that how you sleep at night?" Izabelle asked, incredulous. "That's the story you tell yourself? That it was all you? That I wasn't the one who wrote the business plan, budgeted all the expenses, researched the marketplace? Came up with the *entirety* of the idea?"

"Anyone can do what you did. You aren't special. Clearly the rest of business world agrees with me, or else you wouldn't be crying in a corner with no investors. From where I'm standing, that makes me the idiot for actually investing any of my time in you at all."

Izabelle was dumbstruck. How had she ever cared for such an insufferable human? "You aren't really going to spin this into a pity party for yourself, are you? You're still living off what *I* produced." Izabelle jabbed an indignant finger at him. "Don't you dare for a second pretend that your 'investment' in me wasn't worth your time."

Simon circled his hand dismissively. "Exactly. Now you finally get it. You weren't worth my time. Therefore, I left with the valuable parts of our relationship, which didn't include you. It's not personal. It's just business, darling." He turned with a snide look on his face.

Hearing that line again five years later was more than she could take. A switch had flipped in her. "Fuck you."

Simon turned back around, his face morphing into a sneer. "What did you say?"

"You heard me. Fuck. You. Simon." She wasn't going to let him drop that bullshit line again and waltz away like he had before. He wasn't going to walk away with the satisfaction of thinking he had everything and she had nothing, again. *No. Hell no.* "You can stand here and act like you are god's gift to earth. I am *mortified* to say that I bought that lie for years. But not anymore. I made your company what it is, and but for the fact you tricked an inexperienced girl who loved you into signing it away, it would still be mine. I've spent all this time working my way back up to where you knocked me down to. The worst part is that I was convinced that I had to be like you to do it. Some sort of twisted and detached person that pretended that business wasn't personal. That *I* wasn't what made it all work. I realize now that you didn't do a damn thing on your own. You took your family's money and my company and made me feel like shit for it. You can take your pride, take my old company, take this competition, and shove it up your lazy, pompous ass."

Thirty-Six

JAKE

"Did you watch the livestream of the awards brunch this morning?" Cam flung open his door and marched to his desk, tablet in hand.

I should have firmly enforced the door thing from the beginning. "You know my answer to that question," Jake said, his stormy mood only darkening as she approached.

"Yes, and every person you scared the living shit out of during the watch party yesterday does too, but you're going to want to see this."

"No. I definitely do not," Jake responded curtly.

"Too bad." She hit Play on the tablet. He watched the emcee pull another envelope from the stack in a close-up shot of the podium.

"Fingers crossed, Me-E-O, and here we go!" The emcee read the card. "Well, that doesn't happen too often." The emcee turned the card toward the audience, a shit-eating grin plastered across his face. "It's blank! That's too bad. Me-E-O clocking a big ze-e-ro. That's gotta sting." The camera immediately panned to where Izabelle was sitting alone at a table, awash in bright light. She squinted at the rapid change in brightness, and then her eyes went wide with disbelief. The cameraman zoomed in on her face. Jake could see her pupils darting left and right they were so close to her. The color had drained from her face and hers eyes were starting to water as she fought off tears. After what felt like an eon, Jake heard the voice of the emcee announcing another company, but the camera and the spotlight stayed focused on Izabelle. The spotlight eventually moved off, but the goddamn cameraman kept her in the shot as she shakily stood up from the table and ran out of the room. The camera only cut away once the door had swung closed.

Cam took the tablet back. Jake didn't move.

"Jake?"

He threw his hand across his desk, sending a tower of straightened paper clips scattering, along with every piece of paper and writing utensil that had been on the desktop. He stood and hucked back his chair. Its wheels unable to handle the jerking movement, it crashed to the ground. He stepped over it and went to the window. He couldn't make eye contact with Cam. He wasn't an angry person; he didn't want to be this person, at work or otherwise, but the last two days had caused him to snap. He forced the words out of his jaw, his teeth grinding with every word.

"Everyone. Running. EtaSella. Is. Fired."

∽

"I can't believe I let it get this bad." Jake looked over the documents spread in front of him. He had gathered every single document and piece of information on EtaSella from the past five plus years. He reviewed who had won investments, watched their presentations, and seen all of the ridiculous stunts they were pulling. Once he realized he barely recognized the names of the investors, he called up his father's original investors and asked why they didn't invest anymore. That's when he learned about the "evening mixer" and the hospitality suites. He was sick over it all. He had let this all happen because he hadn't been paying attention. How had he been in such a trance all this time? It was like he came back from vacation and didn't recognize anyone or anything about his own company. He put his head in his hands. "This is beyond saving."

"You can't beat yourself up. You had a lot going on, but it isn't hopeless," Cam replied.

"EtaSella was the one thing my dad didn't want changed. It was the thing he was most proud of, and I let it go to complete shit. It's being run like a goddamn reality TV show." His mind flashed to the image seared into his brain. Izabelle sitting there in the spotlight. The cameraman not giving her the dignity of privacy. The emcee making fun of her company name. "No one even knows what the contest means anymore. Not a single person at the watch party could tell me. They were all too distracted by the damn robots and fireworks to actually comprehend what was going on."

"To be fair, you didn't call on the intern who had his hand raised, and most people don't speak both Esperanto and Latin."

He shot her a withering look. "Not the time, Cam."

Cam shrugged off his look, unfazed. "The question is, what are you going to do about it?"

"There isn't anything I can do," Jake responded, completely defeated.

"That's not true."

"Of course it's true. I could fix it going forward, but why bother? The people that it would matter to are gone."

"That's also not true."

Jake looked at her, incredulous and fuming. "Since you seem to have lost your mind, let's recap the facts." He ticked up his fingers as he elaborated. "One. My dad is dead. I've neglected his legacy to the point where it's a joke. Two. He isn't coming back to fix it. Three. Izabelle never wants to speak to me again. And for damn good reason, considering I lied to her and then the competition, with my company backing it, humiliated her." He steepled his fingers on the desk. "So I fail to see how they aren't both gone or how I'm supposed to do anything about fixing those wrongs."

Cam set her jaw, letting out an exasperated sigh that was nearly a growl. She got up and walked to the corner of the room. She picked up a small leather office chair, a perfect replica of an executive office chair, except the base was normal height, and the chair portion was sized for a child. Heaving it to chest height, she walked back to where Jake was sitting at his desk and smacked it down, right on top of everything Jake was looking at.

"What is this?" she asked.

"My tiny chair."

"Who made this for you?"

Jake scoffed and looked away from her. "I'm not doing this, Cam."

Cam rattled the chair. "Who. Made. This. For. You."

"My dad."

"Why?" she demanded.

"Cam, you know why."

"Why?" Jake was taken aback. She had never shouted at him in all the time they had worked together. "Tell me *exactly* why he said he made this."

"Because he said that even though I was small, it didn't mean I shouldn't have an equal place at the table."

"And *what* did he name his competition?" She stared straight at him. He didn't answer. She raised her eyebrows and rattled the chair again.

"EtaSella."

"What does that mean?" she pressed.

"I don't have time for this."

Cam was visibly pissed, her usually unflappable demeanor cracking. "Oh hell no. We are doing this. Answer the question."

"Tiny chair."

"What language is that?"

"It's Esperanto and Latin." Cam continued to glare at him. "Eta is tiny in Esperanto and chair is sella in Latin."

"And why did your dad name something in two ridiculously obscure languages that no one actually speaks?"

"Because he wanted something that brought together the old and the new."

"Exactly." Cam took the chair off the desk and dropped it on the ground with a clash. "Your dad made a competition inspired by himself and you, and your little, tiny chair. He wanted old investors to be paired with new ideas and for them to all have an equal place at the table, no matter how small the company was. I'll be damned if you keep that chair in here and moan about people not knowing what EtaSella means, only for you to forget all the hard work your dad did in founding the competition and teaching you better than to just accept things as they are."

She kicked the chair out of the way and walked back a few paces. "Your dad hired me when I didn't have anything. I didn't have a business degree. I didn't have a college degree. I didn't even have a secretarial typing certificate. But he gave me a chance. I was fresh out of high school and bold enough to tell him I needed the money. I worked for him for nearly ten years. He let me work my way up and never *ever* made me feel inadequate." Her voice was starting to shake in a way that he had never heard. "So, when you say that all the people it matters to are gone, that isn't true." She paused and gave him an icy stare, her eyes reddening. "He gave a lot of people a chance, and you are not going to let that legacy rot away. I agreed to not tell you how to run your personal life—I am not going to wade into the self-pitying bullshit that is you not wanting to apologize to Izabelle. But you can fix EtaSella. You can make it up to them. You can make sure that what happened this year never happens again. Firing people was a first step. Now actually do something."

She walked out of the room and slammed the door behind her. It was the first time that she had ever bothered to close it.

Thirty-Seven
IZABELLE

BZZZ. Izabelle glanced from her laptop to her vibrating phone. She ignored the text and went back to typing. BZzzZZ, BZzzZZ, BZzzZZ, BZzzZZ. *Really, guys?* She already knew what they were going to say but didn't want to ignore them completely. She begrudgingly picked up the phone.

"Charlie, I told you. I can't come out tonight. I have too much to do."

"Izabelle. Green. We let you off the hook last week. You needed some time. That I can understand. But we are not letting you hide in your house this week," Charlie said.

Izabelle rolled her eyes. "I really have to work."

"You also need to have a life."

"Yeah. That's the problem. I've already wasted a decade of my life, and I have nothing to show for it. I can't let another five years go by, slowly coming up with the next idea. I have to get this next project off the ground way faster than that."

Charlie sounded exasperated. "You have to give yourself a break. You aren't going to get anything done if you burn out."

"Trust me, burnout is not an option. And neither is coming out tonight. I'm sorry."

"Fine. Then we're coming over."

"Wait. What?" Izabelle looked at the phone. The screen was black. *I seriously do not have time for this.* The past week and a half at home had been hell. After she got back, she had given herself a few days to fully wallow. But eventually, the hot baths went cold, the ice cream went runny, and there wasn't anything else she wanted to binge-watch. So eventually, she got off the couch, brushed off the brownie crumbs, and sat down at her desk. She hadn't changed out of her sweat suit though. It was too comfy. New company, new mindset. She wasn't going to be so rigidly formal this time around. But comfy or not, she hadn't been able to brainstorm a single workable idea. Me-E-O had proved to be a dud, but anything new seemed even worse. It was eating her up. Each second that went by felt like an eternity of wasted time.

Her doorbell rang. *Jesus, they got here fast.* She hit the buzzer. "Come on up. It's open." She flipped open the latch and sat back down at her computer. She wanted to cram in as many seconds of work as she could before the chaos arrived.

Knock. Knock. Knock. *Since when did they get so polite?* "I said it's open." She turned back toward her screen. She still didn't hear the door swing open. *Okay. I don't know why you guys are being weird, but I'll get it myself.* She jogged toward the door, sliding the last little bit in her socks. "Seriously, you guys can—" She pulled open the door, and her eyes went wide. "Helena."

Helena van der Court was standing in her hallway, as perfectly crisp as the last time she had seen her. Izabelle had to blink a few times to fully process that she was real and not a figment of her imagination. Helena was wearing a sheath dress and matching jacket this time; the subtle sheen of the tweed definitely looked like Chanel. The diamond studs at her ears and the leather bag on her shoulder made her seem as if she had just stepped out of a board meeting. Which was a complete foil to Izabelle's state of dishevelment. She deeply wished she had brushed her hair and had anything other than her baggiest joggers on.

"Helena. Hello. This is a surprise." Helena strode past her into the room. "Come on in."

Izabelle watched Helena's gaze sweep over her apartment. Izabelle wished desperately to go back in time and not leave her towel in the middle of the hallway after her shower. If Helena saw it, then she didn't comment, and her eyes settled on the desk, where Izabelle's laptop was open. She took in the screen with a hawkish look.

"What are you working on?"

"Um, well, nothing at the moment. I've just been trying to get some new ideas down," Izabelle replied.

"Why?" Helena asked in her usual inquisitive tone.

"After everything that happened at EtaSella, it was pretty clear Me-E-O isn't going to work. So, I'm back to the drawing board."

"And why isn't it going to work?"

Izabelle chuckled awkwardly. "Honestly, I'm out of money. Without outside capital, I can't keep going. No one wanted to invest, so I've got to move in a completely different direction."

Helena nodded solemnly. "Correct me if I'm wrong, but what I'm hearing is that your business is perfectly fine, but you think it's not fine because you're convinced no one wants to invest in it? Or rather, you know the limited pool of investors at EtaSella didn't want to invest."

"Um." Izabelle looked around the room, confused. "I'm sorry, I'm a bit flustered. I didn't expect you."

"You should have. And you should know better than to think that the dingbats at EtaSella can see a good idea if it was stapled to their forehead."

Izabelle couldn't read the woman's expression. There was something that looked like a smile peeking through her stony visage, but it might just as easily have been a sneer. Izabelle stared at Helena, deeply unsure about what was going on.

Helena continued. "My only regret is that I didn't bring champagne this time. We actually have something to celebrate." Her expression tipped into the smile range and Izabelle's stomach lurched.

"Did I hear champagne?" Charlie shouted from the hallway.

Oh dear god no. They could not have worse timing. Charlie, Sabrina, and Ava burst through the door, Charlie in the lead with a bottle of champagne held high over her head, only to come to a skittering halt upon seeing Helena. Their eyes rapidly moved from Helena to Izabelle and back again. The acknowledgment that "Oh, we just fucked up" was written plainly across their collective faces.

Seeing there was no way to avoid this introduction, Izabelle made a sweeping motion with her arm. "Helena, meet Ava, Charlie, and Sabrina, my best friends." She layered the end of her sentence thickly with sarcasm. "Who have an impeccable sense of timing."

Helena elegantly tilted her head in acknowledgment. "Nice to meet you. This actually works out well. Izabelle deserves an audience after she was so cruelly denied one." Helena reached into the structured leather bag on her shoulder, pulling out a manila file folder full of documents. She handed it over to Izabelle. Izabelle took it, expecting Helena to explain. Instead, Helena just looked at her with her signature expression of bemusement.

Isabelle flipped open the top cover. The large, bold font across the top of the first page read:

TERM SHEET FOR Me-E-O inc.

She read down the rest of the page, taking in the facts, figures, and other legal language regarding the potential investment in her company.

"What? No. You can't be serious." Izabelle thought she might pass out. This wasn't possible. She must have fallen asleep and was dreaming, or her stove was leaking gas and she was hallucinating in her dying moments.

Helena chuckled. "I'm generally considered a rather serious person."

"It's just been so long since the competition I—"

Helena now guffawed in earnest. "It's barely been a fortnight. You have to give an old woman a minute to get a few things in order."

"Oh my god. I wasn't trying to suggest—"

Helena smiled calmly at her. "I know you weren't. But unlike everyone else at EtaSella, I like to do my research before I put my money down. Your pitch deck and investor packet reminded me of the last investment I'd made. The tone was the same; it had the same sensible levelheadedness. Which prompted me to do a little digging. I told you I had gotten out of the investment game five years ago when an investment of mine didn't turn the profit it had promised in the business plan. I had always wondered why. It never made sense to me that it had been so brilliant on paper, but the idiot running it never seemed to match the tone of what I had read. It turns out that's because he didn't write up the business plan. You did. I had wanted to invest in *you* all along."

"No fucking way," Sabrina said from the doorway. "You invested in Simon?"

Helena turned to address her. "Yes fucking way. That man couldn't run a business with all the money in the world. I should know. Because I gave him a pretty solid chunk of it."

"Helena, I'm so sorry."

"What in the world are you apologizing for?"

"I feel terrible that you got wrapped up in all of his bullshit. I promise everything I wrote in that business plan was true. I had no idea what he did with it after he kicked me out."

Helena had her questioning face on again. "Kicked you out?"

"More like stole it," Sabrina interjected from the hallway, heated.

Izabelle squinted at Sabrina and then turned back to Helena. "Simon manipulated the board to be all of his family and buddies and then forced a stock split behind my back. By the time he was done, my rightful half of the company had been diluted to pennies."

Helena nodded, pursing her lips in understanding. "Well, that certainly tracks with what I experienced."

Izabelle's stomach dropped. "Please don't tell me he stole your money too."

"Oh god no." Helena scoffed. "My attorneys are way too good for that. As soon as I started to suspect the company's documents and investor deck were not matching how things were actually run, I had my legal team look into it. Simon was driving the thing into the ground. He was doing everything short of directly cooking the books to make it look like everything was fine and well."

"You're kidding!" Ava said, hands clutched in front of her chest.

"Oh, I am very much not kidding," Helena continued. "My attorneys immediately threatened legal action because I'm sure if they kept digging, they were going to find so many instances of fraud you could have stacked them chest-high. I was the only truly independent investor, so Simon's solution to avoid litigation was to sell the company."

"Of course he did, that spineless bastard," Charlie said, looking over at Izabelle, shaking her head.

Izabelle was still confused. "But wouldn't whoever bought it just sue him for fraud themselves?"

Helena arched an eyebrow as she smirked. "Oh, you don't know?"

Izabelle sighed, slightly embarrassed. "I never looked into what he did with it. I was too heartbroken to know."

Helena nodded and continued. "The buyers won't sue you if they are your equally shady parents."

"His parents bought it! Ha! This is the best thing I've ever heard." Charlie was gleeful now, laughing so hard she was bent in half with her hands on her knees.

"It gets better. The deal was he would pay back my initial investment plus interest if I didn't sue. His parents 'bought' the company from him so that he could say he 'sold' his start-up and save face when all that really happened was they liquidated his trust fund to cover his ass. I made sure to warn every respectable lawyer, businessperson, and banker I know the kinds of stunts he and his family pulled and then washed my hands of the whole thing. The entire experience was such a fiasco I decided I didn't need the hassle of direct investing anymore—that is, until I read your business plan."

All of the women, minus Helena, were completely dumbfounded. They were all bouncing looks of giddy disbelief off each other.

Charlie was still laughing her ass off. "Are you telling me that pompous douche is broke?"

Helena was clearly loving this. "Oh, definitely. His parents folded the business for some sort of questionable tax write-off, and he hasn't been able to make a dime on it or anything else since. But all that to say, thank god I still keep my corporate attorney on retainer," she said, gesturing to the folder. "These days, this is usually all done over email, but I'm old-school and wanted to deliver it in person."

All of this was nearly too much for Izabelle to process. "Helena, I-I don't know what to say."

Helena gave her a wink. "I was hoping that you would say yes."

Izabelle opened her mouth to say exactly that, but Helena held up a finger to stop her.

"That is, after you hire independent counsel to review this thoroughly."

Izabelle looked down at the folder and then back up at Helena, then nodded in enthusiastic acceptance of the deal. "Can I hug you?" Tears were starting to well in the corners of her eyes. For once in the past month, they were happy tears.

Helena threw open her arms, breaking with her reserved demeanor. "Yes! I was hoping you would!"

Izabelle threw herself at Helena. This moment was nothing she thought it would be—her tiny apartment, sloppy joggers instead of a fancy dress, hair a mess, friends crowded in her entryway. But it was everything she wanted and loved all in one place. *Almost everything.* She pushed the intrusive thought out of her mind. This moment was too perfect.

"Can we hug you too?" Ava asked from the doorway, where she, Charlie, and Sabrina were all clutching hands.

"Of course!" Helena said in enthusiastic acceptance.

They all immediately joined in, leaping into Helena and Izabelle with a weight-shifting hug.

"This is the greatest girl power moment I've ever been a part of," Sabrina said, her voice muffled from her face being so tightly pressed into Izabelle's shoulder.

After an extra squeeze, Helena pulled away from the group. "Now, young lady, I saw you bring in that bottle. I think it's high time we opened it."

"Yes, ma'am!" Charlie grabbed the bottle of champagne from where she had left it by the door. She popped it open in short order while Ava grabbed glasses from the kitchen. They soon all had a glass of bubbly in their hands.

"A toast," Helena said, raising her glass, "to Izabelle."

Izabelle beamed as her friends lifted their glasses one by one.

"To Simon getting what he deserved."

"To hard work paying off."

"To having everything your heart desires."

Izabelle raised her glass, toasting the moment, and wished that her heart didn't desire one more thing. *Jake.*

Thirty-Eight
IZABELLE

"Now that her term sheet is officially signed, let's raise another glass to Izabelle in celebration of signing her first big investment deal!" Charlie shouted over the din at Buchannan's. The other girls raised their glasses and clinked them together in a group cheers.

"So, how does it feel?" Ava asked.

"It still feels surreal. I can't believe it."

"What?" Sabrina asked, leaning over the table. "I can barely hear you over the freaking TV."

"Ed!" Charlie leaned out of the booth to shout at the bar manager. "It isn't a Giants game, for christ's sake. Can you turn it down?"

He looked at her through his bushy eyebrows with his usual deeply creased frown. "Whaaat?" He shrugged, remote in hand. "It's the news."

Charlie raised her hand in exasperation. "Yeah. We're trying to have a *happy* hour, not a depressing local news hour. We can't even see the screen.'" He waved her off, clearly uninterested in turning it down. Charlie looked at Sabrina. "You talk to him. He likes you better than me."

"Ugh. Fine." Sabrina scooted herself out of the booth to go work her magic on Ed.

"Bend over so he can see down your sweater. It'll help," Charlie heckled as Sabrina went to walk away. She turned and flipped Charlie the bird, eliciting a cackle from all of them. Just as Sabrina was starting to engage with Ed, Izabelle heard the news anchor say, "And finally, in tonight's news from the business world, local CEO Jacoby Masterson has held a press conference regarding his prestigious start-up competition."

"Wait! Stop! Turn it up!" Izabelle shouted.

"Oh, so now you want me to turn it up," Ed said from behind the bar.

Izabelle scrambled out of her seat and crowded behind Sabrina so she could see the screen behind the bar. The news was playing a clip of what seemed to be a press conference. Jake was fully decked out in a suit and tie, standing behind a podium emblazoned with the logo of Masterson Holdings, a step and repeat banner with the EtaSella logo behind him. Izabelle examined his face. Handsome as always, but he looked tired. Her heart twinged. Jake looked directly at the cameras, and the news played the audio.

"Masterson Holdings was my father's business, but EtaSella was his dream."

"Holy shit," Sabrina said, pointing at the screen. "That's Jake? The guy from the resort?"

"Shh," Izabelle hissed as Charlie and Ava squished behind her.

"Woah. He is way hotter than I thought," Charlie said.

"Shut up!" Izabelle said, leaning over the bar and snatching the remote from a surprised Ed. She frantically smashed the volume button so she could hear better.

"He loved an underdog. He founded the competition so scrappy upstarts with great ideas and without connections could have a chance in the business world, without pomp and no matter their circumstance. However, in the years since he passed, EtaSella has forgotten that mission. Forgotten its purpose." Jake paused and looked around the room of reporters, not flinching as the flashes of cameras lit his face. His jaw was tight and clenched in a way she had never seen. "There have been rumors circulating that I fired the executive team who had been managing EtaSella. Those rumors are true." There was an audible increase in murmuring from the crowd. "I take full responsibility for the decline of the competition and for all of those companies who entered, competed, and invested in EtaSella with the ideals of my father, only to be let down by the negligence of his son. In the last few years, I have told myself a lot of lies, that I was fine, that my company was doing everything it should be, that my work fulfilled me, and that my actions didn't impact those around me. It is a deeply regrettable truth that those lies impacted the reality of people I loved and cared about. For those that I speak of, I am forever sorry. I cannot change what has been done and what I did. I let my own emotions cloud my judgment. However, I promise to change what will be done and how I do it."

He paused momentarily to collect himself. "To begin, EtaSella will be canceled for the upcoming year, allowing me time to appoint leaders who understand the legacy of this competition to take the reins and for the rest of us to process the lessons we need to learn." The murmurs of the crowd grew even louder at that announcement. Jake continued over the din of the crowd. "In the meantime, Masterson Holdings will be personally backing and mentoring all of the companies scheduled to compete this year who need our help. No one is going to be left without a seat at the table, now or in the future." Jake took a deep breath and looked straight down the camera lens. Her breath hitched seeing the crisp blue of his eyes, she had missed them so much. "I finally understand what this competition means to those who helped found it and those who poured their entire selves into their companies to compete. To those people, thank you for teaching me what I needed to know. For showing me what it truly means to love what you do and being willing to risk it all. It was at great cost to you, and I will never be able to repay you." Jake looked directly down the lens of the camera. "But I promise you, EtaSella will never be the same because of you. It will forever be better because of you, and the mark you left will never be forgotten. Thank you."

Izabelle watched as Jake strode off the screen, and the news feed cut back to the anchors. She dropped the remote on the bar, processing what she had just heard. Her mind flashed all of the events in front of her—meeting Jake, working on the presentation together, his vulnerability, her pride, her conversation with Helena, how she missed him and wished she could have told him about her recent success. She was mad and hurt, but this hurt wasn't the coal-fired rage of hurts past. This was a longing hurt—a longing for the tired man on the screen who was admitting he screwed up and was trying to make it right. The man who saw her, understood her, supported her. She walked back to their booth in a daze, her friends following closely behind.

Izabelle wordlessly reclaimed her seat, and Ava scooted in next to her. "Why do I feel like that was an apology to you?" she asked.

Izabelle took a full minute to think before she answered. "Because I think it was."

～

She slept on the idea for a week. She wanted to be sure. But she was. She had to try.

The number wasn't that hard to find. She punched it into her phone. *Deep breath.*

"Masterson Holdings, Cam speaking."

"Hi. I just want to make sure I'm talking to the right Cam. I am looking for Ja—er, Mr. Masterson's assistant?"

"Assistant, secretary, knower-of-all. Yes, you've got the right Cam."

"Great." Izabelle took another deep breath. *Here goes nothing.* "You don't know me, but my name is Izabelle Green and —" She stopped when she heard the receiver clatter onto something hard. A brief shuffle followed.

"Apologies. I lost my grip there. I know who you are."

"You do?" Izabelle asked, surprised.

"I *very* much do."

"Oh. Uh. Cool." Izabelle paused. She hadn't been expecting this. "I guess that makes things a lot easier to explain."

"Feel free to skip right to the part where you ask me for my help in reaching back out to Jake."

"You call him Jake too?" Izabelle asked.

"What else would I call him?"

"I don't know. Mr. Masterson or Jacoby?"

"Anyone he likes doesn't call him either of those things. He uses Jake in his personal life. Has since he was a small child, from what I know. Anyway, let's talk ideas."

"Well, we met in the rideshare on the way to the airport."

"Oooh, is that how it happened? I thought you met at the resort."

"We did. The second time. But the first time was in the car, and so I figured if you could get him into a car, then we could have...I don't know, a private moment, maybe?"

Izabelle could hear quiet clapping through the phone. "This. Is. Perfect. If I wasn't sitting at a very open desk right now, I would squeal. Are you free later today? From 4:15 on?"

"Today?" Izabelle hadn't expected this to all fall into place so quickly.

"I don't see a reason not to do it today," Cam responded.

She has a point there. That's what I wanted, isn't it?

Cam continued. "I can send a car around 3:30 and—"

"No. I'll drive myself. But 4:15 is a fine time."

"I can work with that. What kind of car am I trying to get him in?"

"Uhhh." Izabelle hadn't thought this far ahead with the plan. She was going to have to call Charlie after this and hope it worked out. "A Honda CR-V, most likely. I'll call you if anything changes."

"Great. I'll get him outside and at the car at 4:15. Do you know the building?"

"Can you send me the address just in case?" Izabelle heard the keys clacking. "Do you need my email addre—"

"Nope. I just pulled it from the EtaSella files. I've been waiting for this moment. Should be in your inbox by the time you hang up. South entrance at 4:15."

"Wait, do you know what you're going to say to get him there?"

"Please. I've been thinking about it since you mentioned a car. Don't worry about that part."

This woman is on a whole other level. Izabelle took an audible breath. "Alright. Plan made. Is there anything else I should know?"

"Yes," Cam said. "You should know that I am so glad you called."

~

"Hi! What's up?" Charlie asked cheerily from the other end of the phone.

"I need to borrow your car. Actually, no. Scratch that. I need you to pick me up and then drive me downtown. I'll explain when you get here."

~

"Oh god. He's going to be down any second now." Izabelle was in a full-on freak-out. This had all seemed like a very cool, very romantic idea until they pulled up outside of his building. "Shit. Drive! Drive away!"

Charlie looked at her in the rearview mirror. "What in the

hell are you talking about? I took off early today, and this is the man of your dreams, so I will not be driving anywhere but here. You can do this."

Izabelle was furiously crunching her knuckles. "I didn't plan this out. I don't know what to say."

Charlie whipped around in the driver's seat. "What do you mean you don't know what to say? You haven't been thinking about it the whole time?"

"Yes! No!" She slouched in the back seat. "You know I suck at giving speeches." Izabelle frantically tried to wipe the sweat off her palms. "Oh shit. There they are." She looked at the building's revolving doors from which Jake and a tall redheaded woman carrying an iPad emerged.

"Look, I got you here, but you have to do the rest. I'm about to get out of the car and then open the door for him like we talked about. We can't bail now, or else it will look like we were trying to kidnap him or something." Charlie got out of the driver's seat and walked around to the side of the car, where Cam and Jake were approaching.

Why is it so hot? Why did I wear this stupid dress?

"Mr. Masterson, thank you for coming. My CEO is looking forward to speaking with you." Charlie pulled open the rear passenger door.

Jake went to fold himself into the car, giving Charlie a curt "Thank you" as he did so.

It was then that he made eye contact with her. His eyes, those light, entrancing eyes, opened wide in surprise. He spoke in a tone that she hadn't heard before. It was confused and surprised, and his voice cracked with emotion. "Izabelle."

Thirty-Nine

JAKE

"We have to go down now for your 4:15," Cam said, leaning on Jake's door and flipping through her iPad distractedly.

"What? Since when do I have a 4:15?"

"Since this morning when it went on your calendar."

"What's it for?"

Cam smiled with fake sweetness, her personal brand of sarcasm infusing every word. "Had you actually checked your calendar invite, you would have seen it's a test ride with a CEO for the rideshare deal."

"We're still doing that? I thought that deal died."

Cam tilted her head in annoyance. "Yes, we're still doing it."

"Mm. Can't we reschedule?" Jake was not in the mood to talk to anyone today. He was in the same foul mood he'd been in since he'd gotten back. It was very much an "I want to be alone forever" kind of mood. "I'm not prepped for it."

"No. We can't. And you can't keep sitting in here all day avoiding the world. It isn't good for you, and we don't have the budget for the number of paper clips you ruin." She directed her disapproving look to the pile of straight metal rods that had returned to the corner of his desk. "Let's go. I'll prep you on the way down."

He begrudgingly stood up, grabbed his suit jacket, and followed Cam to the elevator. She hit the Down button. Per usual, she waited until they stepped into the elevator and the doors had closed to give him the rundown.

"Alright. As far as I can tell, this would be a really good partnership. They're small but have good outreach. They can network and plan with entities they haven't worked with before. They don't seem intimidated by big problems and generally have a positive attitude."

"Okay. But what are the numbers?" Jake asked as they reached the bottom floor and stepped out.

"I don't think this is going to be much of a numbers meeting. You'll just have to feel it out. When one plus one equals two, it's pretty straightforward."

"What?" Jake asked.

"Never mind," Cam said, looking out at the street, double-checking something on her iPad, and then scanning the street again.

"Where's the car?" Jake asked, scanning the street for the typical shiny black sedan.

Cam began the short walk to the curb and gestured ahead of them at a small SUV. "Trust me. You'll thank me for this."

A woman came around the car and opened the rear door for him. "Mr. Masterson, thank you for coming. My CEO is looking forward to speaking with you." As she said it, she covered her mouth with her hand like she was trying to cover a laugh or something. It was a bit weird, but Jake folded himself into the car with a curt "Thank you" to the driver.

It was then that he saw her, his heart recognizing her in this unexpected place before his brain did.

"Izabelle." His voice cracked as he said it.

She gazed at him with her deep green eyes, and his chest twisted. He had missed them so badly. Missed *her* so badly. He had stared at his dark ceiling every night, kicking himself that the universe had given him second, third, and fourth chances, and he had squandered them all. But here she was, like the world was giving him one last chance. No. That wasn't right. It wasn't the universe—it was her. She was giving him one last chance.

"Izabelle. I am so sorry. I—you deserved to know—I should have told you—but the competition... I-I didn't know and—" He was tripping over himself again. He had thought of everything he wanted to apologize to her for, thought about it in every waking and sleeping moment since she had walked away, and now that he had the chance, they were crashing into each other, creating a multi-apology pile-up in his throat.

Her expression was neutral, like she was trying to get a read on the situation. "I saw your press conference."

Jake's stomach flipped. That was good. At least she has seen some part of an eloquent apology. "Please know that everything I said was true. It kills me that EtaSella, something I backed, treated you the way it did. Especially after I treated you the way

I did. I'm working to fix it. To fix myself. I promise it will never happen to anyone again, and if there is anything that I can do—"

Izabelle held up her hand to interrupt him. "I need you to answer a few questions for me. I just...I just need to be sure." She was crunching her knuckles in the way she did when she was nervous.

"Anything." It was taking every ounce of control he had not to reach out and grab her, pull her into a hug so she could feel the way his heart was hammering for her.

"When did you know that I was participating in EtaSella?"

Jake sighed. She had every right to wonder about this. "I didn't know until you came to my casita for the first time. When you mentioned the competition, I freaked out. It's why I bolted out of the hot tub."

Izabelle let out a small chuckle. "Ohhhh, that makes sense now. And were you really going to leave that night?"

"I was. Or at least I had planned to after you told me. I thought it was the only way I could possibly keep you at arm's length." His eyes searched her face for some hint of how she was feeling.

Another small chuckle from Izabelle. "To keep the personal and professional separate."

Jake nodded, worried about how Izabelle was feeling. "Exactly. I thought it was the only way."

Her mouth twitched to the side. "And so why did you decide to stay?"

Jake took a deep breath. He knew this was what he should have said from the start. "Because I didn't want it to be separate. I didn't want to be apart from you." Jake rubbed at his neck.

The words were coming easier now, but that didn't mean they weren't hard to say. "You made me feel things I haven't felt... well, ever, and you made me feel like me. But I was reckless with those feelings. I let them overshadow what I knew was a risk to you. I knew being attached to me could hurt your business, could undermine what you built, but I didn't fully understand those implications initially. I was more worried that I would be giving you an improper leg up rather than potentially tearing you down. By the time I fully understood, I was so invested in you and your company I knew I would be hurting you no matter what I did. So, I just tried to avoid it entirely. I stupidly thought I could keep things smooth until your presentation, so you wouldn't have one more distraction on your plate. But in trying to avoid hurting you, I made it all so much worse." He looked at her with every ounce of emotion he felt. He clenched his fists next to his thighs to keep himself from reaching for her. "If I could take it all back, I would. I never meant to hurt you, and I will never forgive myself that I did."

She tilted her head, eyes still unreadable. "All of it?"

Fuck. This was the part he knew he wasn't going to be able to say perfectly. Where his words would fail him. But he swore if he ever had the chance, he wouldn't ever lie to Izabelle again.

"No. Not all of it. What I did was wrong. I know that. You deserved to know, and you didn't deserve any stupid action of mine to ever reflect on you, but I wouldn't ever take back the parts that were right." He paused, every part of him wanting to reach for her to steady himself. "And I know that we were right together. I wouldn't ever want those moments with you taken back."

"I hoped so." She smiled. Her perfect smile. It warmed her

face; it went all the way to her eyes and radiated into his core. She blew out a slow breath. "You know how shitty I am at speeches, so know that I'm not saying this exactly right." Jake's heart started to pound even more rapidly in his chest. "I was really mad at you for a while. But then Helena came to visit me, and I started to realize something."

"What? Helena? Helena van der Court? My parents' friend? She's like an aunt to me. How do you—"

"I met her at EtaSella. She came to invest in my company."

"Oh my god. Izabelle, that's amazing! You couldn't ask for a better partner!" He moved to embrace her on instinct.

She put her hand out to stop him. "No. Let me finish. I have to get this out."

His stomach sank. But he understood.

"She came to give me a term sheet. All my friends were there. I had everything I had dreamed about for my company and everyone who had supported me on this crazy journey. Except for one. Except for you."

The little ember of hope he had kept in his heart started to warm. *Is she really saying...?* She reached for his hands, and he took them, the familiar softness gliding into his palms fanning that little ember into a raging blaze of heat.

"Then I saw you at the press conference, and you looked the way I felt. It was then that I fully realized I wasn't mad at you— I was mad at myself. I had sworn I would keep business and my personal life in separate spheres. That I didn't need a man. That I didn't need help. That I didn't need a life outside of my business. I had told myself a lot of things. But turns out I didn't know anything. I didn't even know I was falling for you. Literally. You didn't tell me who you were. But you showed me. You showed me kindness, thoughtfulness, support, acceptance, passion. You showed me love. And I wasn't able to see that. I wasn't able to understand that you were something new and different and wonderful. I'm sorry I didn't listen. Sorry I didn't listen to you, and my friends, and everyone else who tried to help me. I was so mad at the world I couldn't accept there were people who really were on my team, even if I thought I knew." She gripped his hand tighter and she moved toward him. "I made a lot of wrong choices at EtaSella. I felt like you and the competition had burned me, and as a result, my whole business, my whole life, had gone up in smoke. But after all of that anger burned away, I realized, in the end, I was most mad that I let you go. And I wish I hadn't. And that's what I came to tell you today." She looked at him hopefully, a hope that matched his, before her expression turned questioning. "So do you think we could try again?"

Jake launched across the back seat in response. The fire in his heart was burning a hole through him. He pulled her into him, scooping her up with the intention of never letting her go. He hadn't thought it was possible, hadn't thought she could ever forgive him. But here she was. He kissed her so she knew exactly what he felt. What he had felt for so long, ages before he cared to admit it. She met his kiss with equal intensity. She let him know that she was his, and he did the same. He was hers now, and if he had his way, now and forever.

Epilogue
JAKE

"You sure you're ready for this?" Izabelle asked apprehensively, standing in front of the dark dive bar.

"I already interact with two-fifths of this group on a daily basis. How bad could it be?"

She snorted a laugh as she turned and opened the door. "Keep telling yourself that."

Well now I'm nervous. Jake hadn't felt a single ounce of nerves when he first told Izabelle he loved her, or when he asked her to move in. When you know you know, and when it came to Izabelle he knew. She was his world. But standing on the sidewalk outside of Buchannan's he was certifiably nervous. This was the first time he was officially meeting Izabelle's friends, and he knew how much these women meant to her.

She turned around, concerned, when he didn't follow her in. "Hey? You okay? I was just teasing. They aren't going to give you a super hard time. They already love you."

She reached for his hand, interlacing her fingers with his.

The contact smoothed over his anxiety in a warm rush. "As long as I'm with you I am more than okay."

The second they walked through the door the sound of party kazoos and clackers rang through air. Jake's head turned toward the cacophony and immediately saw a giant sign that read:

"CONGRATULATIONS ON LOVING EACH OTHER ENOUGH TO SHARE A BATHROOM!"

Under which Izabelle's friends were sitting wearing party hats. He started cracking up. Of all the scenarios he'd imagined, this had not been one of them.

Izabelle covered her eyes with her hand, her chest shaking with laughter. "Seriously you guys?"

"Yes, seriously!" Charlie shouted, waiving them over. "Anyone who willing signs up to look at someone else's hair stuck to the shower walls from now until the end of time is both certifiably crazy and deserves a sign."

As they approached the group, Jake looked at the sign more closely. "Cam, is that what you had rolled up on your desk today?"

"Hmm?" she blinked her eyes innocently. "I'll have you know that what happens between me and the guys at the print shop during my lunch hour is my business. Thank you very much."

"Well," he said, sliding into the booth. "I am glad to see you're one of the gang."

"Ever since she bet me ten dollars you guys were going to

make up in my car in less than five minutes I knew she was going to fit right in," Charlie quipped.

"And yet, months later, I'm still waiting for you to pay up," Cam shot back.

"Speaking of bets," Sabrina butted in. "How many times did he ask you to pick your towels up off the floor this week Iz?"

Jake looked over at Izabelle quizzically, eyebrows raised.

Izabelle stared at the ceiling with a chagrined expression as she scratched her head. "Yeah...I might have shared one or two things with them."

Jake laughed. This he had expected. "I don't know if my ego can withstand all of you getting together on a weekly basis to rip on me."

"Eh. We can agree to do it on a bi-weekly basis if that makes you feel better," Sabrina responded.

Jake started counting off on his fingers. "Doing the rough math here, I think that would make me feel roughly fifty percent better."

"Ooo, Iz, your man is so good at numbers," Ava joked. "But seriously." She put on her gravest expression, folding her hands on the table top. "What's next for you guys? This basically counts as meeting the family, so I think an engagement is right around the corner."

"Ava! Jesus! Behave yourself. We've been here for two seconds. This is why I didn't bring him to one of these right away."

"Just saying, just saying." Ava put up her hands in defiant surrender.

"It's fine," He leaned over and kissed the top of Izabelle's head. "I deserve all the grilling and more. But the short answer is whatever she wants, she can have."

Izabelle leaned into his shoulder like she always did when she was happy. He loved the way her head nestled into his shoulder and her arm wound its way around his.

"Aw, that's so sweet," Sabina cooed, then abruptly leaned forward with her all-business attitude. "But we're here to tell you what she wants is a princess-cut solitaire on a platinum band."

Izabelle shot her a murderous look, but Jake just smiled to himself. *Good. Because that is exactly what I have waiting for her when the time is right.* He raised his glass. "To the woman I love and all her friends that love her too."

"Cheers!" they all said in unison.

"Jake, the next round is on you," Charlie ribbed.

"Wouldn't have it any other way."

Want more of Jake and Izabelle? Dying to continue reading about this awesome group of friends? Then be on the lookout for Sabrina's love story releasing in 2023!

In the meantime, I would love for you to join my newsletter, where you can get exclusive writing updates and just-for-subscribers bonus scenes.

You can find the newsletter sign up and all things Kallista Kohl at my website:

www.KallistaKohl.com

Thank you for reading!

KALLISTA KOHL
Romance Author

Acknowledgments

When I first had the idea to write a romance novel I figured everyone in my life would think I was a little crazy. I am infinitely thankful that each and every person listed in this acknowledgement not only did *not* think I was crazy, but instead encouraged me, supported me, and helped make this dream a reality. I am eternally grateful to all of you for cheering me on, cheering me up, and not being afraid to tell me when something sucked.

To Red, thank you for reading every single version of this novel. You have always encouraged me to be a reader, and because of you I'm now a writer.

To Kasie, your last-minute edits really came through. Thank you for those and for listening to me read Chapter One to you over FaceTime no less than fifteen times.

To Rachel, Catherine and Megan, you are some of the best friends a girl could hope for. Your questions, feedback and impressions molded this novel in countless ways. Your comments and proof-reads pushed me to make this book better and I cannot thank you enough.

In addition to all of the women above, there is a team of women who I've had the pleasure to meet and work with as a result of writing this story.

To Kristen and Chona, my professional beta readers, thank

you for your feedback, you read a version that wasn't quite there yet, but you helped this novel become what it is today.

To Bailey at Bailey Designs Books, you smashed this cover design. I love it so much I want to have it printed on everything.

To Sandra at One Love Editing, thank you for your patience and your incredible attention to detail. The amount of work you put into polishing this book can never be overstated. Thank you for making it shine.

And lastly to my fiancé, thank you for listening while I talked through plot hole after plot hole, and for having an answer every time I yelled business or grammar-related questions at you from the couch.

Thank you all. For everything.

About the Author

Kallista lives in San Francisco with her fiancé and way too many house plants. She is very proud to report that only a few have died in her care.

Kallista makes her online home at www.KallistaKohl.com and would love to connect with you on her social media platforms listed below.

- facebook.com/kallistakohl
- instagram.com/kallistakohl
- tiktok.com/@kallistakohl

Made in the USA
Monee, IL
05 March 2023